W9-AGH-280

By Andrew Grant

INVISIBLE

INVISIBLE

A NOVEL

Andrew Grant

BALLANTINE BOOKS

NEW YORK

Published in the United States by Ballantine Books, an imprint of Random House, a division of Penguin Random House LLC, New York.

BALLANTINE and the HOUSE colophon are registered trademarks of Penguin Random House LLC.

LIBRARY OF CONGRESS CATALOGING-IN-PUBLICATION DATA
Names: Grant, Andrew, author.
Title: Invisible: a novel / Andrew Grant.
Description: New York: Ballantine Books, [2019]
Identifiers: LCCN 2018038261 | ISBN 9780525619598 (hardback) | ISBN 9780525619604 (ebook)
Subjects: | BISAC: FICTION / Suspense. | FICTION / Action & Adventure. | GSAFD: Suspense fiction.
Classification: LCC PR6107.R366 I58 2019 | DDC 823/.92—dc23
LC record available at https://lccn.loc.gov/2018038261

Printed in the United States of America on acid-free paper

randomhousebooks.com

1 2 3 4 5 6 7 8 9

First Edition

Book design by Caroline Cunningham

For the ninety-nine percent.

INVISIBLE

Chapter **One**

A GOOD PLACE FOR A CLANDESTINE MEETING. A GOOD PLACE FOR an ambush.

Two sides of the same coin. So, heads or tails?

Only one way to find out . . .

I'd done business with Amir Fakhri Asgari—if that was his real name—twice before. Both of our previous meetings had also been in Istanbul. That made good sense. Turkey lies between Bulgaria, where the company I worked for had its factories and offices, and Iran, where Asgari was from. It was easy for me to bring certain items into the country without attracting attention. It was easy for him to take them out again. And the city itself, with its warrens of narrow, twisting streets and countless cafés and restaurants full of secluded alcoves and hidden rooms—it could have been designed specifically for hosting secret rendezvous. They'd been going on there for centuries, and that showed no sign of changing.

Both of my previous meetings with Asgari had been in busy, outdoor places. The first, on the terrace of a restaurant in the shadow of the Blue Mosque where a dervish performed every evening, drawing fervent crowds. The second, at a café on the lawn by the massive outer wall of Topkapi Palace, encircled by an endless line of bustling tourists that snaked its way through the ancient avenue of trees to the security checkpoint for the inner courtyard. So when Asgari nominated the Grand Bazaar as the venue for our next appointment, I wasn't worried. The ancient labyrinth is said to be the most visited tourist attraction in the world. Even on its quietest days it sees over a quarter of a million visitors. The place would be overflowing with jostling hordes of merchants and shoppers from dawn till dusk. And then I read Asgari's message again and another detail jumped out at me. The time he wanted to meet: 2:00 A.M. Not P.M. The stalls and storefronts would be closed up and locked. The chaotic maze of passageways would be deserted. There'd be no potential witnesses. Nothing to convince Asgari it would be in his best interests for me—and the $15 million I'd be there to collect—to leave unmolested.

Of course, there was another explanation for Asgari's desire for privacy. Perhaps he just wanted to examine my merchandise before handing over the cash? Our previous deals had been small beer in comparison. Items he could have procured elsewhere for money that wouldn't change anyone's life. Token transactions, really, designed to establish trust and demonstrate capability. But this time the scale was different. Radically so. Asgari and his bosses were desperate to get their hands on the piece of equipment I'd smuggled out of Bulgaria. No one in Iran could make one for themselves. They lacked the expertise. They didn't have the technology. They couldn't get the raw materials. And they couldn't buy the finished product from anyone else. Not legally, anyway. Supplying it—or any of its component parts or plans—was strictly prohibited by the United Nations. By four separate resolutions. There'd be serious repercussions if we were even suspected of trying to do business. And severe penalties if we were actually caught in the act. I could understand why Asgari wouldn't want to be seen in public poring over such sensitive contraband. I still wasn't happy about it. But there was too much riding on the deal for me to think about pulling out.

There are twenty-two ways into the Grand Bazaar. Officially speaking. Or maybe twenty-three, depending on whom you talk to. Asgari told me to go to one of the largest—the Mahmutpasa Gate, at the northeast corner of the complex—between 1:50 and 1:55 A.M. He said I'd find the gate unlocked between those times, and the security cameras along a specified route switched off. The meeting itself was to take place inside a store. Adnan & Hasan's. They're one of the best-known Turkish carpet dealers in the city. I'd heard of their place before. Word had it that the diplomats from the US Consulate wouldn't buy the rugs they shipped back home from anywhere else.

I arrived at the Beyazit Gate, at the southwest corner, at 11:45 P.M. Yellow light from the surrounding streetlamps was spilling over the Bazaar's vast irregular, undulating terra-cotta-tiled roof, toning down its color and making it look like a battered expanse of dunes after a violent storm. The two rectangular *bedesten*—the oldest buildings at the site, originally freestanding—dominated the center of the complex that had grown up on all sides and absorbed them, the moonlight glinting off the intricate carving that adorned their symmetrical rows of tapered domes. The Gate itself was like something from a medieval castle, which seemed incongruous against the constant hum of traffic and the rattle of a passing tramcar. The structure had been built with huge blocks of solid stone, yards thick, and its pale surface was pocked and stained by centuries of pollution and human contact. The twin gates were made of smoke-darkened wood, iron-hard and lined with metal studs for even more strength. Together the whole thing had survived fires and earthquakes and invasions and insurrections. Now it was supplemented by brand-new, high-security locks and movement-sensitive floodlights. There was no way to get through it without being seen, even at that time of night. But the same couldn't be said for the store on its right-hand side. It sold colorful, hand-woven bags and purses of all shapes and sizes, and by virtue of its location—and some illicit, unauthorized alterations carried out by a former owner—it was one of the very few units that gave access to the inside of the Bazaar as well as the street.

Asgari's warning to keep to his designated route through the Bazaar didn't worry me. I had other ways to deal with the cameras, and no desire for anyone who may be wishing me ill to be forewarned about where I'd be. Or when. I know the Bazaar well, but even so it took me more than ten minutes after leaving the bag store to find the passageway I was looking for. The pale light that filtered in through the high, round-topped windows was just enough to navigate by, though it washed out the colors on the walls and floor, robbing them of the vibrancy that normally showed through despite their peeling paint and crumbling mosaics. I hugged the shadows on the far side of the passage and continued until I found a broad alcove in the lee of a stout stone column that reached up to the steeply vaulted ceiling. The smell of burnt paraffin lingered in the air, and underfoot I could feel something gently crunching as I moved. The residue of crushed sugar cubes. In the pandemonium of working hours this would be the domain of one of the most important people in the whole Bazaar. An old guy, sheltered from the melee by an array of double-stacked brass kettles. He has one, vital job. To repeatedly refill the delicate tulip-shaped glasses carried on swinging silver trays by the dozens of boys who constantly scurry through the crowds. They shuttle to and fro between the stalls and the stores, supplying the merchants who won't entertain the idea of doing business without first drinking tea with their clients. During the day the space was a perfect hub for the brewing operation. During the night, it was a perfect spot for keeping watch over the entrance to Adnan & Hasan's store.

No one entered. No one left. There was no other way into the store. There was no other way out. I stayed hidden until two minutes after 2:00 A.M. Still no one appeared. Asgari had been punctual for both our previous meetings. My instinct told me to walk away. The strange time of night. The weird location. The change in Asgari's behavior. It all felt wrong. But the deal was far too important to abandon over nothing more than a feeling, so I reluctantly broke cover and crossed the passageway.

The store was set into an arch-shaped lot that occupied the entire space between two scuffed, structural pillars. The owners' names were tastefully painted in lowercase gold letters against a sober green background on a wooden panel that fanned out to fill the area below the vaulted roof. Below that, to the right, was a wide window that stretched the rest of the way to the ground. I couldn't see through due to the forest of artfully folded, intricately woven rugs hanging from the ceiling. To the left was the door. It was surprisingly modern. The frame was made of polished aluminum. The glass was spotless and a column of colorful stickers near the handle confirmed which credit cards the store accepted, and proudly announced its most recent TripAdvisor score. I tried the handle. The door swung smoothly open and I stepped inside.

The muzzle was pointing straight at me. It belonged to an AK-47. The shape of the gun is unmistakable. It's so ubiquitous that one country, Mozambique, even has its silhouette on its flag. It's so reliable that there was no point in hoping for a misfire. I've seen fifty-year-old Kalashnikovs that haven't been maintained in decades fire full magazines without a single failure. And the hand cradling the scratched hardwood guard beneath the barrel was so steady there was no hope that whoever was holding it didn't know exactly what he was doing.

I raised the backpack I'd been carrying in my left hand and held it out in front of my chest. Not because I thought it could stop bullets, but because I hoped the guy wouldn't want to risk destroying its contents by shooting me. And I hoped that it might buy me some time. I inched forward, almost imperceptibly, trying to make out who was behind the weapon. All I could see was his left hand. It—and the gun—was roughly at chest height, leaning on a stack of folded rugs maybe one yard wide by two deep. The rest of him was in deep shadow toward the rear of the store. I gained maybe six inches and noticed something that gave me a tiny shred of hope. The fire selector—a crude lever on the right-hand side of the rifle, midway above the trigger—was in the center position. Full auto.

The one real flaw of the AK is that when fired in full auto, it pulls up and to the right. Some newer models have a specially slanted muzzle tip to redirect the gun's exhaust gasses in an attempt to counteract the problem. This one didn't. Which gave me an idea. The only way to deal with someone with a long gun at close quarters is to get in too tight for him to bring the weapon to bear. So I lowered my backpack to the ground, quickly but gently. Dived down to the guy's left, in the opposite direction to the way the gun would naturally try to track when he pulled the trigger. Threw myself forward. Hauled myself upright on the far side of the stack of rugs. Half noted that the gun hadn't fired. Or even moved. Started to lunge for the guy who was holding it. Then realized that I knew him. And understood why he remained frozen.

Amir Fakhri Asgari—the man I was in Istanbul to meet—was

slumped forward against the pillar of rugs. His right hand was still clenched around the gun's grip. His finger was still tensed on the trigger. And a knife was still stuck in his neck. The handle was jutting vertically upward between his hairline and his collar. It was matte black, like its blade. Designed for commandos. Made for killing silently at night. Which is exactly what it seemed to have done.

The skin covering my ribs was tingling with residual, morbid anticipation, but at least now I could be fairly certain that the gun hadn't been aimed at me, specifically. More likely it had just been aimed at the door. Asgari must have gotten wind of an ambush, arrived at the rendezvous point good and early, and set up against the place where he expected the threat to present itself. Only, the threat must have gotten there earlier still, and presented itself from behind. Which begged a number of questions. How had Asgari's assailant known where to find him? Where was he now? And where was my $15 million? Had stealing the money been the objective all along? Or was something else in play? Something much more damaging, from my point of view.

I retrieved my backpack and unzipped its outer pocket, but before I could reach for my flashlight the inside of the store was lit up by a dozen multicolored glass lanterns that were hanging from brass hooks on the walls. The sudden brightness drew my gaze to Asgari's plump face. He looked strangely calm. I guess he'd thought he was in control. He was in place, set up, waiting—and he never saw the blade coming. I wondered briefly why the attacker hadn't retrieved the knife. It was clearly an effective tool. And it had obviously been used by an expert. I couldn't imagine that the resulting blood had put them off, though there was a prodigious amount. Some had spurted from the wound, spraying Asgari's hands and his rifle and soaking into the stack of carpets, ruining the exquisite fabric. More had run down Asgari's torso and legs, plastering his clothes to his body and then pooling around his expensive Italian leather shoes. It had started to congeal, though hadn't yet turned brown. I took a hurried step away from the corpse. I didn't want the man now visible to my left, who'd just pulled his hand back from an elaborate brass light switch, to think I wasn't repulsed.

The man looked about forty years old. He was a shade over six feet tall. In good shape. And wearing the uniform of a colonel in the Iranian army. He was standing next to a younger man, a couple of inches shorter than him, who was also in Iranian army uniform. This guy was a corporal. He was holding a DIO assault rifle, and aiming it casually at the floor between my feet. I'd come across that kind of weapon before. I knew its mechanism was essentially an Iranian copy of a Chinese copy of our own M16. I was pretty sure it was less dependable than Asgari's Kalashnikov, which was still within reach. But not sure enough to try anything stupid. Particularly considering what I could see lined up between the corporal and another stack of rugs. A pair of thirty-inch Zero Halliburton aluminum suitcases, in limited-edition camo. The exact kind and finish I'd specified to carry my money. Maybe there was a chance that the deal was still on . . .

"Mr. McGrath, I presume?" The colonel took a step toward me, and I picked up a slight hint of cigar smoke from his uniform. "OK. Your weapons. Now's the time to surrender them."

"Weapons?" I tightened my grip on my backpack. "Why would I have any weapons? I'm a businessman. I'm here to do a deal. That's all. I'm not armed. I came to meet Mr. Asgari. What . . . who did this awful thing to him? What's going on? And who are you, anyway? Why are you here, at this time of night?"

The colonel took another step, making sure to stay far enough to the side to give the corporal a clear shot at me. "In the circumstances I'm sure you'll understand if I don't take your word for any of that. So come on. Cooperate. Legs apart. Arms out, shoulder height. Right now."

I sighed, placed my backpack on the floor, and allowed him to search me. He took his time, starting with my left arm and running his hands all the way from my shoulder to my wrist. He did the same with my right arm, then moved on to my chest, waist, legs, and ankles. He stuck his fingers down into my socks. Checked my pockets. Felt around my belt. Examined my collar. Then leaned down and reached for my pack.

"Oh, no." I snatched up the pack and stepped back. "No you don't. Not so fast. You want this?" I held up the pack. "Then I want those." I pointed toward the Halliburtons.

"That was your arrangement with the late Mr. Asgari?" The colonel raised his chin an inch.

"Correct." I nodded. "My merchandise is very valuable. You want it, you pay for it, the same as he would have done."

"You're sticking to this fairy tale that you came here to *sell* him something?" The colonel shook his head like a disappointed parent.

"Of course." I looked him right in the eye. "And it's not a fairy tale. You can see for yourself. I brought the goods. He brought the money. What else could this be? Unless—he did bring the money? Have you checked inside the cases? Is it all there?"

"It's a plausible story, I grant you." The colonel tipped his head to one side. "You have the physical evidence to cover yourselves. Implicating yourself in one crime to deflect attention from another. That's clever. But we know what was really going on. How much of the money were you going to give him? Half, presumably, as you apparently asked for it to be divided between two equal packages."

"Are you insane?" I glanced at the Halliburtons again. "I asked for two cases because you can't get one case large enough to fit all the money inside. Plus one case would be too heavy for me to move on my own. Because it's all for me. I've earned it. Why on earth would I give any of it to him? He was getting what he wanted." I patted the backpack. "And if you know what's inside here, you want it, too. It stands to reason. So why don't we . . ."

"We know that *Major* Asgari had grown disloyal to our country." A look of profound sorrow clouded the colonel's face for a moment. "We know that he was selling military secrets to our enemies. To the Israelis, originally. And more recently to you Americans. His scheme was ingenious. It took us a while to figure it out. But now we know how it worked. He was assigned to procure certain pieces of technology necessary for the peaceful defense of our nation, unjustly denied to us by the illegitimate cabal of western infidels, the *United Nations*." He almost spat out the words. "Asgari would claim to have brokered a deal. Our government would provide the necessary funds, however exorbitant the amount. But when Asgari met his contact, who was usually a *businessman*"— the colonel glowered at me—"he would pass on highly classified information. In return, he would keep some of the money. Half? Whatever. Anyway, when he returned to Tehran, it would turn out that the device he had bought was a convincing counterfeit, too sophisticated for him to have known. Or that it had conveniently broken on the journey home. Or that he'd discovered it was sabotaged, and had been forced to destroy it for the safety of nearby civilians. Anything to cover the fact that he was tricking our government into effectively paying him huge sums to betray us all. It's disgusting." The colonel paused and took a long look at Asgari's body, still propped up behind and to the side of me. "If you ask me, he deserved a far more . . . protracted end."

"Now, wait just a second, here!" I stepped away, one hand out in front like a cop stopping traffic. "Forget him. What about me?

That would make *me* the American agent in your scenario. Do you really think I'm in the CIA or something? I've seen those guys, at the embassy in Sofia. They stand out from a mile away. I could never be mistaken for one of them, believe me. No. I'm just a businessman. I'm innocent. Well, not *innocent,* exactly, but you know what I mean. I'm not here to buy secrets. I'm here to sell the thing that Asgari came to me and said he wanted. The thing I'm sure your government still wants. The real thing."

"I don't believe you." There was suddenly a layer of steel in the colonel's voice. "I think you're a spy. I should shoot you. Right here. Right now. Or"—he produced a matte black commando knife from behind his back—"perhaps you deserve the same fate as your comrade?"

"Let's not do anything I might regret." I held out my backpack. "You're wrong, and I can prove it. If I was working with Asgari the way you said, then the device in my bag must be a fake. Right? I mean, an American agent isn't going to hand over the actual technology. No way. I'm sure you're right about that part. So, take a look. My merchandise is absolutely genuine. It's the real deal. Exactly as advertised. Meaning I'm only here for the money. *All* of the money. It's cash that I want. I have no interest in any secrets."

The colonel took the pack and held it up for a moment, as if trying to gauge the quality of its contents by its weight. "So this equipment. Where did you get it?"

"The company I work for makes it. In Bulgaria. We supply it to several other NATO governments."

"Then maybe you should forget these other governments. Forget NATO. Forget Bulgaria. Come to Iran. As our guest. You could make more of this equipment. You'd be very comfortable, I promise."

"You don't understand. *I* didn't make the device. Not personally. It takes a whole team. You need specialists. Technicians. Scientists. All kinds of people. It'll do you no good just kidnapping me."

"Then how did you get your hands on the device, if you didn't make it?"

"I work in quality control. I'm head of the department, actually. Equipment like this, as you know, it has to be one hundred percent perfect. There's no room for error. The slightest flaw, the smallest deviation from the spec, the results can be catastrophic. My job is to sign off on the final testing. It gives me the power to reject any item I'm not satisfied with. So—"

"So this is substandard?" The colonel hoisted the pack up high like a medieval executioner brandishing a traitor's severed head. "You admit you're selling defective goods? Dangerous goods?"

The corporal raised his rifle.

"No!" I held up both hands. "Hold on. You're not listening. Let me finish. The device *is* perfect. It's flawless. I only *pretended* it had failed as a way to account for its disappearance. Then I faked the paperwork to make it look like the device had been destroyed. I'd never have been able to get it out of the manufacturing plant, otherwise. Let alone out of the country."

The colonel gestured for the corporal to stand down. "And if an independent expert examined the device? He'd agree with you? He'd say that it's perfect?"

"Absolutely. Assuming he's competent." I crossed my arms. "I'm totally confident. I stand behind my word, one hundred percent."

"OK, then. Good." The colonel snapped his fingers and after a few seconds another man shuffled out from behind a stack of carpets near the rear wall. He was maybe seventy years old, slightly stooped, and also in uniform. Only his tunic lacked any rank designation or regimental insignia. The colonel handed him my backpack. "Let's see about that."

"Wait a minute!" I took a step toward the colonel. "Who is this guy? Does he know what he's doing? The device is very delicate. If he damages it, and tries to claim—"

The corporal raised his rifle again.

"Relax." The colonel flashed me an icy smile. "If you're telling the truth, you have nothing to worry about. If not . . ." He raised the commando knife to eye level and pretended to use the tip of his finger to test its sharpness.

The old guy disappeared behind the stack of carpets again, taking my backpack with him. I made a drama out of wiping my forehead, as if the heat that was building up in the dusty, enclosed space was starting to bother me, then staggered across to lean against Asgari's pile of rugs. I didn't want the colonel to think I was relaxed about being so close to a dead body, but I had no idea what the old guy's verdict was going to be when he was done with his examination. I wanted to be near the only available cover— and weapons—in case things went south. For a moment I even thought about cutting my losses. The corporal had lowered his rifle. He was within easy throwing range. If the knife came cleanly out of Asgari's neck I could hit the corporal in the throat and rush the colonel before either could react.

If the knife came cleanly out. I rejected the idea. It was too risky. And unjustified. I didn't know what the old guy's level of expertise was, but as I'd told the colonel, my merchandise was good. I had to keep the faith. The best option was to just take a breath and wait it out.

The old guy emerged with my backpack fourteen long minutes later and muttered something to the colonel. I couldn't make out his words, but could tell they were in Persian. For a moment the colonel's expression remained neutral, then the tiniest ghost of a frown played across his face.

"It seems I've misjudged you, Mr. McGrath." The colonel took my pack from the old guy. "Your equipment checks out. The secrets Major Asgari was planning to sell must have been destined for another American. My mistake. Although an easy one to make, when dealing with such a degenerate nationality. Regardless, I trust you'll accept my apologies. You're free to go about your business."

I pushed away from the stack of rugs, moved toward the colonel, and held out my hand. He looked down at it and sneered, as if I were offering him a turd on a stick.

"You seriously expect me to shake your hand?" His voice was heavy with contempt.

"No." I kept my hand outstretched. "I expect you to return my property. As your guy said, it checks out. That makes it extremely valuable. I went to a lot of trouble to get it. And I want it back. So unless this whole thing was a shakedown from the start—unless you murdered Asgari and ambushed me just to stage a robbery, which would be a bit rich given the obnoxious air of moral superiority that you can't even be bothered to try to disguise—I'm not leaving till you hand it over."

"And if I refuse?"

"OK, then. Give me the cash instead."

"And if I refuse that, too?"

I stayed silent, feeding the tension for another fifteen seconds. Maybe twenty. Then I spun around, pulled the knife—which did come out cleanly—from Asgari's neck, and turned back to face the colonel.

"You can't refuse!" I tried to inject just the right amount of craziness into my voice, and to brandish the knife as wildly as a drunk I'd seen outside a Glasgow nightclub the one New Year's Eve I'd spent in Scotland. "That's not right. I came here in good faith. Asgari and I had a deal. I ran a huge risk to bring . . ." I paused for a moment. Pulled a puzzled expression. Allowed it to be chased away by a fleeting smile. Then flipped the knife around and offered it to the colonel, handle first. "You know what? You're right. Forget what I was saying. Take my device. Take the money. Go home. And you know where I'll be? Back in Sofia. In my fabulous apartment. On my balcony, a glass of wine in my hand, looking out over the mountains, smiling to myself. Because I'll be picturing the scene: You'll be in Tehran, or wherever you lurk, and your bosses will come to you and say, 'Wow. That equipment you brought back from Istanbul? It's the best. We want more. Get hold of that nice Mr. McGrath and make another deal, immediately!' And you'll have to say, 'Sorry, Ayatollah,' or whoever it is you report to, 'I can't do that. You see, I totally stitched Mr. McGrath up. I took his device and wouldn't pay him, even though there was no reason not to, given that the money was already signed off and all, and now he won't do business with us anymore.' I wouldn't like to be in your shoes when that happens. And you know it will, because your own expert confirmed my stuff is good, and you can't get it anywhere else."

"Payment isn't the only way to persuade you to cooperate, Mr. McGrath." The colonel's eyes had narrowed slightly. "A phone call to your boss? To the police? The American Embassy? The CIA?"

"Saying what?" It was my turn to smile. "I'm way ahead of you. There's no official record of me ever having set foot in Turkey. And the paper trail showing that the device was destroyed is watertight. It's bombproof, in fact. I know because I designed the system. And yes, the detritus from the incinerator is archived, for this exact kind of situation. But you know what? If the residue from the day in question was to be analyzed, the results would show precisely the correct chemical constituents to be there in exactly the right proportions. So if you ever want to make those calls, go ahead. I'll give you my boss's number. The others you can find online, if you don't know them already."

The colonel said nothing. Behind him the corporal fidgeted awkwardly.

"If you ask me, it's time for some strategic thinking." I kept my voice matter-of-fact. "A couple of cases of cash, for a couple of decades of cooperation? Tell me that's not a good deal."

This was it. The close. I could hear my father's voice: *Just stay silent.*

My father, the great deal maker. The great pacifist.

What would he have thought, if he could have seen me at that moment?

He'd probably have despised me all the more.

US Army Field Communications Center
Fort Huachuca, Arizona 85613

January 6th, 2017

Dear Paul,

A great deal of time has passed since we last spoke, let alone since we last saw each other. Far too much time, if you ask me! But please don't get the wrong idea. I'm not writing to admonish you. I know you're busy, and I know you're likely far away, possibly even on another continent. I know you're doing something you believe in, even if that's something I'm not sure I'll ever be able to fully reconcile myself with. And that's part of why I'm writing to you now.

I've been doing a lot of thinking lately, and I've come to a very important conclusion. It's something I think you should know about. I'd have preferred to tell you in person, but since neither of us can predict when we'll next be together, I thought it was better to at least put my thoughts in writing so you'd be fully in the loop. The background to this epiphany—and I don't think it's an exaggeration to call it that—isn't important. The place where I was when it hit me (Haiti, as it happens) and so on—that kind of detail can wait until we're finally face-to-face once again, which I hope will not be too far in the future. But the salient point is this: I have finally, once and for all, unconditionally accepted that whatever you do with the rest of your life—whether you stay in the army, go to Africa to guard elephants, hunt down Yugoslavian war criminals in South America, or pursue any of your other "crazy" (to my way of thinking) schemes—you won't, ever, under any circumstances be joining me in the business. And that's OK! (I bet you wouldn't have expected me to say that, right?) Because I've come up with a solution. A way forward that I hope will work for everyone concerned.

This is what I've decided to do: take on a partner. (If I'm able to select someone from within the company, that would be my preference.) We'll run the business together for the next few years, until I'm ready to retire. Then I'll sell my holding to him or her based on a valuation formula we both agree on up front. That way the company will continue when I step down, no one will lose their jobs, and I'll still be able to pass on to you the fruits of my life's work (albeit in the form of cash, rather than an ongoing enterprise), which is all I've ever wanted to do.

I must also confess that one reason for wanting to let you know about this new plan (this new mind-set—this new me!) right away is the hope that now you know the days of me dropping hints about working together and you moving back to New York (and I know my hints tend to be about as subtle as dropping an anvil on your head) are over—now that the pressure's lifted, now that the elephant's been let out of the room—you might feel a little more inclined to come home for a visit. Even a short one. The truth is, I miss you, son. And I'd give anything to see you more often.

Love,
Dad

PS—Please write and let me know you've received this, and that you're happy with the plan.

PPS—Please also let me know when you expect to reach town! (Joking!!!)

Chapter **Two**

THE ONLY CONSTANT IS CHANGE.

That's what some instructor told me, way back on my first day of basic training. I had no idea what she was talking about. I had no idea what I was doing there, beyond basking in the juvenile glow of having given a symbolic middle finger to my commerce-loving, military-hating father. I had no idea what the army had in store for me, in those naïve days. And no idea that the instructor's words would turn out to be five of the truest ones I'd ever hear. Certainly in terms of how the army is run. And particularly when it came to commanding officers. It seemed like I had a new one every time I was called back to Group Headquarters, which was in Wiesbaden, Germany.

Soldiers seem out of place in offices, I always think. The uniforms. The standing and saluting when senior officers enter a room. The stilted, acronym-ridden phone conversations. And the furniture. Heavy. Utilitarian. Usually a little beaten up. It's all a world away from the civilian workplaces the army so often sends me to infiltrate. It's a culture shock, every time I return. Like waking up in a freaky facsimile of the real world, the same in substance but light-years away in nuance. The only thing a meeting in an army office has going for it is a kind of cultural early warning system. Coffee. If you're offered some, there's a fair chance your encounter will end well.

Lt Colonel Mark Linn—my new CO—did not offer me coffee.

The Lucius D. Clay Kaserne barracks has seen a lot of change over the last century. It started life as a horse-racing track in 1910, and was transformed into a civilian airfield in 1929. The Luftwaffe commandeered it in 1936, and the 80th Infantry Division captured it in 1945. Now the headquarters of the US Army in Europe, the complex has grown to fill every inch of available space. It was almost bursting out of its site—a broad rectangle with one corner snipped off, bounded on the north side by its military airstrip and by a crazy tapestry of farmers' fields on the other three. Aside from the usual offices and stores and gymnasia and parking garages, it also has a baseball diamond. A bowling alley. A commissary. All manner of imported American vehicles scattered everywhere you look. But despite all the familiar sights, every time I was on a plane that landed there those fields hammered home the fact that I wasn't back in the United States. They're too small. Too chaotically crammed together. And too unevenly shaped to ever be mistaken for the geometric uniformity of our own Midwestern landscape.

My unit—the 66th Military Intelligence Brigade—occupied the last of a half-dozen identical buildings on the east side of the base. They were three stories high, built of plain, featureless brick, and each was crowned with a jagged row of narrow, fussy dormer windows. I don't know what the architect had in mind, but the result made each one look like a bizarre collision between a cheap warehouse and a romantic Bavarian castle.

Colonel Linn's office was at the far end of one of the long, impersonal corridors. I'd never been to it before. Linn was the first of my COs to request a new office, rather than take over his predecessor's. I don't know why he did that. Maybe he liked having to walk farther from the main entrance. Maybe he preferred a more compact workspace. Maybe he was partial to the view from the top floor, although that was hard to judge the morning of our meeting because he had the frayed, steel gray blinds pulled all the way down. My guess was that he was attempting to stage some kind of political game. I'd seen plenty of those play out during my various forays into the private sector. And Linn certainly seemed the ambitious type. Tall, wiry, with the restless energy of a long-distance runner, he was the youngest-looking light colonel I'd ever set eyes on. I was idly trying to figure how much field time he could possibly have under his belt, and wondering if it would be worth calling in a favor to get a peek at his service record, when he finally stopped staring at me across his bare metal desk and decided to get the ball rolling.

"Just back from the Balkans, I see." Linn leaned back and steepled his fingers. "You kept yourself busy. I've been reading your report."

"Sir."

"Some interesting news coming out of Iran, by the way. I don't know if you heard, but we've had word of an explosion. A large one. Just outside Isfahan, near the airport."

"Do we know the cause?"

"The Iranian government's saying it was an accident. At the Mobarakeh steel plant. Something to do with a faulty oxygen injector unbalancing one of the blast furnaces."

"Do we believe them?"

"Our friends in the Mossad certainly don't. They have plenty of boots on the ground over there, as you know. And they're saying the blast came from somewhere else. Somewhere close to the steel plant, to disguise its power requirements and heat signature. But underground. And whatever it is, it's now leaking radioactive isotopes."

I allowed myself a brief smile. "Like the kind of place where solid-state uranium gets converted to gas, and back again. Part of the enrichment process. The plant did exist."

"It did." Linn nodded. "But it doesn't anymore. Thanks to you. The Mossad scientists are saying that losing it'll set the Iranian nuclear program back eighteen months, minimum. Good work, Paul. This is a major result. Success on this level, it's career defining. In any other branch of the service, we'd be giving you a medal."

"Sir."

"There is one part of your report that I have some questions about, though." Linn tipped his head to the side. "I need you to clarify something for me."

"Of course." I settled back in my chair. "What do you need to know?"

"Now, look, Paul. Don't take this the wrong way." Linn held out his hands, palms first. "You clearly did an outstanding job of convincing the Iranians that the piece of equipment you were 'selling' was genuine. They wouldn't have installed it at their conversion plant and blown themselves to kingdom come, otherwise. And the circumstances you were operating in were clearly challenging. Your contact had been caught double-crossing his bosses and was murdered practically under your nose. New players unexpectedly entered the arena, including a senior officer and a technical expert. You had to think on your feet. I get that. But there's one part of the way things went down that . . . troubles me."

"I see." I kept my voice calm and level. "Which part?"

"The money. The belligerent way you demanded it. The fact you demanded it at all, actually. You'd achieved your mission objective, which was to make them trust in the device. So why didn't you withdraw at that point? Why stay in the hot zone? Why risk antagonizing those guys? You could have blown the whole operation. You could have gotten yourself killed. It makes your judgment appear . . . questionable, to say the least."

"With respect, sir, if you think that, you need to reread my report." *Or try spending some time in the field.* "Holding out for the money was the key to convincing them. Everything else was just set dressing. If I'd tried to walk away without it, I'd have gotten a bullet in the back and the device would have ended up in pieces at the bottom of the Bosporus."

"Explain."

"We knew the Iranians were going to be hyper-vigilant. Think of all the success the Israelis have had against them recently. The faulty raw materials they've inserted into the supply chain. The bogus plans. The sabotaged equipment. The computer viruses. That's why the Iranians came looking for an American in the first place. They'd been burned by their usual contacts too many times. So they cooked up the whole scene at the carpet store as an elaborate test."

"Including killing their own guy, Asgari?" Linn attempted a smile. "Or was it a *coincidence* that he turned out to be a traitor?"

"No one in our business believes in coincidences." I kept my expression neutral. "And while killing Asgari would have been hard-core, I wouldn't put it past them. But that wasn't what happened. I don't think Asgari's a traitor at all. And I don't think he's dead."

"You said he was." Linn leaned forward.

"No." I shook my head. "I described the scene. You drew the conclusion. The wrong conclusion. I did, too, at first. Though not for long."

"Why's it the wrong conclusion?" Horizontal creases appeared in Linn's forehead. "What's the problem with it?"

"There are three problems with it." I raised my right thumb, to start counting them off. "First, the blood. There was too much."

"You said he'd been stabbed to death." Linn crossed his arms. "There was bound to be a lot of blood."

"No." I shook my head again. "Not in that scenario. For Asgari's body to be propped up as it was he'd have had to be killed instantly. Otherwise he'd have turned to fight back. Or fallen to the ground, writhing in agony. Or whatever. Which means his spinal cord would have had to be severed, which would have caused his heart to stop beating right away. There should have been no significant arterial spray. And as he was upright, most of his blood would have been below the wound so without his heart pumping, gravity would have kept it inside his body. Plus the blade was still in place, stopping up the hole and reducing any leakage."

Linn steepled his fingers again and scowled.

"Second problem." I didn't wait for him to comment. "The smell. There wasn't any. With that amount of blood, the place should have stunk like an abattoir. It didn't. There was just a slight hint of hessian and sweet tea. I could even pick up the cigar smoke on the colonel's uniform, the air was so fresh."

"I guess only someone who was there would be able to judge that." Linn's scowl deepened. "And the third problem?"

"The knife. It came out of Asgari's neck way too easily. When a blade gets jammed between two vertebra—even the little ones, higher up—you have to really pull to get it back. This one almost fell out. I don't think it had even broken the skin."

"So Asgari was just acting the whole time? He was that good?"

"No one's that good. More likely he was drugged. Something to bring on temporary paralysis. Etorphine, maybe. M99. That's what I'd use."

"I still don't see why." Linn shrugged. "How does any of this help them to evaluate the device?"

"It doesn't. That's the point. How could they evaluate the device? It's based on technology they're not allowed to have. They have zero experience with it. They can't build a test bed for it, because that technology's banned, too. So what would they compare it to? It's an absurd proposition. Does one thing they've never used work the same as another thing they've never used? And it's full of ultra-miniaturized circuitry, remember. There's no way to tell if that stuff's genuine without all kinds of specialized diagnostic equipment. So no. They weren't testing the device. They were testing me."

"How? By throwing a corpse at you, and a bunch of blood, and seeing if you'd blow your cover?"

"In a way. It's like my old sensei used to say. When you attack, never go with one technique. Go with at least three, in case the first couple don't work. And keep the best till last. If I'd fallen for the thing with Asgari's body, then great. That would have been like me walking into a sucker punch. It would have been a bonus for them. They could have gone home early. Same with the accusation about me being an agent, and the old guy who was posing as an expert. But when I parried those blows, it didn't matter. They could back off, leaving me to think I'd survived their onslaught. Get me to drop my guard. Because what they really needed to do was figure out my motivation."

"Wasn't that obvious?"

"No. Not at all." I looked down at the floor for a moment. "Let me tell you something. About my grandfather. He was Irish, so naturally during World War II he worked for British Intelligence. For the section that handled double agents. His team was extraordinarily good. So good that every single agent the Nazis sent to Great Britain was captured, and either killed or turned.

Every single one. Meaning every single report that went back to Germany was planted. The flow of misinformation was vital. D-Day couldn't have succeeded without it, for example. So they were under huge pressure to keep the operation running. But they had a giant problem. Do you know what that was?"

"Trust?" Linn shrugged. "They were dealing with doubles. How can you rely on them?"

I shook my head. "No. It was making sure the enemy agents got paid. You get the occasional spy who's driven by ideology, sure. But as a rule spies are mercenary bastards. If they don't get paid, they don't produce. Now, normally that's an advantage. If you cut off their funds, you cut off the threat. Stopping the money was the first thing the counter-Intelligence guys always tried to do. It was S.O.P. And the Germans knew that. So if the British hadn't gone after the payments, the Germans would have been suspicious. And if they'd received intel from spies who weren't getting paid, they'd have known the information was bogus and wouldn't have trusted it."

"So how did the Brits fix it?" Linn looked genuinely interested.

"It's a brilliant story." I paused for a moment. "You'll love it. But I'll tell you another time. The point is, last week, back in that carpet store in Istanbul, *I* was supposed to be the mercenary bastard. If I'd given them something without at least pushing to get paid for it, they'd have known not to trust me. My goal would have been obvious. Planting the device. Fighting for the money was the only way to disguise that. It was the clincher. I guarantee it."

Linn stood up and turned to the window behind his desk. He pulled the edge of the blind aside an inch, spent a moment gazing through the slender gap, then let it fall back into place.

"OK." He sat back down and laid his hands flat on the desktop. "Let's say I believe you. My next question is, what did you do with the money after they gave it to you?"

"Took it back to Sofia, like I wrote in my report. Why?"

"And then what?"

"I hid it in a storage unit on the outskirts of the city. That's also in my report. Along with the address. Why do you ask?"

"Why take it there? Why not take it to the embassy and have it properly vouchered?"

"The embassy's the last place I could have taken it. I had to assume there'd be GPS trackers in the cases. Maybe even transponders in some of the notes or the bill wrappers. The Iranians aren't stupid. They'd have been fools not to have taken that kind of precaution. It would have given them an extra safety net. They believed the device was genuine after our meeting, sure. But if they'd watched that cash make its way to a US embassy, or an army base, or anyplace we were known to use, the whole ruse would have been blown on the spot."

Linn didn't comment, and I noticed he was doing his best not to look at me.

"Sir, what aren't you telling me?" I leaned forward, trying to catch his eye.

"I was reading your file this morning, as well as your report." Linn raised his head. "Your current tour. It's just about over, isn't it? So I have to ask: Are you planning to re-up?"

"*Why* do you *have to* ask?" I crossed my arms.

"Because we have a problem, Paul." Linn sighed. "When word of the explosion in Isfahan reached us, we sent two guys to the storage unit you listed. Their job was to collect the money. When they got there, the unit was empty. The lock hadn't been forced. There was no sign of any cash. And now I've got a Major Turner and a couple of MPs from the 110th crawling up my ass. They're saying, a stash like that? It would make a nice little nest egg for a newly retired officer . . ."

Chapter **Three**

ONE DAY, A WEEK OR SO AFTER I TURNED EIGHTEEN, I SNEAKED into Manhattan with a couple of buddies from high school. We didn't have much of a plan. We were just thinking we'd hit a couple of bars, drink a few beers, see what the city had to offer . . .

Everything was going fine until the second place we tried. It wasn't the most salubrious of establishments, which wasn't surprising given that most of its revenue seemed to come from selling watered-down drinks to underage kids with sketchy fake IDs. Anyway, a girl latched onto me the moment I set foot through the door. She was tall. Blond. I guess you could say she was gorgeous, although I wasn't interested that way because I already had my eye on someone else. So I bought her a drink, just to be polite. We started to talk. Then a guy came into the bar. He was maybe in his early twenties. He had greasy hair down to his shoulders and a plaid shirt worn open over a black T-shirt with some kind of slogan about the devil printed on it. I didn't pay him too much attention at first. Not until he squeezed by me and walked up to a couple at the next table. He didn't say anything to them. He just stood stock-still between a pair of empty chairs for thirty, maybe forty seconds. Then he pulled out a .38 Special from the waistband at the back of his pants. Shot both of them in the head. Paused for another second. And finally turned the gun on himself.

The sound was stunning in such a confined space. Pieces of skull and brain were sprayed across the table and floor and wall. A fine haze of blood hung in the air, highlighted by the broad shaft of sunlight shining in through the open door. All around me people were diving for cover, shrieking, crying, covering their heads with their arms, or trying to run for the exits. But for some reason the mayhem didn't affect me the same way. The girl I'd been talking to was one of the first to make for the fire escape. I wasn't too interested in catching up with her so I stayed in my seat. Checked my clothes for anyone else's body parts. Finished my beer. Rounded up my cowering buddies. And split before the police arrived.

I thought we'd gotten away clean, but there was one thing I hadn't realized about that bar. It had a security camera concealed high up in the corner near the main entrance. That wasn't something I was in the habit of thinking about in those days. Somehow footage of the shooting made it onto CNN. Inevitably my father saw it. He went absolutely crazy. Not because it showed me sitting in the bar. And not because I had a beer in my hand. But because he thought I looked way too comfortable in such proximity to the violence. He said it revealed a deep flaw in my character. Words like *psychopath* were used. More than once. He insisted that I get help, and ultimately demanded that I sign up for cognitive behavioral therapy.

Instead I got a haircut, and I signed up for the infantry.

My decision to join the army had been impetuous, driven by a re-action to something my father had said, so I guess it was only fit-ting that my decision to leave was made the same way.

There were *some* practical considerations, sure. I couldn't go back to the Balkans—there's no way I could expect to dupe the Iranians twice—so I'd have to wait around for a new posting. That wouldn't happen until the MPs officially signed off on me having nothing to do with the disappearance of the money in Sofia. There was no doubt that they'd clear me. My guess was the Iranians had been tracking it, and came to get it back after their plant exploded, as they'd no longer need to keep me sweet as an illicit supplier. But it could just as easily have been some local guy. Someone who worked at the storage facility. When you deliberately seek out a low-rent, no-questions-asked type of place, you can't be too sur-prised when things blow up in your face. The only issue was how long the cage-kickers would take to process the paperwork. And even when they did, it's hard to wash the stink of something like that completely off your hands. How do you prove you didn't do a thing if there's no concrete evidence that someone else did? Espe-cially when you have years of training and experience in conceal-ing just the kind of underhanded thing they think you might have done. So who knew where my next assignment would be? And while I waited to find out, I'd be tethered to a desk. That prospect did weigh on my mind. But what really swayed me were the words my father had written, two years earlier.

Wedged between a fidgety Buddhist monk and an overweight college student on a flight from Frankfurt to JFK, I pulled the letter out of my jacket pocket for the twentieth time since leaving the Wiesbaden barracks and traced the jumbled series of markings plastered across both sides of the ragged envelope. From what I could make out it had followed me twice around the globe, nar-rowly missing me at a series of postings—London, Sarajevo, Beijing, and a dozen more—until an exasperated clerk at the embassy in Manila sent it back to the center in Arizona that's responsible for vetting mail and forwarding it to operatives working under-cover. It's a necessary process, to ensure that secret locations aren't compromised. I was warned when I first transferred to Military Intelligence that it could cause delays in communications, but a two-year wait for a letter? That had to be a new record. And what kind of letter? A bill? A speeding ticket? No. An olive branch from my father. Something I'd waited decades for. He'd asked for a quick reply, and must have thought I'd blown him off in return. Again. Another strike against me, as a son. And another entry in the debit column of our relationship. I just hoped he'd still be talk-ing to me when I finally reached his house.

The plane banked steeply as it started its final descent, and I caught a glimpse of Manhattan through the window. It gave me the same warm thrill as it did when I was a kid and my father drove us down from Westchester to visit the Bronx Zoo or the Met or go to a Yankees game. I leaned a little closer to the monk and gazed down at the grid of streets, refreshingly modern and uniform after the antique chaos of Sofia and Istanbul. All my favorite buildings—the Empire State, the Chrysler, the CitiCorp—were there, reaching up to greet me like old friends.

Well, almost all my favorite buildings. I hadn't been back to New York since 9/11, so that was the first time I'd seen the city without the World Trade Center and I was shocked by how much the skyline had altered. I was one of the few people who'd liked the Twin Towers, I guess. I was drawn to their elegant simplicity. I appreciated the stark honesty of their design. I'd never been able to stomach the idea of replacing them with something that claimed to be a certain symbolic height but really came up four hundred feet short, and had to hide behind a giant antenna to make up the difference. Seeing the concept fleshed out in metal and glass made it no more palatable.

The rental car I collected at the airport came with GPS, but I didn't use it. That was partly out of habit—why make it easy for people to trace where I've been?—but mainly because I didn't care which route the system thought would be the fastest. I was navigating by nostalgia, not logic. So I ignored the stream of vehicles making for 678—usually the sensible choice—and headed for the Throgs Neck Bridge, instead.

Throgs Neck. I'd loved that name when I was a kid. I had no idea what a Throg was, but that didn't matter. In my mind I pictured it as a hideous troll-like creature lying in wait under the bridge, ready to spring out and lay waste to any cars that dared to pass. When I was very little I'd close my eyes and pray we'd get all the way across without being attacked. When I grew a little older I imagined the Throg leaping out in front of us, causing my father to abandon his pacifist principles and fight it off, hurling its bloodied body over the railing to sink without a trace in the murky water of the East River. Then one day, after some meaningless adolescent argument, I saw myself trouncing the grotesque beast. The fantasies seemed harmless at the time. Nothing more than innocuous diversions to help pass the time cooped up in the car. But later in life they actually served a useful purpose, providing endless fodder for me to torment the army shrinks with at the regular checkups they make all us undercover guys go through.

I made it safely across the river and again ignored the Hutchinson, staying on 95 until it reached the Bronx River Parkway. I continued past the botanical garden, which was having an orchid show that day, cut across Gun Hill, through Van Cortlandt Park, and found my way onto the Saw Mill River Parkway. That had always been my father's favorite route. He preferred it to the newer, faster alternatives. He thought it was more picturesque, with its sweeping tree-lined curves that gave occasional glimpses of the river, and he never missed an opportunity to lecture me about the value of spending a little time in search of the finer things in life. I'd thought he was crazy. To me, the finer things were all in the city. How could you find them by driving in the opposite direction? I remember swiveling around in my seat and staring through the rear window as the faded pavement unspooled in the wrong direction. I used to feel it physically, a tugging in my gut like I was attached to the metropolis by an invisible umbilical cord that was being stretched to the breaking point by the unwanted drive north.

I guess I'd been too young to understand the sentimental attachment my father had felt for our home. To me, it had just been a house. A place to wake up in. To eat breakfast. To play. To come back to after school. Where I'd do my chores. My homework. And all the other mundane activities of small-town life. But to him, I realized later, it had become a shrine to my mother. She'd died there, in an upstairs bedroom, giving birth to a little girl. I was less than three years old at the time. I hardly remembered her. And I never saw my sister. The baby only survived for a few minutes. I'd been too young to understand, even as a teenager, or in the first few years after leaving home. All I'd known was that the bedroom she'd used for the ill-fated delivery was strictly off-limits for everyone except my father. It was kept permanently locked, and he was the only one with the key. Now I could appreciate what it meant to him, and it was clear that my father would never move away. Not of his own free will.

I exited the Saw Mill at the turn for Mount Kisco Country Club, cutting through the leafy streets south of the town and heading toward Bedford. I used to like driving that way because it took me past a house where a girl I liked lived. Marian Sinclair. She was in the class below me in high school. We were inseparable for a while. We went everywhere together. Did everything together. Talked about going to college together. And then the army happened . . .

I knew I must be getting close to my destination, but the area was growing less familiar, not more. There were dozens of houses I'd not seen before. They were larger than the ones I remembered in the neighborhood. Brash. Bold. And closer to the road. It's like they were desperate to be seen, unlike the more discreet, better-mannered properties my friends and I had lived in. Plus these places had no discernible style. They were a shambolic mishmash of components. Oversized. Out of proportion. Screaming money rather than taste. I picked up speed, the warm glow I'd started to feel now sullied by the sight of them, and hurried to find the two right turns that would lead the rest of the way to my father's driveway.

The house looked older than I'd remembered. Its cedar siding was much paler. It had grown silvery, like an aging man's hair. And the structure seemed dated now. The sharp angles of its contrasting planes had become stark and clichéd, rather than sleek and avant-garde. The crunch of the gravel under the car tires still sounded the same, though. I pulled up in the parking area near the path that led to the front door. The driveway broadened out at that point, temporarily, before continuing and sweeping around to the basement-level garage. My father had considered remodeling the yard several times to change the shape of the driveway, but he couldn't find a way to do it without making access to the garage less convenient. That was a deal breaker. He wouldn't tolerate anything that prevented him from getting his car out easily. He had a four-stall garage, but I'd only ever known him to have one car, so that meant he had plenty of space for it. And he always picked something sensible and boring, like a Cadillac. I was always pushing him to get something rare and exotic, even if it was just for the weekends. He kept saying he might, as long as it was American. Like maybe a Duesenberg, or a Studebaker. I remember waiting impatiently each month for the new issue of my classic car magazine to be delivered so that I could trawl through the "for sale" ads. I presented him with plenty of options. But he never followed through on any. As far as I knew.

I switched off the engine and climbed out of the car. I took a moment to stretch and immediately was struck by the smell of the air. It was warm, dry, and heavy with the scent of flowering shrubs and sun-bleached cedar wood. The precise aroma was unlike anything else I'd encountered, anywhere in the world. You could blindfold me and drop me in my father's yard, and I'd know exactly where I was. I smiled at the memories that were suddenly flooding back, resisted the temptation to jump over the white picket fence as I'd done so many times as a child, and carefully opened the gate instead.

I followed the rustic brick path up the gentle slope to the covered porch at the front of the house. A pair of heavy terra-cotta urns stood on either side of the door, overflowing as always with tangles of bright flowers. Carriage lights were burning above them, even though it was bright daylight. That was typical of my father. He was tightfisted about everything, unless it held some kind of symbolic value. I shook my head and pulled the handle that operated the elaborate bell. I always thought the deep clanging it produced wouldn't have sounded out of place in a cathedral.

The low, afternoon sun was warm on the back of my neck as I waited for an answer. A bird started to sing—something small, maybe a sparrow?—and the wind rustled through the few leaves that were still clinging to the trees and stirred the patches of wildflowers and long spindly grasses where my father had long ago tried to restore the area's native landscape. Somewhere in the distance a leaf blower started up. That had been the constant, intrusive, unwelcome soundtrack of my childhood. I'd always said that if I never heard that noise again, I could die happy.

A minute later the door opened and a woman peered out at me. It was Mrs. Vincent. My father's housekeeper. She'd moved in with us a few months after my mother died. I remembered her as being boundlessly energetic. She never had a cross word, for me or any of my unruly friends, and was unfailingly positive and enthusiastic. Now, she just looked small and thin. I guessed the years since I last saw her had taken their toll.

Mrs. Vincent was silent for a moment. She looked puzzled, as if she didn't recognize me. Then she burst into an uncontrollable flood of tears.

"Paul?" She pulled a tissue from her pocket and dabbed urgently at her eyes. "Is it really you?"

"It's been a while, Mrs. V." I reached out to take her hand. "But, yes. It's really me."

She pulled her hand away and took a quick step back. "Have you come to throw me out?"

Inside the house, everything seemed virtually identical to how it had been when I'd left. The paint was fresh, but was the same shade of lemon yellow I'd never liked. The floors had been refinished, but were the same pale oak I was always scared of scratching. Some of the furniture looked a little faded, but the same pieces were still in the same places. There were only a few things that had been added—a floral pattern china bowl on the narrow table near the door for holding keys, a cut crystal flower vase, a recent picture of my father in an ornate silver frame—making them stand out as if I was looking at one of those photographs that are edited to make one color vivid and the others washed out.

I followed Mrs. Vincent through the arch from the hallway to the living room and sat opposite her on one of the white fabric couches my father had always been obsessed with keeping clean. She seemed to need a minute to compose herself, so I passed the time by scanning the familiar spines of the books on the cases that surrounded us, covering all the available wall space.

"You're going to have to talk me through this slowly, please, Mrs. Vincent," I said when her breathing had returned to somewhere near normal. "Why do you think anyone would want to kick you out of the house? Least of all me?"

"Well, Mr. Ferguson—your father's lawyer, do you remember him?—he warned me this arrangement might not last forever." She pulled out another Kleenex and held it on her lap, just in case. "He made it perfectly clear—everything was pending your approval. And this place is a valuable asset, obviously. You never come here. So you probably want to sell."

"My approval?" I held up my hands. "This arrangement? I don't understand a word you're saying. Sell the house? That's crazy. Where's my father? What does he think about all this?"

"Don't you know? Isn't that—" Mrs. Vincent stopped abruptly and turned away. When she turned back, she couldn't look me in the eye. "Isn't that why you came back? Didn't you get Mr. Ferguson's letter?"

"I did get a letter, but it's from my father." I took it out of my pocket to show her. "It's two years old. It got lost in the system. The army—it doesn't matter. The point is, I haven't heard from any lawyer. Why would I have?"

"Paul, I'm so sorry." Mrs. Vincent closed her eyes for a moment. "I thought you knew. Mr. Ferguson's been trying to reach you. There's no easy way to tell you this, so I'm just going to blurt it out. Paul, your father passed away."

Chapter *Four*

Mrs. Vincent offered to make a bed up for me, but there was no way I could stay in that house. Not until I'd gotten things a lot straighter in my head. I did take a look in my father's study, though, before I left.

His study. The room where he died.

According to Mrs. Vincent, my father had a meeting in there less than an hour before he collapsed. She said it sounded like a fight had broken out. At first, it had been verbal. Then it became physical. Voices were raised. Objects were thrown. She said she'd heard things smashing against the walls and on the floor. I made her repeat that part, because anything approaching violence was so out of character for my father. But she was adamant. She said the debris was still strewn around when the police and the paramedics arrived.

I asked her who my father had been arguing with. She said it was a guy named Alex Pardew. His business partner.

She didn't have to add that my father only had a partner because I'd refused to join him in the business . . .

I stumbled out of the house as if I was in a trance and made my way down the path. I went through the gate. Climbed into the car. Started it up. Hit the Return to Depot button on the GPS screen and unthinkingly followed the disembodied directions, street by street, turn by turn, mile by mile, until I found myself bouncing over the vicious-looking one-way anti-theft spikes set into the asphalt at the entrance to the multistory rental lot back at JFK.

I don't remember a thing about the drive. I paid no attention to the route I took. I didn't even feel a pull toward the city as I drew close, before presumably peeling off toward Queens. I just wanted to be somewhere quiet. Somewhere I could be on my own. So as soon as the paperwork was dealt with I grabbed my army duffel from the trunk of the car and wandered through the airport's bewildering warren of anonymous corridors and walkways until I saw a sign for a hotel. I checked in, but only for one night. Trying to think any further ahead at that stage was completely pointless.

The room I ended up with was like any one of hundreds I've been in, all around the world. The carpet was an inoffensive, neutral shade of gray, but the material it was made from was coarse and scratchy. The kind that's designed with suitcase wheels in mind, rather than a tired traveler's feet. The bedcovers were plastered with bright, abstract designs. Which is pleasant enough, until you think about how the real purpose of the patterns is to cover up all the marks and stains left behind by previous occupants. I looked around, appraised every feature, and figured there were only two main things that set the place apart. How much it cost. And that I was there as a private citizen.

I didn't sweep the room for bugs. I didn't map out alternative escape routes. I didn't jam a rubber wedge under the door. I just slumped in the under-stuffed armchair by the window and pulled out my father's letter. Two years it had taken to reach me. My father had died six months ago, according to Mrs. Vincent. If the letter had arrived in any kind of reasonable time, I'd have had the chance to see him. If the army hadn't screwed up the delivery, we could have made our peace. If I hadn't ever joined the army . . .

If. If. If.

A sharp knock at the door broke my chain of thought.

"Mr. McGrath?" It was a man's voice. He was loud and insistent. "New York City detectives. Open the door."

I dragged myself out of the chair, crossed the room, and peered out through the peephole in the door. Two guys were standing in the corridor. Both looked to be in their mid-thirties. They were wearing dark, somewhat shapeless suits. Gold shields were displayed in wallets that were hooked into their breast pockets. Both had pale shirts. One had a striped tie. The other's was plain. One was small and wiry. He was pulsing with energy and couldn't quite keep still. The other was tall. He was broad, without being fat. He looked solid and immovable. I opened the door six inches and glared at each of them in turn.

"I'm Detective Atkinson." The skinny guy nodded toward his partner. "This is Detective Kanchelskis. We have a couple of questions we'd like to ask you."

"Can't this wait? It's really not a convenient time, right now."

"When a person of interest in a case shows signs of fleeing the jurisdiction, we're not too worried about their convenience." Kanchelskis took a step toward the door. "Not as a general rule."

"I'm not very interesting. Trust me. And I'm not fleeing anything. I'm arriving. I have no travel plans at all. Why don't you check with the airlines and leave me alone?"

"We just have a couple of questions." Atkinson's tone was more conciliatory. "They're important, or we wouldn't be bothering you at your hotel like this. They won't take long. And it would be a lot more *convenient* to talk in your room, rather than having to relocate to our station house."

I sighed, then opened the door the rest of the way and gestured for the detectives to come inside. Atkinson flashed a smile at me, then slid past, pulled a chair out from under the desk, turned it around, and sat down. Kanchelskis stayed by the door, his hands in his pockets. I returned to the armchair near the window.

"Is this about my father?" I leaned back against the unsupportive cushion.

"Why would you assume that?" Atkinson glanced at his partner.

"Well, here's the thing, Detective." I straightened up again and rubbed my spine. "I've been a civilian for less than eighteen hours. Nine of those I spent on a plane. Four, in a car. One, talking to an old lady. And say another one dealing with rental cars and airport bullshit. That leaves under three hours, and there's a limit to how much trouble a person can get themselves into during that length of time. I mean, it's conceivable that I broke a couple of speed limits earlier. Maybe ran a red light. But are those the kind of things that would bring a pair of detectives running to my doorstep?"

Atkinson raised an eyebrow.

"And there's the fact that only one person knew I was going to stay at an airport hotel tonight. Mrs. Vincent. My father's housekeeper. I was just with her, up at his home. I did nothing suspicious while I was there. Nothing to make her think a call to New York's finest was necessary. Which means she was acting on instructions. I'm guessing yours. Look, I get how this works. A man suddenly dies. You have to rule out funny business, so you play the percentages. You talk to the family. Which in my father's case is just me. And you can add to that the fact that I wasn't around in the aftermath of his death, so you didn't get the chance to question me before."

"That's right." Kanchelskis glared at me and folded his arms. "You weren't around. You and your father were on bad terms. You had been for years, from what we hear. Plus you were in the army, meaning you have the kind of know-how to make someone disappear. If you had the correct motivation. Which you did, because you stood to lose a lot of money if your father went ahead and sold his company on the cheap to his partner, instead of leaving it to you."

"Oh, cui bono?" I nodded as if I'd been hit by a profound revelation. "Who benefits? You are playing this by the book, aren't you, Detective? But you're way off the mark. My father wasn't going to sell on the cheap. The reason he brought in a partner was to guarantee a fair price, and to ensure the company would continue in good hands. He knew I had no interest in the business, but was going to leave me the proceeds anyway. I had absolutely nothing to gain by killing him. Here, let me show you something."

I reached for my pocket, and right away the detectives went for their guns.

"Settle down, gentlemen!" I held up my hands. "They do say the pen is mightier than the sword, but there's no need to panic. I have a letter here, from my father. You need to read it. Then you'll understand the background to the whole situation."

I handed the letter to Kanchelskis. He read it slowly and passed it to Atkinson.

"That thing's two years old." Kanchelskis's expression was hovering somewhere between suspicion and disgust.

"I know. But I only just got it. The army has a system for—the details don't matter. Long story short, the letter got sent to all kinds of places around the world before it reached me. I came as soon as I could after finally getting it."

"It's ancient history. There's nothing in it we didn't already know. But one thing does really jump out." Kanchelskis narrowed his eyes. "You don't show up for your father's funeral, and then come running as soon as there's a mention of money?"

My father's funeral. What was wrong with me? I hadn't even thought about that. Where had it been held? When? Did anyone come? We don't have any other family. Did anyone speak? The sudden rush of questions was bad. But worse was the knowledge that my father must have gone into the ground still believing I'd forsaken him.

"It wasn't like that." I shook my head and dragged my mind back to the present. "I didn't even know my father was dead. If there was a letter telling me, then that was delayed, too. I only found out just now, when Mrs. Vincent told me."

"Really?" Kanchelskis's voice was heavy with disdain. "You were waiting for a letter? What century are you living in? No one could call you? Send you an email?"

"Actually, no. I was posted to some sensitive areas overseas. The only kind of permitted contact was snail mail."

"I can believe that." Atkinson cleared his throat. "My brother's in the navy. He's a weapon systems techician. We're never allowed to know where he's stationed, either. We can't call him. Or use email. Not even his wife can. And if any of us want to send him anything, like for his birthday or whatever, it has to go via some central place. It can take ages to reach him. Two years for a letter is extreme, though."

"The army mail system is not the issue here." Kanchelskis scowled. "Tell me, Mr. McGrath, where were you on March 5th?"

"Why?"

"Because that's the day your father died."

My father died on March 5th? I hadn't known the exact date. It was like I was being crushed beneath all these unknown details.

I could feel them like a weight on my chest. I took a moment and focused on continuing to breathe. Then I thought back to early March. I'd been in Afghanistan the whole first week. Most of it bivouacing in a cave. I'd been waiting for a contact to show up. He was supposed to bring me a "borrowed" laptop. I was there to make a clone of it, so that we could unscramble the data and read the contents without the owner knowing.

My contact was days late. I waited for him way longer than procedure dictated I should. But the kid did appear in the end. I ran the copying process as quickly as I could, but by the time the kid left to return the laptop he knew he'd have to hurry so it wouldn't be missed. Its owner was due back from a trip to Kabul on March 8th, which was cutting things close.

I was surprised to see the kid retracing his steps ten minutes later. Then I understood. He realized he'd just then picked up a tail, so had started back toward the rendezvous point in the hope that whoever was following him would think he hadn't delivered the laptop yet, meaning the contents weren't compromised. It was a crazy plan. The only way for it to work was for him to be killed before he reached the cave. It was agony, watching him weave his way through the rocks and gullies at well below his previous pace.

The kid's plan worked. He took two rounds in the back. So when I returned his attacker's fire, I made sure to miss. I needed the guy to report back that he'd foiled the delivery, or the kid's death would have been in vain. In the end I made sure it was worth something, though. The information we pulled from the cloned computer saved at least a dozen other lives.

"I can't tell you where I was on March 5th." It took a conscious effort to push away the memory of the kid's body sprawling between two giant rocks, his blood soaking into the sand from the gaping holes between his shoulder blades. "Only that I was deployed overseas."

"How convenient." Kanchelskis's lips twisted into a sneer.

"Not really." I turned to stare at him. "How is it convenient? It would be convenient if I'd been at Disney World with a bunch of witnesses and miles of security footage to prove it."

"Claiming you were overseas isn't good enough." Kanchelskis folded his arms. "We need more."

"OK." I nodded. "I'll have my ex-CO get in contact with you. He can vouch that I was on an operation, outside of the United States, on the relevant date."

"That's still not good enough." Kanchelskis shook his head.

"It's the best you're going to get."

"Give us your CO's contact information. We'll get in touch with him."

"Fine." I held out my hand. "Pass me that pad from the desk. I'll write it down."

"And we'll be back if we have any more questions. So don't leave town." He nodded to Atkinson. "You ready?"

"Mind fetching the car?" Atkinson drummed his fingers on the desktop. "I'll meet you out front in a minute."

Kanchelskis grunted, then left, and Atkinson waited for his footsteps to die away along the corridor.

"I apologize for my partner." He shot me a weak smile. "Kanchelskis was born extra suspicious, I guess."

"That's an understandable trait in a detective." I nodded. "You're telling me you're not suspicious, as well?"

"Maybe I am." He looked away. "But in a different way."

"Different how?"

"Kanchelskis, he thought maybe you had something to do with your father's death, and then stayed out of sight till the dust settled. Me, I come from a military family, too. I know how long it can take to hear news, and then get away from your posting. And I know how some army people think. They can get used to coloring outside of the lines. And to finding violent solutions to certain kinds of problems. So I thought, maybe you'd come back to look for your father's partner, given what happened."

"What did happen, exactly?" I paused. "You've got to understand, when I came back—today—I thought my father was still alive. The fact that he's not is news to me. I'm still processing it. So why would I look for his partner? I don't know anything about the guy. All I heard is that my father apparently had a screaming match with him on the night he died."

"The screaming match part is correct." Atkinson's fingers drummed a little louder on the cheap wood. "OK. I'll give you some background. You've read your father's letter, so you know he was planning to sell his company to his partner. The price was going to be based on a formula they signed up to at the outset. Now, from what our finance guys tell me, your father was pretty old-school. These days, most businesses try to avoid owning too many assets. They prefer to lease their buildings and equipment and so on, to keep the value of their balance sheets as low as possible. That way, all the things their shareholders care about, like return on investmest or whatever, appear much greater. Your father wasn't like that."

"I can believe that." I could hear my father's voice in my head. "I remember his lectures, from way back when he was still hoping I'd join the business. He didn't have any shareholders, so he could run the company whichever way he wanted. He thought those accounting tricks were bullshit. And to him, it was always better to have something than not to have it. He was like a handyman with a garage full of nails and screws and nuts and bolts. If you have the spare parts, you can use them somewhere down the line. If you don't, then you can't."

"That makes sense." Atkinson closed his notebook and slipped it back into his pocket. "But it was a problem for Pardew, his partner. I guess he hadn't done his due diligence very well because the company had a lot more assets than he expected. Meaning the purchase price was going to work out a lot higher, too. So Pardew started cooking the books. He was moving fringe assets between old subsidiaries—your father apparently bought lots of other companies over the years, and never officially closed any of them down—and recording the transferred assets at much lower values. Here's an example. There's a brownstone in Hell's Kitchen. Your father acquired it years ago as a sweetener for another deal. He never did anything with it, but its value skyrocketed with all the development that's going on. It's now worth north of thirty million dollars. Pardew moved it to a different subsidiary and booked it at twelve million. The discrepancy came to light when your father heard about a developer sniffing around for properties to buy in the area and thought about off-loading it. He started looking, and found lots more examples. That's why he summoned Pardew to the meeting at his house. It's what led to the confrontation they had. After Pardew left, your father dismissed his housekeeper for the night. He demanded to be left alone. Then he collapsed. He was dead thirty minutes later. Now, it's theoretically possible that someone else—you, in Kanchelskis's version of events—was there and finished your father off once they were left alone. In Kanchelskis's version, that would be to stop him selling the company at the cheaper rate Pardew's scheme would have resulted in. But if you ask me, that's unlikely. To me, it all falls on Pardew. Covering up a multimillion-dollar fraud is a powerful motive. He wanted to stay out of jail, and probably hoped to still buy the company from your father's estate at a knock-down price."

"This Pardew guy sounds like a twenty-four-karat asshole. I'm surprised my father ever hooked up with him. Did he have any priors?"

"No. He was a big shot at a rival firm when your father brought him on board. His nose was completely clean. No red flags after they became partners, either, except one thing last year. A DUI bust."

"My father hated drunk drivers. I can't believe he didn't cut him loose. The old man must have been getting soft."

"There was no cause to dissolve their partnership. The case was dropped. It never went to court. Your father might not even have known about it."

I moved to the window and pulled back the curtain, but all I could see was the white outside wall of a parallel wing of the hotel. It was glowing unnaturally bright in the paranoid glare of the airport's security lights. "Where's Pardew now? I'd say he has a lot to answer for."

"That's exactly how I thought you'd react." Atkinson nodded. "But no one knows where he is. We arrested him after the autopsy was complete. The ADA agreed to charge him. She was hoping for murder in the second, but was sure that manslaughter at least was a lock. The case went to court. It was tricky—fraud always is, even when it's just to establish motive—but everything was going well. Then, right before the prosecution was due to rest, some critical papers went missing. As far as anyone knew, they were there at the courthouse. But no one could find them. So the judge declared a mistrial. And two days leter, Pardew disappeared."

"This asshole got off because some papers were lost?" I took a step toward him. "Are you serious?"

Atkinson shrugged. "That kind of thing happens more often than you'd think. What can I say? The system's not perfect."

"Something needs to be done about it."

"I agree."

"What do you suggest?"

"First thing, we need to find those papers. They're the key. The ADA won't waste time trying to re-file the case without them. And given that they contain most of Pardew's financial records—a lot of which he deleted online when he realized he was going to be arrested, so we can't get them anywhere else—they might give us a clue as to where he'd run to. If we're lucky."

"Have you looked for them?"

"Of course. The best we can. It's complicated, jurisdiction-wise. We need the cooperation of the court guys. No one's got the manpower to search the place, top to bottom. And a lot of the people who work there aren't too happy talking to cops."

"Why not? Surely judges and lawyers talk to cops all the time?"

"They do. But I'm not talking about them, so much. I mean the people who really know what's going on. The invisible guys. The clerks. Security guards. Janitors. Guys who make the cappuccino at the coffee bar, and spend all day chatting to everyone who passes through."

"You really think they're the guys to talk to?"

"I do. If someone outside of the NYPD could spend some time down there, bend a few ears, you never know . . ."

I turned back to the window.

"Let me give you an example." Atkinson stood up. "A while back, there was this case that hinged on getting DNA evidence off some clothing that had been taken to the courthouse as an exhibit in a trial. The problem was, the box of evidence had disappeared. No one knew where it had gone. The place got turned upside down. No one could find it, and the case was about to get kicked out. Then a janitor heard a couple of lawyers talking about the problem, and he led them to one of the judges' chambers. There the box was, right on a shelf. Of course, that time it led to the ac-cused guy getting cleared. But you see what I mean?"

"I do. Still, it sounds like a long shot." I thought for a moment, then held out my hand. "All right. If it's the only angle we have, give me your card. I'll spend some time at the courthouse. Keep my ears open. And if I hear anything, you'll be the first to know."

Chapter *Five*

INNOCENT UNTIL PROVEN GUILTY.

That's an important assumption in civilian life, from what I've heard. Most of the time. But in the army—in the Intelligence community, at least—we lived by a different mantra. *Lying, cheating bastard until proven otherwise.*

The importance of this principle was hammered home about nine months into our initial training program. It came with our first ICT, or Integrated Competence Test. The idea was that up to that point the instructors had taught us a number of separate skills, so the next step was for them to see if we could put these together under mission-like conditions. To find out, we were taken one at a time from Fort Huachuca to a small town in New Mexico. The first task was to interpret satellite photographs to determine the location for a dead drop. Next we had to retrieve the message from its hiding place and decode it. The decoded message gave the specifics for a covert rendezvous, which meant we had to not only show up at the correct place and time, but also dress and act in such a way as to win the confidence of the contact who'd be waiting there. The guy was playing the role of an aerospace engineer who'd been approached by a Russian spy who was trying to steal the engine design for the next generation of US stealth fighter. Once his trust had been established—which wasn't easy, given his twitchy, paranoid geekiness—he dropped a pair of bombshells. Another technician had sold out and was preparing to hand the plans over to the Russian, that night. And one of our handlers—he didn't know which one—was a double agent, so if the information was passed through our regular channels, it would be compromised and the opportunity to capture the traitor and retrieve the plans would be lost.

The guy said he knew where and when the treacherous deal was set to take place, and begged for help to stop it. A couple of the recruits took his pleas at face value and showed up, ready to save the day. They were rewarded with a paintball between the eyes and a one-way ticket to Fort Gordon, Georgia, for reassignment. They complained that this treatment was too harsh, since verifying the engineer's information via other, improvised means wasn't part of the brief. Their whining didn't get them very far. Our instructors took the view that you can teach a skill—how to pick someone's pocket, clone their cellphone, bug their office, follow their car in heavy traffic—but you can't teach an instinct. And you can't teach initiative. You either have those things, or you don't.

I wasn't one of the recruits who got reassigned. It's not necessarily an attractive characteristic, but I guess I was born naturally distrustful. So the next morning I didn't rush to do what Detective Atkinson had asked me to. Instead, I started by making a couple of phone calls.

The AirTrain system had been little more than a line of semi-completed concrete columns sprouting between the lanes of the Van Wyck Expressway the last time I was at JFK, so after checking out of the hotel I decided to give it a try. The Federal Circle station was clean and bright and I was happy to see a train already waiting at the platform when I arrived. I took a spot in the corner and looked down on the lines of traffic creeping along and choking in a pall of gray-blue exhaust fumes as we swept past high above them on the elevated track. It was a great vantage point for watching the planes—so elegant in the sky as they roared away from the earth or came in to land; so cumbersome on the ground as they crept between the runways and the terminals—for the few minutes it took to reach Howard Beach. Then I had to change to the subway. I was disappointed that the new trains didn't go all the way to Manhattan. I was sure I remembered talk of a new terminal being added for them at Penn Station. I guess it must have been canned to save money. At least I was traveling on my own, and only had my army duffel to carry. I was glad not to be caught up in one of the ragged knots of slow-moving tourists, weighed down with incomprehensible amounts of luggage and zombified by jet-lag.

I emerged at Chambers Street to find that the bright fall sun I'd enjoyed in Queens had given way to gray clouds and drizzling rain. I hurried past the library and city hall, cut between Foley Square and the courthouses, and found my way to the district attorney's office on Hogan Place. It was a pale building with smooth, elegant stonework and plenty of restrained art deco detail, spoiled only by a rash of air conditioners sprouting from every window.

I told the frowning receptionist that I was there to see ADA Sonia Dixon. She glowered at me over her steel-framed glasses and gestured toward a woman standing just inside the doorway. I'd noticed her hurrying along the street a few yards behind me. She was pushing six feet tall even in her flat shoes, and had been holding a plastic document folder over her head to keep the worst of the rain off her deep red hair. I hadn't realized she was going to follow me inside, or that she was the person I wanted to meet.

Ms. Dixon waited for me to sign in, then led the way to her office. It was on the second floor. She took the stairs, moving with the purposefulness of a person who doesn't like to waste time. Something about her manner reminded me of Marian—the second time something had in two days. Marian had talked of becoming a lawyer, too. I wondered if she'd done it. She'd tried to persuade me to go to law school with her. I was hit by a sudden flash of what life could have been like if her campaign had been successful. The two of us could have come to work together. Met for lunch. Maybe ended up opposing each other in some high-profile trial. That would have been something. As things were, it was just another *what if*. I was starting to hate *what if*s. I hadn't encountered one for years, but all of a sudden they were coming at me from all sides.

The last office I'd been in was Colonel Linn's, four thousand miles away. It was about the same size. It also had a single window. But that's where the similarities ended. His was so antiseptic you could have used it as an operating room. Dixon's felt like a graveyard for office furniture and fixtures. Her blind was stuck halfway down at a drunken angle with several of its slats caught up in its grimy, twisted cord. Not that it made much difference to the amount of light entering the room, the window was so filthy. Dog-eared folders were heaped up on the windowsill. There were dozens more on the row of mismatched metal filing cabinets that were lined up against one wall. There were still more balanced precariously on the battered wooden desk. It struck me that if the Pardew file really was missing, it could easily be in this office. Papers could be lost in here for years. Unless she'd developed a bizarre method for organizing everything not previously understood by science.

Dixon walked around to her chair and sat down. I noticed that the desk wasn't lined up straight with the walls. Was that deliberate, I wondered, or was she just too busy to fix it? The law school certificates hanging on the wall behind her were perfectly level. So was a row of twelve playbills from college productions of Shakespeare plays.

"So." Dixon indicated that I should sit on one of a pair of visitors' chairs and took a yellow legal pad from her top drawer. She leafed through it until she found a blank page and secured the rest with an elastic band. "Mr. McGrath, you have information about the Alex Pardew case?"

"No." I shifted my weight on the metal-framed chair. It was hard to find a comfortable position. "Not me."

"You said you did." Dixon's pen was poised in the air above her pad. "That's why I agreed to see you right away."

"No." I shook my head and tried to pull a disarming smile. "I said I'd heard you needed information about that case, and that I wanted to talk about it. I'm sorry if that led you to the wrong conclusion."

Dixon threw down her pen. "You know where the door is. If it hits you in the ass on your way out, I'll take that as a bonus."

"Don't be like that, please." I held up my hands. "I'm sorry if I misled you. I'm not myself right now. I'm not thinking straight. I'm way behind the curve. You see, Alex Pardew was my father's business partner, and my father's dead. I only found out yesterday. I was in the military, serving overseas. We had some stupid beef between us, going back years. I came home to reconcile with him, but there was some communications problem because the army—it doesn't matter. Last night the police came to my hotel. They told me that Pardew had been arrested, but then got let off somehow before he was convicted of anything. I don't understand what happened. If he had something to do with my father's death . . . ? I was hoping, if you could spare two minutes, maybe you could bring me up to speed?"

Dixon retrieved her pen and set it down next to her legal pad. "Thank you for your service, Mr. McGrath. I'm sorry for your loss. Since you're here, I'll try to answer your questions. But I must warn you, there's probably not much I can tell you."

"As I understand it, my father was suing his partner for some reason?"

"What?" Dixon leaned forward in her chair. "Who have you been talking to? No. What happened is that your father discovered that Alex Pardew was engaged in fraudulent activities. They argued, which seems to have led to your father's collapse. That brought in the police, who uncovered the extent of Pardew's criminal activities. He was on trial for financial crimes, which was a slam dunk. I was also going for felony homicide, though that was a lot harder to prove. I had a medical expert ready to testify that the stress of the fight triggered a previously undiagnosed heart condition, but that part's not entirely clear-cut. It would have been a lot easier if Pardew had killed him with a knife or a gun." Dixon's eyes flickered from side to side as if she were reading something on the wall behind me. "Oh, I'm sorry! That's a horribly insensitive thing to say."

I kept my expression neutral. "What kind of fraud was Pardew into? Only give me the layman's version, OK?"

"OK. It was like this. Pardew had signed an agreement with your father to buy his company at a price set by a formula. He was attempting to reduce that price by using illegal accounting maneuvers."

"You said the case was a slam dunk. So you liked your chances?"

"Oh, yes." A hungry smile spread across Dixon's face, but she quickly chased it away. "Of course, nothing's ever guaranteed when a jury's involved. But the case was running like clockwork. I was expecting his lawyer in my office any day, trying to plead it out. And then—a file containing some critical evidence disappeared. Didn't the police mention that?"

"You didn't keep copies?"

"Working copies, yes. But they're inadmissible as evidence. There's no chain of custody, and unless documents are original or certified copies, the defense could argue reasonable doubt that they're altered or faked."

"So do you think there's a connection between the ice under Pardew's feet growing thin and the file disappearing? It seems like very convenient timing."

"Mr. McGrath, I'm an officer of the court." Dixon closed her eyes for a moment. "Even if I thought that, I couldn't start throwing accusations around without solid evidence."

"But it was a fortunate coincidence, from Pardew's point of view?"

"Certainly. And while this is also not admissible, it's not the only time Pardew's skated on solid-looking charges. Six months before your father died—so a year ago, now—Pardew got in a car accident. He was breathalyzed at the scene and found to be DUI. But a judge ruled out the evidence on some bogus technicality. The defense claimed the BAC kit could have been subjected to excessively low temperatures in the officer's squad car due to a freak cold snap there'd just been, so the calibration couldn't be guaranteed to be accurate. Now, I know the cop. He's been on the job twenty years. There's no way he'd screw something up like that."

"So it was another *coincidence*?"

"I couldn't say." Dixon shot me a wry smile. "But first evidence is ruled out, and then evidence disappears? Do you like baseball,

Mr. McGrath? A hitter gets walked in consecutive at bats? You've got to wonder if that's intentional. And if it's not, we need to find Alex Pardew on the double and get him to tell us his lottery numbers."

"Sounds like a plan. But tell me. Does evidence disappear from the courthouse often?"

"Not often, no. But it does happen."

"So the file could have gone missing by accident?"

"It could have." Dixon crossed her arms. "And Elvis could have moved into my grandmother's basement. He could be running rock 'n' roll classes for seniors. Teaching them to gyrate, so they wouldn't need physical therapy after getting their hip replacements."

"What an image. But back to the courthouse. How could anyone get Pardew's file out of there? Wouldn't that be a big risk? Don't they have pretty tight security?"

"They do. But you wouldn't need to remove the file. Have you ever been to the courthouse? It's a massive, rambling old place. You could hide any number of files there, if you had the access. That's what I'd do. It's like when I dated a detective, right when I was starting out in the department. He had a case where a car was stolen, and it got used in a kidnapping. They found it burned out under the Williamsburg Bridge a few days later. I thought he'd be pissed, but he wasn't. It was the opposite. He told me they'd got lucky. The forensics guys could still harvest all kinds of evidence, despite the fire. And it showed them that the perps they were looking for were amateurs. He said the pros would have dumped the car in long-term parking at JFK. It would have stayed there for months on end before anyone noticed. I've dealt with criminals for years since then, and I've learned he was right. Good ones don't draw attention to themselves."

"So you think the file's still at the courthouse somewhere?"

"I have no idea."

"But if you were a betting woman?"

"That's where my money would be, yes."

"How would you go about finding it?"

"I don't know if it can be found. The police already tried. They came up empty. It might be a question of waiting for it to turn up on its own."

"That's one approach." I stood and held out my hand. "But who knows? There may be others."

Chapter **Six**

I MUST HAVE BEEN IN THE NEIGHBORHOOD OF THE NEW YORK County Courthouse dozens of times when I was a kid, when I only had eyes for skyscrapers. It must have been one of the buildings I passed on my way to meet ADA Dixon the other day, but I didn't pay much attention because I was hurrying to get out of the rain. That was a shame, because it's a magnificent structure. The kind of building that wouldn't have seemed out of place in the center of Rome.

It looked like an ancient temple with a flight of solid stone steps, maybe a dozen feet high, stretched across its whole width. Above them, a parallel row of ten massive Corinthian columns rose up to support a symmetrical triangular pediment, complete with classical sculptures and a neatly carved inscription. Taken altogether, it could be the Pantheon's younger, smarter brother. But when I paused in the center of Foley Square for a moment and closed my eyes and listened, I knew the only place in the world I could be was Manhattan.

I was surrounded by the urgent drumming of footsteps on the sidewalk. The pulsing of car engines as the morning traffic stuttered and surged through the clogged arterial streets. The angry, blaring horns. Taxi doors slamming closed. Tires squealing as drivers vied for the smallest gaps between other vehicles. Sharp staccato outbursts from commuters who got blocked off as they rushed to work. Softer, part elated, part exhausted exclamations from tourists who were desperate to tick off one more landmark before their vacations came to an end. The rhythm was unique, like a manic, hyperactive heartbeat. And even after all the time that had passed since I was last there, it still sounded like home.

Behind me a TV crew was setting up to record an episode of a cop show. Fraught twenty-somethings were bustling around in black clothes, barking questions and commands into handheld radios. Bored security guards were scanning the area for unruly fans to hold back. A pair of real cops looked on, unimpressed. A lawyer with a wheeled briefcase that was almost as big as my army duffel was struggling across the uneven stone surface.

Everywhere I looked people were rushing and hustling, except for one other guy. He was standing on the other side of Centre Street, right in front of the courthouse, gazing up at the statues. He was leaning on a cane. It was made of aluminum, and was adjustable like the temporary kind people borrow from the hospital. The guy turned and shuffled away. Then he stopped, turned back, and paused again. It was like he wanted to start up the steps but an invisible force was preventing him. I watched him for another few moments, then crossed the street and almost got hit by a guy on a bicycle. There were way more of them in the city than I remembered. Maybe the rash of bike lanes that had appeared since my last visit was encouraging them.

"That one's *Truth.*" I paused on the sidewalk next to the old guy.

"What?" He shook his head and squinted at me, as if coming out of a dream.

"The statue." I point up to the tip of the pediment. "The one you were staring at. I read about it, once. He's *Truth,* and his friends are *Law* and *Equity.* I guess they put them up there so you know what you can expect, inside."

"Are *you* going inside?" He sounded suspicious.

"I have to. I work here."

"What's it like?" His eyes narrowed. "I've never been in a place like this."

"I'm not totally sure." I shrugged. "It's my first day, actually. But I doubt there's anything to worry about."

"So what are you?" He took a step away from me, like he'd detected a foul smell. "A lawyer or something?"

"Me?" I smiled. "No. I'm just a janitor."

I helped the old guy up the steps and along to the main door, then left him to join the security line and made my way around to the back of the courthouse. If you could strip away the ornamentation, you'd see the building was really a series of geometric shapes. The front was a rectangle with a triangle on top, and the main section was a hollow hexagon with a circle in the center, joined by six narrow rectangles like the spokes of a wheel. The entrance I'd been told to use was at the rear of the hexagon. I had to go down a flight of steps to reach it, not up, and then head through a pair of glass doors. One of the doors was boarded up with a sheet of coarse plywood. I wondered what had happened to it. Had there been a break-in? Had someone been fired and then taken out their anger on the glass? Or maybe a prisoner had escaped? I asked the guy manning the security station about it, but he just shrugged.

I passed through a metal detector, retrieved my wallet and keys, and headed down a short dark corridor that led into the basement of the main hexagonal section of the building. The circular central core was walled off, but I could see through a door that it was used as a filing room. A woman was sitting at a desk near the entrance, nimbly sliding her computer mouse across a copy of last month's *New Yorker*. Behind her, the space was filled with row after row of gray metal shelves. All but one were crammed with white cardboard files, their pink edges showing varying degrees of fade.

I turned right at the end of the corridor and followed around two faces of the hexagon until I found the Janitorial Services room. It smelled of dust and disinfectant. Metal shelves ran down the whole right-hand side, holding rolls of paper, mop heads, spray bottles, plastic garbage bags, towels, and all kinds of other supplies. A section at the far end was fenced off and locked with a padlock on a chain. Straight ahead, in the center of the room, there were four round tables like the kind you'd expect to find in a staff canteen. These were surrounded by two dozen chairs. They were of varying styles, and several looked like they'd been rescued from a Dumpster. Beyond the tables were two couches, which weren't quite lined up. They were covered with a threadbare, furry material, with green and yellow stripes that were garish even in the room's patchy artificial light.

The cleaning carts were stored on the left-hand side. They were lined up between stripes on the floor like cars in a garage. There was a number painted on the wall by each one, which I assumed referred to individual janitors. It reminded me of a parking structure I'd once seen in Chicago. It was underground, beneath Millennium Park. The FBI and the Secret Service had taken the place over for the duration of an international economics conference. I was there to make contact with a potential defector. He'd nominated the garage for our rendezvous, but I struggled to find the guy because the whole space was filled with lines of shiny black Suburbans. Only those were all parked facing out, ready for quick get-aways if needed, not shoved in haphazardly like the carts at the end of a shift. And the SUVs had been identical. On closer inspection, I realized the carts were all set up differently. They'd been customized to varying degrees. Someone had strung plaited black trash bags between the handles of the two bins on the cart closest to me, to hold longer items like mops and brooms. The next in line had a yellow cloth bib strung around one bin, with pockets for spray bottles and aerosols. It looked homemade, but effective.

The door opened behind me and a guy came into the room. I guessed he was in his mid-thirties. He was wearing gray coveralls, and had long blond hair tied back in a ponytail and a scruffy goatee. I could see the tips of several multicolored tattoos peeking out from his collar and the ends of his sleeves.

"Can I help you?" The guy sounded suspicious.

"I hope so." I took a crumpled piece of paper from my pocket and studied it for a moment. I could remember the name that was written on it perfectly well, but I've found people are always faster to trust you if you seem a little disorganized. "I'm looking for someone. Frank Carrodus."

"That's me." His voice relaxed a notch. "Are you McMahon? If so, you're early."

"Sorry about that." I held out my hand. "I'm keen to get started. And please, call me Paul."

When ADA Dixon's version of events had borne out Detective Atkinson's story, I'd decided that I would spend some time at the courthouse to see what I could find out about Pardew's missing file. But why stay on the outside, picking up scraps of hearsay, when you could be on the inside, seeing things for yourself? And if a janitor had found a box of lost evidence recently, as Atkinson had told me, I figured a janitor was the thing to be. Faking the credentials for the job application was new—I was used to having that done for me—but it still took less than an afternoon with the public computers at the central library. I wasn't planning on being there long—it wasn't going to be my second career—so I didn't have to worry about blowback from the IRS or anything like that. And I could have used my own name, but old habits die hard. I stuck to the usual formula. You use your real first name, so you'll reply if someone calls to you. And you pick a different second name. I always liked something else Irish. There was no good reason, but I'd done it so long it had become a superstition.

Carrodus looked me up and down, then crossed to the shelves, took down a new coverall—still in its cellophane wrapper—and handed it to me.

"The locker room's through there." He pointed to the back of the room. "Go get changed. Then we can start the tour."

Carrodus had a cart waiting for me when I came back out in my new uniform. He ran through the basics with the equipment, then led the way to the door.

"Have you had much experience with this kind of work?" Carrodus paused before pushing the handle. "Be honest. You wouldn't be the first to exaggerate on your application form. And if you need extra training, I need to know, 'cause it's down to me to get it set up."

"Don't worry." I smiled. "I know what I'm doing. I worked at an army base before this. Over in Germany, actually. You wouldn't believe the kind of messes I had to clean up in Europe and other places over the years."

"Yeah?" His voice relaxed a little. "Why don't you tell me about it sometime?"

"I'd be happy to." I nodded. "We could swap war stories. I bet there's plenty going on around here that people don't know."

"Too right." Carrodus winked. "Let's get a beer sometime."

"Sounds like a plan."

"What brought you back to the States?" Carrodus opened the door and held it for me. "And why New York? It's not the most affordable place to live. Not if you do an honest day's work. If you were a banker or something, that would be different."

"The short answer?" I wheeled the cart out carefully, not wanting to cause any damage on my first day with my boss watching. "My father. We'd been on the outs for a while—years, to tell you the truth—and then he got sick. All of a sudden. Anyway, I came back hoping to patch things up."

"I'm sorry to hear that. How's it going?"

"Let's just say I don't expect us to be getting much closer any time soon. Unless things take a radical change, of course."

"Well, if you've got family issues, this is a good place to work. You're pretty much free to come and go as you please. You'll have your own allocated area—I'll show you yours on the plan of the building—and as long as you clean it thoroughly every day, including the restrooms, how you plan your time's up to you."

"Sounds good."

Carrodus stopped next to a bank of bronze-colored doors. "OK. First thing to learn. See these elevators? They're not elevators. They're closets. It's only every other set that's real. They made it that way to look balanced or something, with the building being symmetrical. Anyway, remember which is which. You don't want to be stuck standing outside the wrong ones, looking stupid."

We continued to the next bank. The shiny brass door opened the moment Carrodus hit Up, and after he helped me steer the cart inside he pressed the button for the third floor. The elevator started moving with a bump, but stopped again almost straightaway. The door opened, and I saw we were on the first floor. A woman with a gigantic stroller started to come in, but she quickly reversed away when she saw my cart.

"Look at that asshole." Carrodus pointed at a guy who was standing on the blue-gray marble disc in the center of the floor. He was taking pictures of the mural that covered the inside of the rotunda's domed ceiling, which depicts the evolution of justice from Assyrian times to the foundation of the United States. "Photography's not allowed in here. You're supposed to check your camera at the desk, over there."

"Should we do something about it?" I took hold of the cart, ready to wheel out onto the shiny floor. The guy had moved to the outer circle of the floor design now, and was standing on one of the signs of the zodiac. Taurus. My sign.

"Leave it." Carrodus put his hand on my arm. "He's not our problem. Just a jackass with a camera. Not worth losing your job by starting an unnecessary ruckus. Security will deal with him. Eventually."

The third floor was hexagonal, like the basement, only instead of a solid central core there was a wall lined with tall, old-fashioned leaded windows. They faced the hollow center of the building and overlooked the domed roof of the rotunda. I stopped to scope it out, but Carrodus grabbed the front of my cart and pulled it toward one of the spoke-like corridors that led toward the main part of the building.

The courtroom on the left at the end of the corridor was in use when we arrived, so we turned our attention to the one on the opposite side.

"Brace yourself." Carrodus pushed the heavy wooden doors and held them open until I'd wheeled the cart inside. "You won't believe the kind of crap people leave behind. They treat this place worse than a movie theater."

Back in the janitors' room four hours later, Carrodus slapped me on the shoulder. "Good job so far today, Paul. I think you're going to be a good fit here."

"Thanks." I lined my cart up in its bay. I'd been given #12. "I enjoyed myself. I hope I'm going to find what I'm looking for."

"Working here's not just a job." Carrodus moved to the door and casually leaned against it, arms crossed. "It's like being part of a family, too. Which leads me to something they might not have told you at your interview. We look after one another on this job. Kind of like an informal union. To help out, where needed."

"Sounds interesting." I pursed my lips as if I was carefully weighing his words. "That's something I could maybe get behind."

"It's not a voluntary situation." His voice had gained what he probably thought was a harder edge. "I'm the treasurer. Ten percent of your take home kicks back to me. Also, you'll *volunteer* to cover extra shifts as needed. Any questions?"

"No, Frank." I flashed him the friendliest smile I could muster. "That's OK. It's perfectly clear what I need to do."

Chapter Seven

I WAITED FOR CARRODUS TO LEAVE, LETTING HIM THINK HE HAD A new recruit for his *union,* then pulled my cart back out of its bay and headed for the elevator. I wanted to take a look at room 432. That was the room where Alex Pardew's trial had taken place.

I could set my own pace, without Carrodus breathing down my neck. I swept my way slowly around the inner hexagon of the fourth floor until I reached a corridor leading to the main building. There were glass-fronted booths on both sides, where the passageways joined. I guessed they originally housed pay phones. I could see an ancient wire poking out from a heavily overpainted junction box near the skirting board in one of them. I could picture manic reporters in striped suits and trilby hats racing from the nearby courtrooms to phone in juicy details from the most scandalous trials of the day. Now they'd use their cellphones. Or just email their stories directly to their editors. There were Wi-Fi repeaters at regular intervals along the ceiling. Though strangely no CCTV cameras. That was a shame. It was a pain in the ass to sift through hours of footage, but it was sometimes the easiest way to catch someone who was up to no good.

Room 432 was on the right at the end of the corridor. It was square, maybe thirty feet by thirty, with a knee-high fence that divided it sideways across the center. The area closer to the door was for spectators, with six solid wooden benches for them to sit on. The jury box was beyond the fence, to the right. Tables for the lawyers were in the center. On the far wall, below the flag, the witness stand was tucked in at the side of the judge's bench. Next to that was the door to the judge's chambers. And in the far corner, the clerk's desk and a couple of low filing cabinets.

There was nothing wrong with the place, exactly. Everything about it was perfectly adequate. Yet as I stood there, I couldn't shake the feeling of disappointment. Of betrayal, almost. The building's extravagant exterior drew you in with a promise of elegance and ceremony. The central rotunda seduced you with its sumptuous marble and gilt. The paintings of Moses and Hammurabi, literally elevated above you, implied that you were in the presence of age-served wisdom. Even the entrance to the courtroom spoke of old-world grandeur with its foot-wide, gray-veined marble frame and brass-studded mahogany doors. But inside, everything was worn. Every surface was dusty. Every fixture, every fitting was dulled with the patina of bureaucratic routine. If that was the reality of practical, institutional jurisprudence, then it was deeply unsatisfying. If I'd been there to experience the defining moment of my life—as a defendant, or a plaintiff, or even a spectator in the trial of the man accused of killing my father—I'd have wanted more. Regardless of the verdict, the surroundings didn't live up to the proceedings they hosted. They should have been more profound. More magnificent. More dignified.

Given the workman-like mood that had descended on me, I figured I may as well take advantage of the opportunity that had presented itself and take a look in the judge's chambers. Maybe I'd get lucky and find the missing papers on my first try. I was about to stow my broom and make my way through the gap in the center of the fence when I saw that I wasn't alone after all. There was someone else in the room, at the far end of the last spectators' bench. An old guy. I recognized him. From the sidewalk outside the courthouse, that morning. Now he was completely still. He was slumped slightly forward with his cane resting against the arm of the bench to his side. For a moment I thought he might be dead. Then I stepped closer and saw he was breathing. Very shallowly. His eyes were open. They were staring, though unfocused. He was obviously unaware I was there. I could have gone ahead, through the door and into the chambers, but old habits die hard. The guy could wake up at any time. He could see me come back out. Why invite some stranger to be a witness? I decided it would be better to wait until no one was there.

I started to sweep the wide, black-paned floor tiles between the benches, to pass the time as much as anything, when the old guy suddenly coughed and sat bolt upright. He struggled to his feet and took a couple of unsteady steps toward the door, then noticed me. He nodded a vague greeting with an expression on his face that lay somewhere between confused and heartbroken.

"Sir?" I stopped sweeping and leaned on my broom. "How's it going? Is everything OK?"

The old guy seemed to stare in my direction, but his watery eyes were struggling to focus. His mouth opened and closed, but his words wouldn't come. Instead, he shook his head.

"We met outside, earlier. Do you remember?" I took a step toward him. "We talked about the statues on the roof. I was wearing regular clothes then. My name's Paul, by the way."

"Bob." The old guy held out his hand, which was bony and

cold. "Bob Mason. Paul? How can I explain this to her? What just happened? I don't understand."

I gestured to the nearest bench. "Want to sit for a minute, Bob? Talk me through it? Maybe we can figure things out between us."

He looked me slowly up and down as if he was noticing my coveralls for the first time. He seemed hesitant, but he did sit. I leaned my broom against my cart, then joined him.

"I don't know where to start." He slumped forward again, resting his elbows on his knees.

"I'm guessing you came to watch a trial?"

He nodded slowly. "I knew I shouldn't have come. I knew there was no point."

"What was the case about?"

"The asshole who hurt my wife. Who left her in a wheelchair. He was supposed to get thrown in jail. The cops said there was no doubt. They promised us. They said he was going down for a long, long time, after what he did."

"But that didn't happen?"

"No." Mason straightened up and turned to look at me, with a hint of fire appearing in his eyes. "They let him go. Just . . . let him go." He clicked his fingers. "Just like that. The guy's free as a bird. It doesn't matter what he did."

"What did he do? Was it an auto accident? A DUI? A hit and run?"

"No." Mason looked down at the floor. "The guy's an animal. He beat her. With a wrench. He hit her head. Her back. All over."

I paused for a moment, then kept my voice as soft as I could. "Where did this happen? On the street somewhere?"

Mason shook his head again. "In our apartment."

"Was it a home invasion?"

"The guy said he was there to do some repairs." Mason scowled at me. "He was wearing an outfit like yours. He had a box of tools. Lydia was so happy when he arrived. We'd almost given up hope of getting the pipes fixed. We haven't had any hot water for nine months. The super quit on Christmas Eve. He hasn't been replaced, so we've been calling the landlord ourselves every day. Or trying to. We can't get past his secretary."

"What are you thinking? That the landlord sent this guy to do the repair, but for some reason he went crazy and beat your wife instead?"

"Our landlord sent him." Mason nodded. "I'm sure of that. But not to do any repairs. To shut us up. And get us out of the building. All the other tenants are having problems, as well. After the super quit, Lydia started making a list. She started calling on everyone's behalf. She thought it would be easier if there was just one list of issues. I guess, instead, the landlord thought it would be easier to shut one person up."

"You're sure the landlord's behind this?"

"He denies it. Through his secretary, of course. But I'm sure. If something looks like a turd, and stinks like a turd . . . Here's the thing, Paul. We live in a rent-controlled apartment. It's a small building. Most other units in it are rent controlled, too. And the area? New buildings are springing up all over the place. If he could get rid of us and redevelop, or sell the land, he'd make a fortune. That's why there were problems in the first place, if you ask me. The asshole doesn't want to spend money on a building he wants to demolish. And he sure doesn't want old folks like us in the way of his gold mine."

"So who was actually on trial? The guy who attacked your wife?"

"Right. The animal. He should be put down."

"And what about the police? Couldn't they connect the guy to your landlord?"

"No." Mason's hands balled into fists. "The filthy animal came up with some cockamamie story about it being a burglary gone wrong. He said it wasn't planned. He just took the opportunity when he saw the door to our apartment standing open. The cops didn't believe him, but they couldn't prove anything. Then they thought he'd do a deal when he saw how badly the trial was going. Roll on the landlord in return for less jail time."

"Is that what happened? They let him go for giving up the landlord?"

"No." Mason banged both palms against his forehead. "I don't understand it. They just let him go."

"They don't just let people go." I took Mason's wrists and eased his hands back down to his lap. "Did the guy come up with some other defense? Some last-minute trick? What did the lawyers say? The judge?"

"The lawyer—the one on our side—a guy from her office came in and passed her a note, and she suddenly asked to make some kind of special statement. A motion? Something like that. The judge said OK, so she stood up. She sounded real mad, and said there was a problem with the evidence. That something was broken. The chain of command?"

"Chain of custody?"

"Right. That was it. And with this chain broken, she said the evidence was no good. It couldn't be used. And that was all they had. There were no witnesses. Not even Lydia, because he hit her from behind. They only had the wrench, with her blood on it." Mason paused. His breathing was fast and shallow. "And the guy's clothes. And shoes. They had her blood on them, too. Little droplets, that had sprayed on him when he . . ."

"The lawyer." I gave Mason a moment. "Did she say exactly what had happened to the chain of custody?"

He shook his head, then turned to look at me. "What am I

going to tell Lydia? How am I going to explain that they lied to us? That the animal who attacked her is out walking the streets? That our landlord, nothing happened to him, either? How can she go back to that apartment? Even if she wanted to? It's on the second floor. There's no elevator. Lydia's stuck in that damn wheelchair. But if she doesn't go back, where else can we go? We can't afford regular rent. The situation's hopeless."

Behind us the courtroom door opened and a judge came in. He didn't give us a second glance. He just strode past and disappeared into his chambers, whistling "Ride of the Valkyries."

"Situations are never hopeless, Bob, if you look at them the right way. What's your landlord's name?"

"George Carrick."

"Maybe Mr. Carrick's luck is about to change."

"The police couldn't change it. The lawyers couldn't. So who's going to? You?"

"Me? No. I'm just a janitor. All I'm saying is, don't give up hope. You never know what might happen."

I rode down to the first floor with Bob Mason and saw him to the exit, then continued to the basement to return my cart. I changed back into my regular clothes. Made my way to the rear corridor. And stopped dead. Frank Carrodus was standing at the far end with the security guard. He went to slap the guy on the back, and at the same time slipped him a fat white envelope with his other hand. It was a practiced move. Easy to miss if you didn't know what to look for. But one thing was for certain. I'd be keeping a close eye on Carrodus—and the guard—from that point on.

Chapter *Eight*

I LEFT HOME WHEN I WAS EIGHTEEN, AND SINCE THEN I'VE ONLY lived in two types of accommodations: places owned by the army, and hotels. I've never had a house of my own. And I've never had any direct experience of dealing with landlords. But somehow, despite that, I've managed to inherit my grandfather's very Irish attitude toward them. One of instinctive hatred. For him it stemmed from a historic prejudice against English landowners. For me, there was an added dimension. I'd spent my entire adult life fighting for those who couldn't fight for themselves, and that left me conditioned to kick the ass of anyone who preys on the less fortunate.

I supposed it was theoretically possible to come across a conscientious landlord. It didn't sound as though George Carrick fit that bill, though. And it was also conceivable that the attack on Lydia Mason—Bob Mason's wife—really was a coincidence. Conceivable, but unlikely. I was still mulling over the odds when Detective

Atkinson finally arrived for our breakfast meeting the next morning.

Atkinson had chosen the place, deep in the Village. It was called the Green Zebra. It was named after some kind of tomato, apparently. I hadn't heard of it before. It hadn't existed the last time I'd been in the city. Despite being new, the exterior was designed to look almost derelict. The woodwork was only half painted, and what paint was there was artfully distressed. The lettering on the sign was hand-drawn and already faded. The sign itself was hanging above the window at a drunken angle, its boards cracked, and the ends of crude galvanized nails were showing at each corner, as if someone had hammered them in with the heel of their shoe.

Inside, the idea seemed to be that nothing matched. Part of the floor was wood. Part was covered with scuffed linoleum. Part was carpet. The tables—there were twenty-two—were all different sizes and styles. The chairs were even more of a mishmash than the ones in the courthouse janitors' room. The pictures on the walls—some framed, some not—were all at odds. The only aspect with any kind of uniformity was the clientele. It was like someone had called central casting and asked for three dozen hipsters, stat. They all seemed happy, though, nibbling on their small portions of exotic, healthy food and sipping their fancy single-origin cappuccinos and lattes. All in all the place was about as far from a stereotypical cops' donut shop or greasy spoon breakfast dive as you could get.

"I hope you heeded my warning not to interfere with a police inquiry, and to stay away from the courthouse." Atkinson winked at me and tested his chair to make sure it would take his weight before he sat down. Given his skinny build, that seemed like an unnecessary precaution.

"I'd say I've treated your advice in the appropriate way." I smiled and picked up the menu. "Incidentally, have you guys made any progress finding Pardew?"

"Nada." Atkinson shook his head. "That's why we need those papers. The Eggplant Benedict's really good here, by the way."

"I'll stick with coffee, thanks." I put the menu down. "Regular coffee. With nothing foamy in it. And I have information for you. Something I came across. I think it would be worth a second look."

"Is it about Pardew?" Atkinson signaled to the nearest server.

"No. It's something else."

"Your message said you were on to something connected to Pardew." Atkinson glared at me across the table.

"No." I shook my head. "I said I might be on to something. I have come across a lead. I'll follow it up. And I'll let you know if it pans out. In the meantime, I have something else for you."

"OK." Atkinson crossed his arms. "What?"

"So I met this guy. He may or may not have been at the courthouse. There was an apparent attempt to run him out of his apartment, and his wife was assaulted so badly she's in a wheelchair. Maybe permanently. The guy who attacked her was caught. There was enough evidence to get a conviction. He claimed it was a random burglary gone wrong, but the police think he was working for the landlord, a guy named George Carrick. They were hoping the guy would roll on Carrick. But there was a screw-up with the chain of custody, the asshole got a walk, and Carrick was untouched."

The server arrived with Atkinson's food and my coffee.

"That does sound fishy." Atkinson took a bite. "But what do you want me to do? It wasn't my case."

"An innocent woman was attacked, probably on this guy Carrick's orders. The police department fumbled the pass. That's not good enough. Mrs. Mason deserves justice. And if it wasn't an honest mistake—if Carrick can reach out and arrange for evidence to be tampered with—you guys could have a major corruption problem on your hands. Someone needs to do something."

"OK, OK." Atkinson took another mouthful. "I'll ask around. See what I can do. Meantime, you need to concentrate on finding the Pardew file. You need to make that your number one priority. And forget about the amateur social work."

Chapter *Nine*

IT WAS TWENTY-EIGHT BLOCKS FROM THE GREEN ZEBRA TO FOLEY Square. The sun was out, but it wasn't too warm. Wispy clouds were spinning their ever-changing patterns across the sky. I was facing a day cooped up in the courthouse. So I decided to walk.

It took a little over half an hour, though I didn't have much control over the time. I just let myself be carried along by the tide of people, moving at its speed, regulated only by lights at crosswalks, feeling like I was moving even when we were still. Being on foot in other cities just doesn't feel as electric, and I hadn't realized how much I'd missed it.

In Foley Square they were still busy with the TV show. They must have been expecting some actors to show up soon, because a boisterous crowd had gathered. The security guards kept herding people back and sending clouds of pigeons flapping into the air. Then the director threw a fit when a bunch of worried-looking guys in cheap suits clutching bulging files of forms and photographs wandered in front of the cameras. A cop stepped in, calmed the director down, then steered the group toward the INS building on Worth Street. I skirted around the craziness and crossed Centre Street. A knot of photographers was waiting at the foot of the fenced-off section of steps leading to the courthouse's main entrance. Maybe some big case was set to conclude that day. I was tempted to wait and see whether it would be a triumphant ADA who emerged, or a vindicated defendant. But I had urgent work to do, so I carried on around the side of the building without pausing.

The glass was still broken in the staff entrance door. The guard granted me a tiny nod of recognition this time, but he still wasn't ready for conversation. I made my way quickly to the janitors' room. Punched in. Changed into my coverall. Collected my cart. Checked my supplies. And took the elevator to the fourth floor.

Room 432 was empty this time. I double-checked for semi-comatose geriatrics, then pushed my cart through the gap in the fence, wheeled it past the lawyers' tables, and left it blocking the doorway to the judge's chamber with my broom balanced precariously so that it would fall and warn me if anyone tried to squeeze by.

The chamber turned out to be a triangular shape. I guessed that was so it would tessellate with the adjoining segment of the hexagonal building. It had a single window that looked out over the roof of the portico. I could see the back of one of the statues. *Truth*. Its crude metal support was visible from that angle, bent and rusted but still doing its job. That seemed appropriate, somehow.

The judge's private desk was sitting under the window. It was made of old, battered mahogany with a green leather top. I searched its drawers. I love how desks are almost always left open in civilian offices. I did come across one that was locked once, in Luxembourg, on an early case. I assumed that must be where the important stuff was kept. It took me four days to get enough uninterrupted time to pick the lock. And when I did get it open, I found . . . sugar and powdered creamer for the guy's coffee. I guess it's just a question of priorities.

This judge's priority seemed to be opera. His drawers were full of programs and tickets from the Met, and he had a signed photograph of James Levine on the wall, so I figured he wasn't much of a #metoo guy. His shelves were stacked with masks—his tastes clearly ran to the grotesque—and a bunch of stage props I guessed he'd bought in charity auctions.

The only other piece of furniture in the room was a leather Chesterfield-style couch. Its surface was cracked and thoroughly beaten up, like it had been taken from the stage set for a London gentlemen's club. There was a plain white pillow at one end, and it was long enough for a person to sleep on. A short person, anyway.

Next to the couch was the door to a closet. Inside it four spare shirts were hanging on a rail, along with four ties. There was a pair of dress shoes on the floor, and behind those, three pairs of women's pumps. Each had four-inch heels. One was black. The others were scarlet. They were all a smaller size than the men's. There had to be a story there. Any other time I'd have been consumed with curiosity, but that morning I couldn't get past the feeling of disappointment at finding nothing more than some incongruous footwear. I knew it was unrealistic to expect to unearth Pardew's documents in the first place I looked, and in a way it wouldn't have been right. It would have been an insult to my father's work ethic. He valued nothing that came too easily. I remember being in disgrace one time because my school report card came back with an A for achievement in math, but a five—the lowest score—for effort. I savored the memory for a moment—more bitter than sweet, but capturing my father's character in a nutshell—then doubled my resolve to search every room in the building if I had to. And as many other buildings as necessary, if it turned out the documents had been smuggled out somewhere.

On my way back to the basement I decided to pause on the first floor. I wanted to watch the security operation for a while, and assess its effectiveness. With the current emphasis on terrorism I expected it to be capable of stopping people from smuggling items into the building. But what about the other way around?

Sometimes systemic weaknesses can stem from inadequate equipment, but usually human error is to blame. Most often, habit. People stop thinking about what they're doing or looking at their results, and instead just rinse and repeat. Take the World War II Enigma machine as an example. My grandfather was one of the first to see an example after a prototype was stolen by the Polish resistance. The machine was soon passed on to another part of British Intelligence, because cryptography was not his strong suit. But he did hear that the key to cracking the code was the way the German operators used to set the machine's first rotor. Their operating procedure called for it to be changed every day. If this had been done at random, there'd have been no way to decipher intercepted messages. Even with the latest breakthroughs with computers, there wouldn't have been enough processing power to try all the possible permutations in the time that was available. But one of the analysts came up with a theory. What would happen if every morning the operators just advanced the first rotor one position? That would be the easiest way to conform with their instructions. The code breakers tested the possibility and their success rate skyrocketed, because they'd cut the number of potential combinations by a factor of ten.

Eliminating random behavior was key to defeating Enigma,

and it was a similar story here. Clear patterns were emerging in the guards' actions. There were two of them on duty. One of them was pulling every fifth person for a closer inspection. The other, everyone with a metal briefcase. If you wanted to avoid a detailed search for any reason, all you'd have to do is watch. Whether that had any implications for the whereabouts of the Pardew file wasn't yet clear. It would require further evaluation. But the camera-confiscating guard was doing a better job that day, at least. I watched a guy emerge from the line, hand over his form, wait, then get his GoPro back and leave. There'd clearly been no unauthorized selfies for him.

When the elevator door opened in the basement I caught a glimpse of Frank Carrodus. He was walking fast, turning the corner into the corridor that led to the rear exit. I left my cart by the wall—one of its wheels had developed a squeak—and followed him. I reached the corner. Peered around. And could see nothing. A folding screen had been pulled across the whole width of the corridor. I crept closer to it, stood still, and listened. At first there was only silence. Then a door opened. I heard footsteps. Something being carried out? Followed by more footsteps. I counted six sets. Then a seventh. I heard breathing. It was light and fast, but not nervous. There was no sense of panic or urgency. It was more like some kind of established operation was under way. I heard the exterior door scrape open. Most of the footsteps trailed away. There was a sound like hands slapping together. Then the door closed again. There was only one set of footsteps now. And they were coming my way.

Chapter *Ten*

I SCUTTLED BACK TO MY CART AND DRAGGED IT TO THE ELEVATOR. Hit the Call button. And waited.

Ten seconds crawled by. No one caught up with me from behind. Another ten seconds ticked away. And another ten. No one approached me. Then the elevator door opened. No one was inside. I checked over my shoulder one more time, then set off backward as if dragging the cart out of the elevator car. Then I swung it around. Headed for the janitors' room. And dumped the cart in its bay.

I hurried back toward the rear exit. From the end of the corridor I could see an extra guard was there. I realized it was time for their shift change. The two guys looked like they were friends. They were standing close to each other, chatting happily. I could hear snippets about baseball. Girlfriends. Cars. But nothing about smuggling or bribes.

I slowed down and took a look around. There was a spare X-ray machine, marooned in the middle of the floor. A ramp for wheelchair users. A long folded table leaning against the wall. Opposite that was a door. Its burgundy paintwork was worn and scuffed. A sign attached to it read *Staff Only*. And based on the layout of the corridor, it was the only place the people I'd heard could have come from.

The guards' conversation had moved on to basketball. It was becoming heated, so they were paying no attention to me at all. I moved over to the door and tried the handle. It turned easily. I pulled. I hadn't heard any hinges squeak earlier, but I braced myself, anyway. Then relaxed. The door moved silently. I opened it just wide enough to slip through. Then eased it closed behind me and started cautiously along another corridor.

The walls were painted cream, with a slight chalkiness showing on the surface. The wood on the skirting boards and doorframe was faded green. Chunky iron radiators were spaced out along the right-hand wall. Most were dented and rusty. The floor was covered with large, speckled beige tiles. At the far end of the corridor I could see a staircase, leading down. There was a sign on the wall above the top step. It had three joined yellow wedges in a black circle, very similar to the radiation warning symbol, but with an added circle at the six-o'clock position. This was labeled "Capacity," but I couldn't read the number. "Fallout Shelter" was written in yellow on black in a rectangle at the bottom. Below it, a downward arrow had been painted on the wall using a Cold War–style stencil.

I followed the arrow down the stairs. There were two flights. They descended maybe thirty feet, and opened onto another corridor. This one was shorter. The colors gave it the same '50s vibe, but there were no iron radiators on this level. And the far end was blocked by a metal door. Another, larger *Fallout Shelter* sign was attached to it, but this one had a red band stuck across at an angle that read *Decommissioned. Do Not Enter.*

The door was held ajar by a concrete block wedged between it and its frame. The door itself was thick and solid, like a bank vault's, only it was completely smooth on the outside. The design would allow it to flex in a blast and return to its original shape, and not jam or snag on fallen debris. I'd seen a film of one being tested, years ago, and wouldn't want to be stuck on the wrong side. I moved closer, and when I was less than six feet away the door began to swing back. A woman appeared. She'd be in her late twenties, I guessed. She was wearing jeans, Nike sneakers, and a faded Yankees hoodie. Her hair was dark, and she had it tied up in a bun. She had large, blue-framed glasses pushed up onto her forehead, and was holding a Star Wars mug in her left hand. She dropped the mug when she saw me and it shattered, splashing her shoes with the final dregs of her coffee.

"Frank!" The woman scowled, and planted her hands on her hips. "You better get out here."

A few seconds later Carrodus appeared in the doorway. He was holding a clipboard, which he clutched to his chest when he recognized me, and as he stared, deep lines spread across his forehead.

"It's OK, Jane." Carrodus touched the woman's elbow. "You head up. I'll take care of this."

"My mug!" She turned and glared up at him.

"Don't worry about it." He nudged her gently away from the mess on the floor. "I'll clean it up. And I'll get you another one. I promise. Now go."

The woman glared at him for another couple of seconds, then started to move. Carrodus and I stood and listened to her footsteps receding up the stairs.

Carrodus crossed his arms and pressed the clipboard tighter against his chest to make sure I couldn't read any of his papers. "You shouldn't be down here, Paul. The best thing you can do is go back upstairs and forget you were ever here."

"I can't do that, Frank."

"Why not? This is none of your business."

"It might be. It depends what you've got hidden behind that door."

"I've got nothing hidden."

"OK. Then it depends what you just smuggled out of here."

"I didn't smuggle anything out."

"Oh come on, Frank. I saw you hand an envelope to the guard last night. Today, he screened off the exit. People went out. I heard multiple footsteps. Don't tell me there's nothing going on here."

"What are you?" Carrodus frowned. "Some kind of narc?"

"No." I shook my head. "My interest is purely personal."

"Are you undercover? Who are you working for? The INS? The DEA? Because there's nothing here for you. Please, Paul. Trust me. Walk away."

"I can't do that. And I'm not undercover. I'm just a janitor. The same as you."

"Then why do you care what's behind this door?"

"OK." I paused. "I'll level with you. I told you I came back to reconcile with my father. Well, I can't do that. Because he's dead. He had a fight with a guy, then collapsed. The guy was ripping him off, big-time. He was most likely responsible for my father's death. And he walked away from a trial in this courthouse because some critical documents went missing."

"I'm sorry to hear that, Paul."

"If those documents went missing because you're running some kind of operation here, smuggling files out to order, then you're going to be more than sorry."

"You think . . . ?" Carrodus shook his head. "OK. Fair enough. I can see why you might come to that conclusion. But you're wrong. So this is what I suggest. I'll show you what we're doing here. And when you've seen it, I'm going to ask you to keep it to yourself."

Carrodus turned, pushed the door, and gestured for me to go in. I knew that would be a stupid thing to do, given that I'd just shown him all my cards. It was crazier than going into that carpet store in Istanbul. But there was more at stake this time, at least for me personally. And I didn't have to justify my decisions to anyone but myself anymore. So I went in.

I found myself in another long, narrow corridor. Plumes of concrete dust rose from the floor as I walked. There was peeling beige paint on the walls, and wide ventilation pipes hung from the ceiling. I couldn't tell if they still worked. A line of water barrels along the left-hand side formed a kind of inner wall. "Office of Civil Defense" was stenciled on their sides, along with instructions for filling and storing them. As well as reusing them as commodes when empty, by adding a plastic seat.

"Seventeen and a half gallons per drum." Carrodus brushed his fingers against their metal sides as he walked. "Five people to each one. That gives you an idea how many could shelter down here."

I turned back and looked at the door. There were three tempered-steel bars evenly spaced across the inside, operated by a central lever. I imagined the scenes on the stairs and in the outer corridor if the bomb sirens ever had gone off. People would have been fighting to get inside, whether they were on the list of authorized personnel or not. Eventually someone would have had to make a decision. They'd have had to close the door. It would have taken several people, probably, to force back all those left outside. I wondered how soundproof the door was. Would you have been able to hear people banging and scraping, desperate to get in? Knowing you'd have to step over their dead, irradiated bodies, if you were ever in a position to leave? I suddenly felt even better about the Istanbul mission. I couldn't believe the human race was stupid enough to stampede toward the nuclear abyss once again, but at least I'd played a small part in trying to turn the tide. I'd rather push the idiotic multitude back from the brink than a few desperate souls from a bunker, given the bigger picture. But the only issue right then and there was, what was Carrodus doing with the place?

"Paul?" Carrodus had kept walking and was now waiting for me at the end of the corridor. "Through here. Come on."

I followed him into a rectangular space. It was large. Maybe fifty feet by eighty. Our footsteps echoed as we moved toward the center. Pools of light came from round lamps in eighteen-inch shades that hung at regular intervals from the pale concrete ceiling. About half the floor was covered in rugs and a bright patchwork of carpet offcuts. The walls were painted with vivid murals. One was a jungle. One, outer space. Another, the ocean. The last, a city. Four armchairs were lined up at the far end of the room. They had wooden frames, low backs, and pea green vinyl upholstery. They looked like original government issue. And they were solid. Built to withstand any outbreaks of cabin fever that occurred while the surface of the planet was busy getting devastated. To the side, there was a portable coatrack with one small jacket hanging on it. And in the center, toys. A motley collection of Barbies and G.I. Joes, plus heaps of metal tins. There were two sizes, and some were stacked up into towers and forts.

"So you see: No hiding. No smuggling." Carrodus held his arms out wide. "Instead, welcome to Doomsday Daycare, as we like to call it."

"You bring kids down here?" I sniffed the stuffy air. "Is the ventilation working? What if there was a fire? Where's the—"

"Is it perfect?" Carrodus took a step toward me. "No. But can you give me a better alternative? Where else are the kids supposed to go? No one who works here can afford to live in Manhattan, obviously. We all live in the boroughs. Or Jersey. And even so, both partners still need to work to put food on the table and keep a roof over their heads. Assuming you're not raising your kid alone. Then it's even harder. Trust me on that."

I realized I was out of my element. This hadn't been a common problem in my old unit. Although I had seen fancy child care facilities at some of the companies I'd been sent to infiltrate. "What about the employers? Can't they help with this kind of thing?"

"Oh yeah." Carrodus rolled his eyes. "Employers can help. And they're happy to if you're a lawyer. Or a banker. Or a senator. Which is stupid, because if you were any of those things then you could afford regular daycare, anyway. Which we can't."

"Have you asked?"

"A hundred times." Carrodus flung his clipboard onto one of the armchairs and jammed his hands into his pockets. "And we always get the same answer. A flat-out refusal. No one's going to help us, Paul. So we do it ourselves."

"This is what the ten percent kickback is for?"

"Basically." Carrodus nodded. "Some goes to the guards, to help get the kids in and out unnoticed. Some goes for supplies. Although we reuse everything we can." He picked up a piece of paper from a pile by a pair of easels near the "space" wall. It was olive green, and about eight feet by five. "Like this. Do you know what it is? Or was? A bedsheet. One of the originals from down here. Somehow they left a lot of stuff behind when they decommissioned the place at the start of the seventies."

"These, too?" I picked up a pair of tins from the top of a precarious tower. The larger one had a label saying *"Office of Civil Defense. All Purpose Survival Biscuits. Packed: Dec '69."* It rattled as I moved it. The smaller one was *"Carbohydrate Supplement #2. Flavor—fruit. Packed: May '68."* It was lighter, and made no sound.

"We had to empty the fruity ones." Carrodus took the tins and set them down, one on top of the other. "We couldn't risk the kids eating the contents. They looked like candies, but it turned out the food dye they used back then gave you cancer. Imagine that. You survive Armageddon, only to get killed by the food they gave you to last through the nuclear winter."

"That's crazy." I pointed at the tins. "There's still something in that larger one. Want me to grab it?"

"No need." Carrodus held up his hands as if surrendering. "The biscuits are harmless. They're made out of bulgur wheat. It's the same as what the archaeologists found stored in the pyramids. That stuff was still good, so the government scientists figured if it could last from Egyptian times, it was a safe enough bet for down here. They don't taste too good, though."

"You've tried them?"

"Maybe once." Carrodus shrugged. "And if some of the kids aren't getting enough at home . . ."

"Who was that woman?" I turned back toward the doorway. "The one who left when I arrived?"

"That was Jane. Our teacher. Or room mom. Call her what you like."

"You pay her?"

"No. She's a janitor, like us. That's why we ask people to do extra shifts. To cover for her while she's down here with the kids."

I stopped and took another look around the place. If I had kids, I wouldn't want them cooped up in a windowless, subterranean chamber like this. But as Carrodus said, it was better than nothing. And at least they were doing something to help themselves.

"Frank?" I hurried to catch up with him. "I'm sorry I jumped to the wrong conclusion before. You're doing great work here. I'm happy to chip in with the cash and cover Jane's shifts. And if there's anything else I can do to help, just ask. Within reason. I'm not changing any diapers. Or teaching anyone to paint. No one would be happy with the way that would turn out."

Carrodus stopped and held out his hand. "Thanks, Paul. I'm sorry I wasn't more open, but I didn't know you. I can't take any chances with this place. And I'm also sorry about the situation with your father's trial. But listen. Usually when something gets screwed up around here it's chaos that's to blame, not conspiracy. Give me the names and dates, and I'll keep an eye open for the file. I could ask a couple of the guys to do the same, if you like. Just the ones I trust. And I don't have to go into detail about why."

I made my way back up from the shelter and went to the janitors' room to collect my cart. I felt bad about mistrusting Carrodus, and knew what my father would have wanted me to do about it. Redeem myself through work. So I thought I'd head back to the fourth floor. I needed to develop a more effective system for eliminating rooms and chambers. That wasn't easy, given the unpredictable timing of the trials and the preliminary work that went on inside them. But I knew I'd figure something out with a little effort.

The elevator stopped on the first floor again. This time an old guy with a walking frame wanted to get in. A younger guy—his son?—held the door while he inched forward into the car. Behind them, I could see six people heading for the exit. They were moving together as a group, as if they were familiar with each other. I wondered if they were part of a jury, leaving for the day. And if so, which courtroom were they from? I watched as they approached the security station and saw one of the guys peel off. He crossed to the camera table. Pulled out a receipt. Retrieved a serious-looking SLR. Slung it around his neck. And hurried after the others.

It took me a moment to realize the significance of what I'd seen.

And that I would have something to give Atkinson tomorrow, after all.

Chapter *Eleven*

ATKINSON HAD NOMINATED THE GREEN ZEBRA FOR BREAKFAST. Again.

It was a poor choice, I thought. Not because of the food, which I couldn't comment on, as I'd only tried their coffee. Or the décor. Or the preponderance of hipsters. But because it went against every one of my instincts to go to the same place twice. Particularly at the same time of day. In my previous life that kind of behavior would have been unthinkable. I knew that now I was a civilian I'd have to let that mind-set go. I'd understood when I turned in my papers that I'd have some adjusting to do. I just hadn't expected a guy like Atkinson to keep lobbing grenades in my path.

Atkinson was late. I wasn't happy about having to wait, but at least that meant I could pick a different table. I went for one at the rear of the section with the wooden floor so that I could sit with my back to the wall. The tabletop was covered with metal ceiling tiles that had been sprayed with metallic purple paint. My chair was a curvy 1960s creation in beige vinyl. It didn't match—obviously, or they'd probably have thrown it in the trash—but it was surprisingly comfortable. High on the wall behind me someone had hung a framed, six-foot-wide collage of Emily Dickinson poems juxtaposed with cuttings from a 1950s Sears catalog. It was for sale. The artist was asking for $7,000. I had no idea what he was trying to communicate, but he clearly wasn't short of nerve.

It took Atkinson a moment to spot me when he finally showed up. Then he weaved around a group of eight bearded guys who were taking an inordinate amount of time to strap their various infants into a selection of complicated slings and backpacks, and sat down opposite me. A server happened to be passing, so he ordered the Eggplant Benedict again without waiting to look at a menu. I ordered tea, more for the sake of change than because I wanted any.

"What have you got for me, McGrath?" Atkinson seemed to be finding it harder than normal to sit still. "That lead you mentioned. Did it pan out?"

"No." I shook my head. "That was a dead end. There was nothing to it at all. But I did stumble on something else. And this, it could be huge."

"The location of the Pardew file? Who took it?"

"No." I felt a physical jolt at the mention of Pardew's name. In the army each mission's priorities were clearly defined at the start. Now my life felt like a game of Whac-A-Mole, with a flurry of shifting targets popping in and out of view. I wanted to catch the guy who'd ripped off my father, and maybe caused his death. Obviously. That had to be my main focus. But I couldn't turn my back on the Masons. And neither could I ignore a possible threat to public safety. "No. This is something else. Something I uncovered at the courthouse. I'm worried about the security procedure. There could be a major breach."

"Which is how the Pardew documents went missing?"

"I don't know. There may be a connection. There may not be."

"If you don't know, why are you telling me about it?"

"Because if I'm right, something's seriously out of line, and someone has to do something about it."

We paused while our server delivered our food.

"How familiar are you with the security arrangements at the courthouse?" I inspected my tea. The color was passable so I fished out the bag and set it on the non-matching saucer.

"Been there a thousand times." Atkinson's mouth was full of eggplant. "Pretty familiar."

"So you know that photography's not allowed?"

"This better not be about some random tourist taking unauthorized pictures." Atkinson stabbed the air with his fork to emphasize his point.

"It isn't." I took a sip of my tea, and immediately wished I'd stuck with coffee. "It's not just that photography isn't allowed. You can't even take cameras into the building. You have to surrender them at a dedicated desk near the entrance. You get a receipt, and claim them back on your way out."

Atkinson grunted, and waved his fork impatiently.

"Yesterday, I saw a guy coming into the building." I set my cup down. "He went all the way through the security line, the metal detectors, the whole nine yards. Then he collected a camera. Then he went straight back out."

"So?" Atkinson took another mouthful.

"So the guy was going the wrong way. It made no sense. If he left his camera on his way in, he should have been going the other way—out—when he collected it."

Atkinson laid down his fork. "Maybe he forgot to collect it on the way out. Didn't remember till he was already outside. Then he'd have to go all the way back through security to get it."

"Maybe." I risked another sip of tea. "But imagine this. Say someone you know hypothetically checked the camera receipt stubs. Say he could only go back two weeks, so as not to attract attention. And say he found that the same guy we're talking about left a camera eight other times. And that it was always signed for by the same guard, even though the guy came at different times of day. Would that be a coincidence?"

"It could be." Atkinson picked up a sliver of English muffin and used it to chase the last of his egg yolk around his plate. "It's a little weird, but it doesn't prove anything. And how did you get your hands on the receipt stubs, anyway?"

"I didn't say I did. But here's what I think. The guy's set up a kind of dead drop routine. He writes a message. Takes a picture of it. Leaves his camera with the one specific guard. The guard hands the camera to his contact, who reads the message off the memory card. He writes a reply, or gives instructions, or whatever, again by taking a picture. Then he returns the camera to the guard, ready for the outside guy to pick it up."

"What kind of message? Or instructions?"

"Who knows? The balance of opinions in the jury room during deliberations? Offers of bribes? Whatever it is, it can't be legitimate. It looks like the system is compromised. If I'm right, some kind of action's required. Urgently."

Atkinson was silent for a moment. "What did you do in the army, McGrath?"

"I was in logistics. Why?"

"Your mind works in a weird way. Do logistics guys have much experience of dead drops?"

"Not as a rule."

"And here, has any harm been done?"

"How could I know? But it could be a major problem, and it should be investigated."

"How do you know about this, anyway? If you're poking around the security station at the courthouse all day someone will end up getting suspicious of you, and you'll blow any chance of finding the Pardew file."

"Don't worry. If the documents are there, I will find them. If they've been taken, I'll find who took them. In the meantime, I thought you'd want to know about this."

"Right." Atkinson drummed his fingers on the purple tabletop. "My workload's just so light that I'm dreaming of more cases landing on me. Listen, McGrath. This is not my area. It has nothing to do with me."

"But it's someone's area, right? Can't you pass it on to them?"

"All right." Atkinson flopped back in his chair and was finally still for a moment. "I'll make some calls. But I'm not making any promises."

"Good." I nodded. "And I'll let you know if I find anything else."

Atkinson wiped his mouth with a napkin, threw down a twenty, and got up to leave.

"Wait." I grabbed his jacket. "What about Mr. Mason and his wife? Any progress on their case?"

Atkinson looked blank.

"The guy from the courthouse. Whose wife was attacked? Bob Mason? We spoke about him yesterday."

"Right." Atkinson threw up his hands. "That guy. With the landlord you like for being behind the attack. Look. I've done some digging. And I've got to be honest with you. With this one, I can't help."

"Why not?"

"It's not my case. It belongs to a detective at a different precinct. My lieutenant won't cut me any slack to waste time on it."

"It's not a waste of time. Look, give me this detective's information. I'll talk to him. See if—"

"You'd be wasting your time, McGrath. Without any admissible evidence, the case is dead in the water. It stinks, but that's that. Accept it, and move on."

"Could you at least call Bob Mason, then? He feels betrayed by the system. He needs a boost to get his life back on track. It would mean a lot, a detective taking the time to talk to him. And maybe you could tell him you'll help—or the other detective will—if more evidence ever turns up."

"Fine." Atkinson balled up his napkin and flung it on the table, next to the money. "I'll call the guy. I'll have one conversation with him. One, singular. And that's all."

Chapter *Twelve*

I TOOK THE SUBWAY BACK TO THE COURTHOUSE THAT DAY.

I like to ride underground railroads whenever possible. They can tell you a lot about a country. Take the Tube in London, which creakily reflects England's faded glory. The Metro in Paris, with its quiet, elegant efficiency. The Moscow metro, with its impossibly grandiose stations and ticket halls. But my favorite system has always been New York's. I love the simple efficiency of its stations. The no-nonsense ticket barriers. The trains, with their distinctive sound and rhythm. I could ride them for hours, just watching the people. Standing. Swaying. Reading. Talking. Listening to music. Hustling. Or if you're on the wrong line at the wrong time, sizing you up for a mugging, or worse.

I took the 2 Train from Sheridan Square to Fulton Street, then headed north on Broadway before cutting across to Centre Street. The bulk and heft of the buildings all around me felt reassuring, and I was happy to let the relentless flood of pedestrians carry me forward. I was still troubled by Atkinson's attitude, though. His approach was so compartmentalized, it frustrated the hell out of me. A couple of weeks ago, if I'd picked up on a threat against a navy ship or an air force base, I'd have passed it on to my opposite number as a matter of urgency. And I'd have followed up, to make sure the information was acted on. There's no way I'd have just blown it off because it affected a different branch of the service. No one I worked with would have done something like that.

As I approached the southwest corner of Foley Square I came across a security booth at the edge of the sidewalk, next to a set of raised yellow-and-black bollards on chains that controlled vehicular access to the street. A guard was on duty inside. It wasn't clear which agency he belonged to, because there were so many active around there. But what would he do if he overheard people plotting against the Empire State Building, for example? Ignore it, because he didn't work there? I hoped not. Maybe Atkinson could swap jobs with him for a couple of weeks. Maybe that would change his focus.

I continued through the square and paused for a moment next to its giant abstract granite statue. The courthouse looked small from that angle, squatting next to its federal cousin. With the position of the sun at that time, it was literally in the larger building's shadow. I felt my hope seeping away, like a sixth sense when a mission was about to go sideways. I shook it off, crossed the street, and made my way around back.

The guard at the employee entrance was much friendlier to me this time. He mentioned his kids. We shot the breeze for a few minutes. Then I asked him about the broken glass in the door.

"Nothing *happened* to it." He shook his head at the naïvety of my question. "It just broke."

"Glass doesn't just break." I kept any hint of an accusation out of my voice. "Something must have broken it. Or someone."

"The wind, maybe." The guy shrugged. "Or a drop in the temperature. The door has a metal frame. It expands, it contracts, and *bang*!"

"I guess." I tipped my head to one side. "But shouldn't glass be strong enough to withstand that kind of thing? The weather's the same all over, but you don't see broken doors all around the city."

"It *should* be strong enough. If it's the right kind."

"You think this isn't the right kind?"

"I know it isn't. The glass in a door like that? It should be laminated. Like a car windshield. You should be able to beat on it with a baseball bat and not get through. But this? It's regular glass. It's too weak. You can tell by the little decals in the corner of the pane. The day they installed it I told my wife, you better get me a coat and scarf for Christmas, because that glass ain't lasting till the new year. And I was right. And the joke is the glass they replaced— 'cause of some kind of city-wide *proactive maintenance initiative*— there was nothing in the world wrong with it."

"You're saying the door's been broken like this since before the end of December?"

"No. They fixed it in January. It broke again in February. And it's broke a couple more times since then."

"So what happens? They keep using the wrong kind of glass? Why would they do that?"

"'Cause if they used the right kind, it wouldn't keep breaking." He gave me a look that said he was struggling to believe that I couldn't see something so obvious. "And then they wouldn't be able to keep coming back and charging for more repairs."

Carrodus was on his way out of the janitors' room just as I arrived.

"Got to run." He slapped me on the shoulder as he hurried past. "I'm late picking my kid up from school. Any luck finding that file?"

"Not yet."

"Sorry. Me neither. But I'll keep looking."

"Thanks, Frank. Hey, before you go, I have one quick question. Is there any information anywhere about the building itself? Plans. Specifications. That kind of thing?"

"Probably. But how's that linked to your dad's case?"

"It isn't. This is something else. It's probably nothing, but it's got me curious."

"Well, there should be something. Maybe in the maintenance supervisor's room? Go clockwise, and take the second spoke. His is the last door on the right. There's no sign. Just a picture of a pit bull. It's not meant as a welcome."

I'd planned to get straight on with my search for Pardew's file. The thought of it—the absence of it—was hovering over me like a specter and the nagging vision had only become more insistent since my conversation with Detective Atkinson over breakfast. I'd finished searching the fourth floor and was itching to start on the third, right away. But I figured taking a few minutes to scratch an itch wouldn't hurt my overall plan. I've learned over the years to follow my instinct in this kind of situation. The route to a goal is rarely a straight line. So I followed the directions Carrodus had given me. I found the maintenance supervisor's room. Knocked on the door, and got no answer. It was locked, but in name only. It took me less than thirty seconds to open it. Cleaning equipment isn't all you can carry on a janitor's cart, after all.

The air in the room was heavy with the stench of tobacco. Not any regular kind, though. Something heavier, more potent, not unlike the cigar smoke that had lingered on the Iranian colonel's uniform in Istanbul. I closed myself in with the fumes and took stock of the room's contents. There were two deep-drawer cabinets, wide enough to hold building plans. Four regular file cabinets. A plain metal desk with a dusty computer and a wilted potted plant, its spindly stalk straining desperately toward the weak glow that spilled in from the light shaft in the ceiling.

The architect's plans seemed like a good place to start, but I found nothing in them that gave any specifics about glass or doors. Next I worked my way through the regular drawers until I found copies of repair orders. They were filed chronologically and went back six years. I jumped to the most recent ones. There were twenty-seven for the last month. Most were for fixing broken lights. A couple covered the aftermath of overflowing toilets. Various elevators had malfunctioned, with differing degrees of severity. An air conditioner had leaked. And the last one in the batch confirmed the replacement of the glass in the rear door.

I checked the specification. It was clearly stated: laminated. The kind of glass that the guard said should have been used, but wasn't. Because it wouldn't break and require a subsequent repair. I went back another month in the records. I found details of similar incidents—and another order for glass replacement. For the same door. And the same kind of glass. Laminated. Not regular. And from the same contractor.

I found four other orders for the same work since Christmas. I took photos of all of them. And while I had my phone out, I googled local glass suppliers. I found three companies serving the Manhattan area that had the right kind in stock. And when I checked their prices, I noticed something else. Their quotes were all less than a fifth of what the courthouse had been charged.

Chapter **Thirteen**

CIVILIAN LIFE IS ANOTHER COUNTRY. THEY DO THINGS DIFFER-
ently there . . .

. . . *and that's OK*, I told myself. Over and over. Atkinson had
nominated the Green Zebra as our meeting place for the third day
running. He was a detective. He was experienced. He knew the
city. If he thought it was safe to show up at the same time in the
same place, day after day, I had to trust him. Even though that still
wasn't easy.

Atkinson was even later than he'd been the previous day. The
place was even busier, which gave me the choice of only two tables. I picked one in the carpeted area. It was different in terms of
its location within the restaurant. Its size. And its design—this one
had a garish paisley tablecloth, a vase of multicolored tulips,
patchwork cloth napkins, and knives and forks with rainbow-
striped plastic handles. But all of the waitstaff were the same. Eight
of the customers had been there on both our other visits. Eleven of
them had been the day before.

It's all right, I kept telling myself. *Civilian life . . .*

Atkinson spotted me the moment he walked through the door. He headed straight over and plonked himself down on a heavy pine farmhouse-style chair opposite me, a little out of breath. He glanced at the menu, shrugged, then dropped it back on the table.

"All right, McGrath." He ran his fingers through his hair. "What have you got for me this time? Have you found the file yet?"

"Not yet." I was watching him and laying mental odds about whether he'd order the eggplant again.

"What exactly are you up to at that courthouse? Do you go there every day? You were in logistics in the army, right? So do you even know how to do this kind of work? Listen, I have to ask you something. Here's the bottom line, Paul: Are you wasting my time?"

He was worried about his time being wasted? That was a little rich, coming from a guy who dragged me twenty-eight blocks out of my way and then kept me waiting for over fifteen minutes.

"*I'm* not wasting *your* time, Detective." I lowered my voice. "You need to learn a little patience."

"Don't lecture me about patience." Atkinson leaned back in his chair. "I'm being plenty patient. But my lieutenant isn't. He wants to know, which means I need to know: Can you do this, or not?"

"That depends." I crossed my arms. "Is the file actually there?"

Atkinson drummed his fingers on the table, causing the cloth to wrinkle up a little. "As far as I know it is. But that's the problem with things that are lost. No one knows where they are. Not for sure. Otherwise they wouldn't be lost."

"You're a philosopher, as well as a detective. That's impressive." I leaned toward him. "Listen. I'll promise you this: If the file is in the building, I will find it. If it's not, you need to help me figure out where else it could be. I wasn't even in the country when this all happened, remember."

"All right." He pinched the bridge of his nose for a second. "I'll do what I can to buy you some time. I really, really want this guy. I'm sure you do, too. But you keep getting my hopes up with these meeting requests, and it's frustrating as hell when you're not giving me anything."

"I told you. Some things take time. That doesn't mean I'm not working my ass off. And meanwhile, I'm giving you plenty. And I've got something new today. Something big. The kind of thing you'll definitely want to jump on right away."

Atkinson took out his notebook and leaned forward. "Sounds good. Go ahead. Shoot."

"OK. Here's the issue. There's this contractor, Highstead Property Solutions. They were hired to replace the glass in the rear door at the courthouse. Did you notice it was broken the last time you were there? Anyway, they've replaced the glass six times since last Christmas. Why so often, you ask?"

"No, I really—"

"Because they're using regular glass when they should be using something much stronger. Laminated glass. And they're charging for laminated glass, which is more expensive. Every time. I've seen the invoices. And not only are they charging for laminated, they're charging five times the going rate."

Atkinson flung his notebook down on the table. "Seriously? This is what you freaking called me here for? Because some repair guy is gouging? Welcome to New York City, pal. Get used to it."

I shook my head. "Listen. This is more than just gouging. This is stealing from the city. From your city. Our city. Taking money that could be used for more cops. For new squad cars, or better equipment. Hell, for child care for city workers, even."

"Things don't work that way, McGrath." Atkinson covered his

head with his hands for a moment. "Who knows which budget the money for this glass comes out of? You need to know that before it can be reallocated. Even then there'd be a line of other departments with their hands out, trying to get it. And the cost of a couple of extra windows? How significant could that be? It would probably cost more to get it back, by the time the lawyers get their noses in the trough."

"The amount doesn't matter." I banged my palm on the table. "Guys are stealing. That's wrong. It should be stopped."

"What world do you live in, pal?" Atkinson shook his head. "Cloud cuckoo land? Wake up. You're not in the army now. You're not in some nice cozy logistical bubble where everyone follows the same rules. You're in the real world. And in the real world, things happen that suck. They happen every day."

"It doesn't matter what world you're in." I waited until the guys at the next table turned their attention back to their food. "Theft and fraud are wrong. And if you sit on your hands when someone does wrong, you're only inviting more trouble. That can have serious consequences. Like the first time I was in Iraq. We were based out of an old school. The area around it had been flattened and it was fenced off to make an exclusion zone. After a few days the locals had picked holes in the wire. They started coming through at night and poking around, looking for metal fragments they could melt down and reuse. They should have been stopped right away, but the commander turned a blind eye. To be fair, the rules of engagement needed a little refinement back then. But anyway, the following week three guys sneaked through with mortars. Twenty-seven soldiers lost their lives."

Atkinson sneered. "You're not in Iraq now, McGrath. And no one's going to start World War III over a couple of windows."

"It's not just a couple of windows. I did some research. Highstead Property Solutions has six other active contracts with the city right now. How much are they skimming off those? And that's not all. The word on the construction blogs is that Highstead's in pole position to be the lead contractor for the governor's new affordable housing initiative. That's worth, what, billions of dollars? And it's not just money that's on the line there. It's people's homes. Their lives. If the new properties aren't built right because the contractor's cheating, anything could happen. Remember that apartment building that went up like a bonfire in London a couple of years back? People died because someone skimped on the external cladding. You want that to happen here?"

"OK." Atkinson spoke slowly, like he was dealing with a moron. "Maybe there's a bigger problem. You're probably right to report it. But not to me. Fraud cases are not what I do."

"What about the guard at the courthouse and the security breach I told you about yesterday?"

"I don't think you get—"

"So you've done nothing about that, either. What about the Masons and their crooked landlord?"

Atkinson sighed and shook his head.

"Tell me you at least called Mr. Mason, like you promised."

Atkinson clenched his fists and leaned in closer. "Listen, McGrath. Let me tell you how this works, once and for all." His voice dropped to a low, insistent whisper. "I'm a detective. I investigate major cases, which are allocated to me by my lieutenant. Exclusively. I don't run around the city following up on rumors and random complaints. If you help me find Pardew's file, then good. If you find anything else, I don't want to know. So don't bother me again with bullshit about cameras or windows or landlords. And talk to Mason yourself, if he's so important to you. You're the one who built up his hopes. Not me."

I set off to the courthouse on foot after leaving Atkinson at the café. He still hadn't ordered so I never found out if he chose the eggplant, but by then I didn't care. I just wanted to walk. Fast. I was angry. At Atkinson, for his miserable can't-do attitude. At the army, for delaying my father's letter. At my father, for dying before I got home. At Pardew, for maybe killing him. At whoever had lost Pardew's file, and consequently screwed up the case against him. But mainly I was mad at myself. Every decision I'd made since leaving Istanbul had turned to shit. Nothing had panned out the way it should have.

By the time I reached Foley Square I figured I was finally calm enough to call Bob Mason, even though I really wasn't looking forward to it. He answered right when I thought I was going to be dumped into voicemail. He was cautious at first, then surprised when he remembered who I was. I asked after his health, and his wife's. We chatted about the courthouse for a minute or two. And then, without mentioning his case, I suggested we should get together to chew the fat some more. There was a pause, then Bob agreed. He proposed Madison Square Park, that afternoon. He said he liked to sit there for a while on his way home from the hospital after visiting his wife. It was just about halfway to his building. And there was a place that sold good milk shakes.

I just nodded to the guard on the door at the courthouse on my way in because I didn't feel like making conversation. The janitors' room was empty so I got changed and restocked my cart as quickly as possible and headed up to the third floor. I was still feeling cranky when I grabbed my mop and started in on the tiles. But then something unexpected happened. With each pass I felt the tension ease in my shoulders. I could see a tangible result for my efforts. My mood lightened. My thoughts regained a degree of clarity.

Detective Atkinson's words were still fresh in my mind as I traded my mop for a polishing cloth. He'd said I needed to decide which world I was in. And he was right. I was caught in a kind of limbo. I no longer fit in the military. And I didn't yet fit in as a civilian. Would I ever fit? Perhaps a better question would be, had I ever really fit? Anywhere?

I certainly hadn't when I was living at home with my father. I'd always been an outsider in his world. At basic training they'd deliberately kept everyone off-kilter to try and unsettle us. To me that hadn't been a problem. Someone must have noticed because I was soon reallocated to Military Intelligence, eventually winding up in the 66th and being stationed in Europe. I was the only one from my intake to be sent there. And from then on I was a permanent, professional outsider. I was never who I said I was. I was always playing a role. Deceiving everyone I met. Using anyone who could help me. That put me in mind of a store window I'd walked past on my way from the Green Zebra. A guy was there, setting up a new display. He was dressing the mannequins. Styling their hair. Posing them in little tableaux. The scene seemed like a metaphor for my life. The only question was, which was my role? The dresser? Or the dummy?

After I finished cleaning my allocated area I had time to search four more chambers and two storerooms, but there was no sign of Pardew's file. I could feel the frustration cloaking me like a shadow as I returned my cart and headed for the exit. The upcoming conversation with Bob Mason was weighing heavily on my mind, as well. I couldn't remember looking forward to anything less in my life. Disappointing a guy who was trying to buy illegal parts for nuclear weapons? Fine by me. Letting down an old guy? An innocent victim, who was only wanting justice for himself and his wife?

No wonder Atkinson had refused to go near it. Maybe he was smarter than I'd given him credit for.

I jumped on a 4 Train at Chambers Street and got off at Union Square, because I was running a little early. I swept across Fourteenth Street in the midst of a throng and cut through the square, heading north. All kinds of detritus from the farmers' market they held there was blowing around. I kicked a cabbage leaf aside to avoid treading on it. Sacks of garbage had been heaped up next to the sidewalk, and they were starting to smell. A rat was sitting on one, nibbling away on a pizza crust, as bold as brass. A woman walked by with a dog on a leash. It was a timid little thing, wearing orange booties. It made me think of Istanbul. Cats and dogs live wild there, throughout the city. They fend for themselves. And there aren't any rats.

I emerged from the park in front of Barnes & Noble on Seventeenth, then strolled half a block west to Broadway. There were more stores open than when I'd last been there. Some trendy ones, like Bonobos and Lululemon. Quirky ones, selling offbeat china goods and cute gifts. Expensive ones, like Design Within Reach and Restoration Hardware. Plus a selection of bars and restaurants. Music was pulsing from their dark interiors, and they already looked pretty full. I was glad Bob Mason had opted to meet outside.

I continued past the Flatiron Building and watched a succession of people skirt around a short, bald guy who was lying passed-out on the ground, clutching a book about baseball. Not one of them did anything to help him. That seemed to be the theme of the day. A guy with a sandwich board was wandering around near him, yelling about how the Russians are replacing us with communist sleeper clones. No one was taking any notice of him, either.

I watched the crazy guy wander away, then waited in the crowd to cross Twenty-third. The Flatiron was behind me. The Empire

State ahead and to the left. The Chrysler peeking out above the Venetian-style building, straight in front. The Met Life, like an Italian campanile, to the right. Each had been the tallest building in the world, at one time. I closed my eyes, knowing they were there. I listened to the traffic and the blaring horns and the muffled rap music spilling out from some random guy's headphones. I breathed in and smelled hot dog smoke and exhaust fumes.

New York. How can you not love it?

I entered Madison Square Park at its southwest corner, near the statue, and followed the path through the shrubs and toward the fountain. Bob Mason was sitting on a bench to the side of it, both hands on his cane, stooping forward a little. He struggled to his feet as I approached. We shook hands, then sat down in unison.

"Mr. Mason. It's good to see you again. How are you feeling today?"

"A little better, thank you. And please, call me Bob. It was nice of you to get in touch. It's good to see a friendly face."

"It's good to be here. How's your wife doing, Bob?"

"She's having a rough go." Mason paused. "She's stuck in her damn wheelchair. It makes her feel like she can't leave the hospital. It's too hard for her. But honestly, Mr. McGrath—"

"It's Paul. Please."

"Honestly, Paul, it's not just the physical harm. It's not just the injuries I'm worried about. The psychological side of it—I think that's hit her even harder. She was making a little progress, knowing the guy who'd hurt her was arrested, and believing he'd be going to jail. When they let him go, it really knocked her back."

"What are the doctors saying?"

"Not much. There's not much hope." Mason's words dried up for a moment. "The way things are headed, Lydia'll be in that chair for the rest of her life. One doctor's talking about some new treatment he knows about, but it's only done at another hospital. It's very expensive. And we don't have the right coverage. As far as I can tell. It's just so complicated. There's Medicare part this and part that, and gap insurance, and deductibles and lifetime limits. If I'd joined a bank instead of the army . . ."

"You served?"

"A long time ago." Mason nodded. "Vietnam. Two tours. You?"

"Iraq. Afghanistan. A few other places."

"I thought so. I can see it in you, Paul."

"I haven't been out long, actually. It's taking me a while to adjust."

"Tell me about it."

Neither of us spoke for a moment.

"It was nice of you to talk to me the other day at the courthouse. The news about the case collapsing had knocked me on my ass. It was you who got me back on my feet. You were wrong, though."

"I was? About what?"

"The police. The authorities. I've heard nothing. No one's doing anything."

This was the moment. It was time for me to pass on Detective Atkinson's message. To confirm Bob Mason's fears. That's what I'd come to the park for. To do him the courtesy of spelling it out. Putting an official seal on it. I wouldn't be breaking any news. He'd already reached the conclusion for himself. And it wasn't my decision. It wasn't the outcome I'd wanted, or argued for. I was little more than a bystander. But somehow the words just wouldn't come out of my mouth.

"Do you hear me, Paul?" Mason slumped a little lower on the bench. "No one cares."

"I don't think that's true, Bob." I swiveled around to face him. "I'm pretty sure that someone is on your case now."

"Who? Why haven't I heard anything?"

"You will. When the time's right. Justice has a way of catching up with guys like Carrick. And the guy who did the attack. What was his name? Davies?"

"Right. Norman Davies. But what makes you so sure something's happening?"

"I keep my ears open at the courthouse. Specially around the police. I heard they brought in a new guy. It's strictly on the QT, though. He's an outsider. Some kind of independent contractor. He has his own way of doing things. That can be more effective in certain types of situations."

I shook Mason's hand and watched him make his way slowly toward Broadway. After a minute he disappeared from view, absorbed by the crowd waiting to cross the street, so I turned and walked the opposite way on Twenty-third. I'd heard there was a good burger place nearby. I was suddenly feeling hungry. And there'd be no more trips to the Green Zebra for me. I'd finally realized there could be advantages to not fitting in. To living in your own world. By your own rules.

The penny had finally dropped.

Some things, if you want them done right, you've got to do them yourself.

And the more important the things, the truer that becomes.

Chapter *Fourteen*

I'D HEARD ABOUT STORIES IN THE PRESS, STARTING AROUND THE time of the second Gulf War, suggesting that in Military Intelligence circles we represented human targets as playing cards with their suit and rank indicating their value and priority.

The truth is, the playing card analogy is a technique we've used for decades, but the media coverage gave a very misleading impression of how it's implemented. A king might have been an ultimate target, but that didn't mean you could go out, wander around the ruins of some Iraqi city, and expect to snatch the guy straight up. You had to understand the enemy's command structure. Their hierarchy. The way our system worked was more like solitaire. We started with the lower value cards and worked our way up until the board was clear. We learned as we went. We gathered evidence. Dug into the background of the characters who were involved. Built a stock of information to make it less likely that we'd walk into a trap.

That approach had kept me alive for a lot of years, so tempting as it was to go straight after George Carrick, I formed a more pa-tient plan. I needed to start at the bottom of his organization and work all the way up to the top.

I finished my burger, which was excellent, then continued east on Twenty-third. I took First Avenue to Tenth, then zigzagged through the East Village, past Tomkins Square Park, all the way to Sixth and Avenue D. That put me at the northwest corner of the Lillian Wald Housing Project. According to the file I'd sneaked a look at before leaving the courthouse, the place was home to Nor-man Davies. The guy who'd attacked Mrs. Mason.

I continued east on Sixth, then made my way around and up onto the pedestrian bridge over the FDR. It gave me a good van-tage point to scope out the development. It was a dark, inhospi-table place. The shadows left by the broken streetlamps were exaggerated by the light spilling down from the highway. I counted sixteen apartment blocks. Their exteriors were all stained a can-cerous black by the exhaust fumes of the relentless stream of ve-hicles that rumbled past. The buildings themselves were scattered around like hulking, hostile jigsaw pieces that had been abandoned because they didn't fit together properly.

Perching on the bridge was a disorienting experience. There was nothing but noise and light and movement behind me, and only stillness and silence and darkness in front. It took me more than five minutes to identify Davies's block because all the signs around the site were either missing or too defaced to read. I even-tually figured out which one it was, then tried to trace the structure of the buildings. There were lamps over the communal doorways, but they were mainly broken. The stairwells appeared only spo-radically lit. There were dim, yellow lights showing in maybe ten percent of the other windows. It was hard to believe the place had been built with the best of intentions. Its architects had conceived it as a pleasant place to live. By all accounts it had been, when it was new. Now it looked like the ground had been split open and the overflow from purgatory regurgitated through the gap.

I crossed the rest of the way over the bridge, followed along the east side of the FDR on the bike path, then came back across another bridge at Houston. I passed a school, which had done its best to insulate itself from its surroundings with fences and razor wire. Then I turned north again onto Avenue D. It wasn't the world's greatest recce, but it was the best I could do in the circumstances. I was probably being overcautious, anyway. But then, as I kept finding, old habits die hard. And overcautious beats under-alive any day.

I took a breath and entered the project. I couldn't see anyone, but right away I felt eyes watching me. I stayed in what little light there was, looped around an adjacent building, and approached Davies's block from its front. An intercom had been installed next to the double glass door, but now it was just a jumble of components—a speaker, a microphone, a keypad—hanging impotently from its wires. I pulled on a pair of thick blue latex gloves that I'd taken from my janitor's cart—old habits—and tried the door. Its lock was also broken. The oil-starved hinges put up a valiant fight, but I soon got it open.

I immediately wished I hadn't. Going through that doorway was like walking into a latrine. One that was long overdue for a cleaning. The stench was almost overpowering. I forced myself to pause, despite the unpleasantness, and wait for my eyes to adjust. Details of my surroundings gradually became visible. I saw that the floor had once been tiled with bright blue and white squares, but now more than half were missing. There were beer cans strewn all around. Vodka bottles. Burger wrappers. A pile of dried vomit in one corner. Three syringes discarded in another. The outer wall was badly stained from a water leak, and the others were a patchwork of overlapping blocks of varying shades of cream. I guessed that was the result of graffiti being repeatedly painted over. There were also two elevators, but you couldn't have paid me to go in either of them. In a place like that, they would basically be coffins on steel cables, if they even worked at all. So despite having to go up nine floors, I took the stairs.

I climbed slowly, because you never know who or what might be waiting on the next landing. At least the smell eased with each floor I passed. I reached the ninth unmolested and found the fire door. I had to lift the handle to get through because only the bottom hinge was still attached to the frame. The door led to a corridor that cut the building in half. There were windows at either end, but they were covered in grime. Three lights were evenly spaced out along the ceiling. Their cloudy glass globes were covered with wire mesh. Only one was working. I took out my pocketknife, unscrewed its cover, and loosened the bulb until it went out. Then I approached Davies's door.

I stood to the side and knocked. There was no reply. I knocked again, harder. There was still no answer. Leaning across from the side in case Davies was shy but trigger happy, I started to work on the lock. It took fifteen seconds to pick. I stayed crouched, covered by the wall, and held my flashlight up high and to the right. No shots rang out, so I risked peeking around the doorframe. I could see that the entrance foyer, at least, was deserted.

The foyer was small. Its off-white paint was dirty and marked. There were five coat hooks, and all were empty. A pair of filthy sneakers lay on the floor. The floor itself was covered with cheap vinyl, which was bubbled and blistered in places. That was probably just due to its low-quality materials, but I took care not to tread on any of the raised patches, just in case. You don't have to be house-proud to know how to set a booby trap.

I moved into the hallway. There was a thin brown carpet on the floor. A signed Mets team photograph on the wall. And doors leading to four other rooms. Three were on the left-hand side, and one was on the right. Two of the doors on the left opened into bedrooms. One was completely empty. The other had a queen bed with a knot of nasty turquoise sheets on the floor next to it. There was nothing under them, or beneath the bed. Nothing was in the nightstand drawer, but I found tape residue on the back of the unit. That would be a good place to conceal a gun. It would be in easy reach if you were surprised in the night. A bunch of wrinkled clothes was shoved over to the left-hand side of the closet, next to six empty Nordstrom hangers. Two more pairs of worn sneakers had been tossed on the floor, and there was an empty John Varvatos shoe box on its side at the front.

The shower curtain in the bathroom was covered with mildew. There was a toothbrush on the side of the sink—only one, not surprisingly—with worn, splayed bristles. The basin was plastered with dried toothpaste stains. A Burberry cologne box was alone in the trash. It was empty. A thin, beige bath towel lay crumpled on the floor. And the toilet was like something out of a bacterial warfare experiment. I pulled on a second pair of gloves—you can't be too careful—and checked the cistern. Nothing was stashed inside or wedged down behind it.

The final room was a combined cooking and living area, and it took up half the apartment's overall floor space. At one end, a couple of the kitchen cupboard doors were missing. I could see cheap, mismatched plates stacked up haphazardly on their flimsy interior shelves. A door was hanging off another cupboard. The countertop was caked with grease and dust for most of its length, but a section in the center had recently been cleaned and now housed a new microwave and a shiny chrome Nespresso machine.

At the other end of the room a sixty-inch Sony TV had been mounted on the wall. Someone had made a clumsy attempt at wiring it to a Bose surround-sound system with little black cube-shaped speakers dotted around on spindly metal stands. A new-looking leather couch was positioned in front of it, and a ratty fabric armchair had been shoved to the side. Its cushion was all askew. Its base had been slashed open, but I couldn't find anything hidden inside.

There was nowhere left to check so I considered switching off the lights and settling down to wait. That wasn't an attractive prospect, given the surroundings. And I figured the odds of Davies returning any time soon were low, so I nixed the idea and headed for the exit. There'd be other ways of getting to Carrick. More sanitary ways. I was confident of that.

There were four guys waiting for me in the lobby when I emerged from the stairwell. Two were standing directly in front of the exit door. Two were on either side, a yard farther forward, forming a C shape. All of them would be in their early or mid-twenties. They were short and stocky, with sneering expressions on their faces. One had a bat. Two had pickax handles. And the other, a crowbar.

The crowbar guy took a step forward. "You a cop?"

I stayed where I was and smiled pleasantly. "Me? No. Listen carefully and I'll explain what I do. And how you're going to help me."

Chapter Fifteen

I arrived at the courthouse early the next morning. Images of the Pardew file turning to ash before my eyes had plagued me all night, disturbing my sleep, and I wanted time to search at least four more rooms on the third floor before it got too late to go and take care of another piece of business.

The janitors' room was the busiest I'd ever seen it when I walked in. There were half a dozen guys in a circle by the line of carts, caught up in some kind of animated conversation. Frank Carrodus was in the center. After a moment he saw I was there and beckoned me over to join the group.

"You've got to hear this, Paul." He shook his head like he didn't believe what he was saying. "My sister works as a civilian aide for the cops, at the Fifteenth Precinct. Last night they get this 911 call from one of the projects. There was some kind of disturbance, late in the evening. Nothing unusual there, right? Wrong. Some officers responded—not too quickly, would be my guess—and do you know what they found? Four local hoodlums, all beat up. One had to go to the hospital. He'd been whacked in the head with a crowbar, they reckon. The other three just had cuts and bruises. But get this. They said the guy who hurt them made them break into a supply closet, take out a bunch of brooms and trash bags, and start cleaning up. The building. The courtyard outside. All over the place. And the best part? When they asked the guy what his deal was, he wouldn't tell them anything. He just said he was a janitor. A janitor! Like us. Have you ever heard anything like that?"

"Me?" I shrugged. "No. It sounds crazy. The guys were probably on drugs. They probably imagined the whole thing."

By the time I left the courthouse three hours later I'd discovered that one judge liked to bring more than coffee to work in his thermos. And that another was planning a surprise trip to Jamaica for her husband's birthday. But I'd found no sign of Pardew's file. I was disappointed, but I know what my father would have thought. It was too soon. I had to work for it. I had to keep looking.

I took the subway to Forty-second Street, made my way across to Eleventh Avenue, and turned north. The place was a maze of scaffolding and portable generators and closed sidewalks. I guess it was true that the neighborhood was hot. Taller buildings were going up south of Forty-third. New ones were being squeezed in, and old ones replaced, north of that. I wondered where exactly my father's building was. The one that had led him to discover Pardew's fraud. I wondered who wanted to buy it. And what they wanted to do with it. I'd have to check. I wasn't too enthusiastic, though. Hell's Kitchen had never been my favorite area. I think that stemmed from the first time I'd visited it as a kid. My hopes had been high for evidence of demonic activity, or at least something good to eat, but I hadn't seen a single devil or the first sign of cooking. False advertising sucks, especially when you're young and pedantic.

The building the Masons lived in was on Forty-ninth Street, between Eleventh and Twelfth. It was a six-floor walk-up, frayed around the edges but oozing old-school charm. I went up the short flight of outside steps. The front door was the original wood. Its white paint was chipped in places, and several of its stained-glass panels were cracked.

There was an intercom to the side of the door. It had twelve buzzers. There was a card next to each, but they were all hand-written and too faded to read. I tried each buzzer in turn. There was no reply from any of them. I tried the door instead, and it opened. Inside, the hallway smelled damp, and there was a hint of raw sewage in the air. It was like an old people's home I'd investigated in England one time, which was involved in raising money to send recruits to terror training camps in Syria. That operation hadn't ended well. I hoped it wasn't an omen.

The wooden floor in the hallway was in desperate need of a polish, and in some places, repair. Several of the blocks were raised, I guessed by damp. The walls were paneled, and four lighter sections revealed the places where pictures had recently been removed. A modest chandelier hung from the ceiling, with several crystals missing. There were two doors, offset, so that neighbors couldn't see into each other's apartments if they came out at the same time. I listened at both of them, and heard nothing.

Next I made my way to the staircase. It was nicely proportioned, from the days when form was as valued as function and both were more important than price. The banister was made of rich mahogany, but four spindles were missing and the top of the newel post was loose. Deep scratches ran down its length, and the carpet on the treads was threadbare. The iron was also missing from the bottom step.

I decided to start at the top of the building and work my way down. I made my way slowly upward, and when I reached the highest landing I saw the source of some of the dampness. The roof had been leaking. The floor on that level was simpler than in the hallway. It was made of planks rather than blocks, and many were now warped and twisted. Gaps had appeared between them and they creaked alarmingly when stepped on. The wallpaper was peeling, too, and there were chunks of plaster missing from the ceiling. The place was going to need some serious TLC to get it back in shape.

I was about to head down to the fifth floor when I heard a scraping sound behind me. I looked around, and an apartment door abruptly closed. I went over to it and knocked, but there was no answer.

"Hello?" I knocked again. "Would it be OK to speak with you for a second? Don't worry—I'm not selling anything."

There was no response.

"My name's Paul McInally." I knocked a little harder. "I'm working for your landlord, Mr. Carrick. He asked me to put together a quote for building renovations. For the common areas, mainly, plus—"

The door jerked open and a woman appeared. She'd be in her seventies, I guessed. Her hair was steel gray. Her face was deeply lined. Her eyes were blazing. And she was wearing a giant thick cardigan, blue slacks, and pink furry slippers. "Finally!" Her eyes narrowed. "Wait. You don't look like a contractor. Let me see some ID."

I took out a black leather wallet that contained a generic gold shield—one of the little souvenirs I'd kept from my time working undercover—and showed it to her. "You're very perceptive, Mrs. . . . ?"

"Milner."

"Well, Mrs. Milner, you're right. I'm not a contractor. I'm a consultant, and right now I'm assisting the NYPD. Specifically, I'm looking into what happened to your neighbors, the Masons. Could you tell me, how well did you know them?"

Mrs. Milner took a step back. "OK. You better come in."

I followed Mrs. Milner to her living room. She had a low, sleek couch with mustard-colored upholstery. Two matching chairs. A glass-topped coffee table. A long, low wooden media unit. Everything was beautifully coordinated, and all the items in the room—apart from the flat-screen TV—could have been lifted directly from the '50s. They looked strangely familiar, and I realized they were the original versions of the items I'd seen the day before in the store windows on Broadway.

"Have you lived here long, Mrs. Milner?"

"All my life." She nodded. "My parents lived here, and we stayed on after they died. Me and my husband. He's not here right now. He volunteers at a center for seniors. He's older than half the people he helps, but that's Bryan. He can't keep still."

"You must like it here."

"I love it!" There was no missing the passion in her voice. "The building. The view. Look! You can see the Hudson. The river changes all the time. It's better than television. And the ships. There aren't as many as there were, but I still love to see them coming and going."

"Have things changed much over the years?"

"Oh yes." She looked down at the floor for a moment. "It used to be wonderful, with our first landlord. Mr. Cumbes. It was the same with his son. Nothing was too much trouble for those guys. Everything was always pristine. Then young Mr. Cumbes died, and his daughter sold the building to Mr. Carrick. It's been downhill ever since. Look at the place now! It's getting almost unlivable. Mrs. Graydon, who lives opposite—she got hit on the head by a huge hunk of falling plaster after the heavy rain last year. Mrs. Leonard, on the second floor, her baby wound up in the hospital. The poor little guy couldn't breathe because of the mold spores. She's staying with her mother now, in Florida, until things improve around here. Mr. Nicholl, who lives on one, his wife died, then on the day after her funeral he woke up and found that the toilet had overflowed in the night. His whole bathroom floor was covered in—you know what. He still can't shift the smell all the way. And poor Mrs. Aitkin. She has the other apartment on one. Her daughter came to visit, with her brand-new baby. And do you know what? The little girl got bitten in the night by rats. She had to go to the hospital. They gave her rabies shots."

"Have you tried talking to the landlord about all this?"

"We can't. No one knows how to reach him."

"So how do you report your maintenance issues?"

"That used to be easy. We had a super who lived in the building. Old Mr. Cumbes hired him. But the guy retired, and he still hasn't been replaced. Now we have to call a number if we have a problem. And we always just get a machine. I've never actually spoken to Mr. Carrick. Sometimes I wonder if he even exists."

"If you leave a message, do you at least get a response?"

"Hardly ever. Basically all he does is take our money."

"Why don't you stop paying him. That would get his attention."

"Are you crazy?" She stood up. "This apartment's rent controlled! We want the building fixed up, not us kicked out."

"Do you think with all this neglect, he could be trying to drive you out?"

"That had crossed my mind." Mrs. Milner moved to the window. "I'm sure he could make a lot more money if he got new tenants. Or sold to a developer. Or demolished the place and started again. You've seen all the construction work around here.

The neighborhood's trendy now, all right. You should have been here in the seventies. I tell you, I survived that, so I can survive anything. If someone wants me out, they can carry me out in a box."

"Do you think Mr. Carrick could have had anything to do with what happened to Mrs. Mason?"

"That had crossed my mind, too." She came back to the couch and sat down. "I hope not. But . . ."

"But?"

"Lydia Mason and me, we're the same. We're obstinate. Some of the others were starting to waver. Lydia was worried. She thought, if they start leaving, that'll make it harder for us to stay. So she offered to be our spokesman. To represent all of us. To make a nuisance of herself till we got a result. She'd been doing it about a month. Calling. Leaving constant messages. Saying we'd get a lawyer if we had to. She'd made a little progress, too. She found the number for Mr. Carrick's secretary. He's a man—and European—but that's still better than an answering machine. Then the attack happened."

"Had you seen anyone loitering around near the building?"

"Me, no. Nothing like that. But Bryan thought he had. He told me he'd yelled at a young guy a couple times. After the attack, I begged him to stop doing things like that. It's asking for trouble."

"Did he say what the guy looked like?"

"Kind of. He said he was white. Skinny. About five foot ten. And he had close-cropped ginger hair."

"Well, thank you for your time, Mrs. Milner. You've been very useful. I need to head out now, but I'm going to leave you a number. If you have any further problems in the building I want you to call it and ask for Detective Atkinson. He'll take care of you."

Mrs. Milner's description of the guy her husband had seen loitering in the neighborhood certainly was very useful. Because a skinny white guy, about five-foot-ten tall, with cropped ginger hair, was standing diagonally opposite the building when I left, clumsily pretending not to be watching out for me.

Chapter Sixteen

I MADE MY WAY BACK TO ELEVENTH, THEN HEADED SLOWLY SOUTH, checking the reflection in the angled windows I passed to make sure the ginger-haired guy was following me. He was, a constant twenty yards behind. I turned east on Forty-third, maintaining the gap between us until I reached a pair of old apartment buildings that were being torn down, presumably to make room for something taller and larger. The closer building was already in ruins. It offered no cover whatsoever. The next one was fenced off. Its windows were boarded up, so I slipped through a gap where two posts didn't quite join and hurried around to the rear.

The ground had been completely cleared. The surface was smooth, obviously done by a machine, except for a pit that was directly at the back of the building. It was about eight feet deep and twelve square. Maybe I'd been wrong. Maybe they were rehabbing the building, or putting up an addition. But whatever the reason, I wasn't going to argue. This setup was better than I could possibly have hoped for.

"Hey." The ginger-haired guy appeared around the side of the building and puffed himself up, thinking he had the advantage when he saw that I was cornered. "I want to talk to you. Stay where you are."

I took a step toward him. "Have you got any weapons on you? Any hard objects in your pockets? Anything sharp?"

The guy looked confused. He didn't answer, but I saw his right hand brush across the back pocket of his jeans.

"I'll take that as *no,* then." I snaked my left leg around the guy's ankles and shoved him hard in the chest. He fell back, and landed square in the center of the pit. There was a hollow squelching sound as the dirt knocked the wind out of him, so I gave him a moment to catch his breath before I continued. "Age before beauty, my friend. I'm going to be asking the questions. Starting with, why were you following me?"

The guy hauled himself to his feet, rage distorting his already unfriendly face. "What the hell? What'd you do that for, man? I'm going to kill you. Get me out of here!"

"If you're going to kill me, that's not much of an incentive for me to get you out, is it? No. So this is how things are going to work. If you want out, you have to answer my questions first."

"Screw your questions." The guy paced up and down, looking for handholds in the wall. The dirt was smooth and slick. He tried to dig his fingers in and kick footholds with his toes, but the sides of the pit were as hard as cement. Eventually he gave up and tried another tack. "Help! Help! Somebody? Get me out!"

The guy yelled for nearly two minutes straight. Then he stopped in the center of the pit, his fists by his sides and the veins bulging in his forehead, glaring up at me. .

"It's no good shouting *help*." I shook my head. "This is New York. No one cares. Usually *fire* is your best bet, but you're in a construction site. Who's going to notice? It's like I said. Your only way out is to answer my questions. So. Why were you following me?"

He didn't answer.

"If you don't talk to me, I'll leave. How long will it be till anyone finds you? Will it be tonight? Tomorrow? Next week? I hope you had a good breakfast . . ."

The anger on the guy's face suddenly turned into a smirk. He reached for his back pocket. Started to look worried. Tried his other pockets. Then began moving around, staring intently down at the ground.

"Are you looking for this?" I held up the slim flip phone I'd removed from his pocket as he fell.

The guy punched the earth wall in rage, then whimpered and tried to shake the pain out of his hand.

"Why were you following me?" I kept my voice gentle.

"Look, it's my job, OK?"

"Your job is to follow me?"

"Not just you. I work security. At that building you were poking around, with no business being there. We've had problems recently. So the landlord promoted me, and sent me to protect the residents."

"In that case I feel even worse for the residents. What's the landlord's name?"

"I don't know. He never said."

"Is it usual to get a job and not know your boss's name?"

The guy didn't answer.

"I guess that's not a fair question." I softened my voice a touch. "It's probably not usual for you to get a job at all. What does the guy look like?"

"I don't know." The guy scowled. "I never met him."

"So how did he hire you?"

"Over the phone. A friend introduced us."

"What's your friend's name?"

"Norm."

"Norman Davies?"

The guy nodded. "How did you know?"

"It's a small world. Where's Norman now?"

"I don't know. He said he was going away."

"When did you last see him?"

The guy shrugged. "Couple days ago."

"So if Norman introduced you, he must have worked for the same guy?"

"Right. But he got fired. A few weeks ago."

"Fired, why?"

"He got arrested. He was in jail. I don't know why."

"But then he got out?"

"Right. The police screwed something up, he said. He was lucky."

"What if it wasn't luck?"

"I wouldn't know anything about that."

"So, your job. You provide *security*. Does that mean you're at the building twenty-four/seven? Do you live there?"

"No." The guy leaned on the pit wall. "I get paid to stay in the area. *On call*. I can't be more than ten minutes away. So I hang out on Eighth. In the bars there. If there's a problem, I get a call."

"How does your boss know if there's a problem?"

The guy shrugged.

"Did he call you just now, and tell you I was a problem?"

"He said you might be. He wanted you checked out."

"Was that the last call you took?"

The guy nodded. I checked the call log in his phone. Found the last incoming call. The number was withheld.

"How do you get in touch with your boss?"

"I don't."

"How do you get paid?"

"In cash. Sometimes it's waiting for me at the building. Sometimes it's dropped off at home. Sometimes it's at the bar. He calls and tells me where it'll be each week."

"One last question. What's your name?"

He didn't reply.

"It can't hurt to tell me. And if you want to get out . . ."

"It's Jonny. Jonny Evans. What's yours?"

"My name's not important. I'm just a janitor. I clean up dirty buildings. Now I'm going to check on what you told me. If it's true, I'll come back for you. Or at least send someone with a ladder. Like maybe the cops."

I went directly back to the building where the Masons lived, let myself in, and stomped upstairs to the top floor. Then I came back down, making no effort to be quiet. I was on the bottom step, about to turn and head back up, when the phone in my hand started to ring.

"Mr. Carrick?" I kept my voice bright and cheerful. "It's good to finally speak."

"I don't know who that is." It was a man's voice on the line, hesitant and cagey. "Who are you?"

"Let's not play games." I sat down on the stairs. "I was just speaking with Jonny, your security guy. He said this was the best way to get in touch with you. My name's Paul McNaught, Mr. Carrick, and I'm here to buy your building."

"It's not for sale."

"Let's not be hasty. I'm very sentimental about the place. My aunt Jenny used to live here. So here's the deal. I'll pay twenty percent over market price, which can be independently verified. That gives you a very generous premium. Plus it saves you the cost and aggravation of making all the outstanding repairs. And it means you'll be able to avoid a whole bunch of lawsuits. What do you say?"

"The building's not for sale."

"Let's at least meet. We should talk. Try to find a way forward. You see, Jonny gave me some interesting information about his friend Norman. Did you know they'd met after Norman's release from jail? Evidently they're very close, because Norman told Jonny all about how you ordered him to attack one of your residents. They seemed like just the kind of details the police would love to know."

"That's complete crap. Let me talk to Jonny."

"Jonny's not here right now. It seems he's gone underground for a while."

The line went silent for a moment.

"Listen. For the record, I don't know this Norman guy. But from what I've heard, you're too late. He was tried for this alleged assault already, and he got acquitted. So now he's safe. Double jeopardy protects him."

"That's an interesting theory. But here's the thing. Norman wasn't acquitted. It was a mistrial. Which means the whole double jeopardy thing doesn't apply. The DA can re-file the charges at any time. And he's pissed as hell about what happened. If my information gets into his hands, you're screwed. So. Does 8:00 A.M. Monday work for you?"

Chapter *Seventeen*

WHEN I WAS A KID THE EMPIRE STATE BUILDING WAS PRETTY MUCH the center of my universe. I must have gone to the observation deck with my father at least two dozen times. Security wasn't as crazy in those days, and the lines moved much more quickly. Even without fast passes. Not that my father would have let me get one, had they been available. He'd have said it was wrong for some people to pay extra and jump the queue.

I always walked around the outdoor platform clockwise, starting with the view to the north. I'd take my time and study the city from all four sides. My father would stand behind me, and tell me all about his favorite architects and the buildings laid out around the grid below us. As I grew older he'd quiz me. He'd check what I remembered. And test to see if I noticed which buildings had gone up or had been demolished or altered since our last visit. I was always right. It was one of the few things that pleased him about me. Afterward, if there was time, we'd eat at the diner on the first floor. That made the building a very nostalgic place for me. I'd often pictured going back. Maybe taking my own kids, on a weekend or during a school vacation. But I'd never imagined starting my working week there with an early-morning meeting.

George Carrick's office was on the twenty-fifth floor. The area outside the elevator was like a little time capsule. All kinds of fine art deco details had survived around the doorframes and light fittings and windows. I gazed around at them, so distracted that it took me a moment to realize that Carrick's was the only suite on the corridor that had a nameplate.

Carrick's reception area was a reasonable size, but it was completely dominated by a museum-style display case standing in the center of the space. It was full of scale models of new buildings. A couple looked familiar—ones that had recently sprouted in billionaires' row—but it wasn't clear if ground had ever been broken on some of the others. There was an expensive-looking leather-and-chrome couch against the wall to the right, with framed black-and-white photographs of buildings above it. The reception counter was on the opposite side of the room, between two pale wooden doors. A guy was sitting behind it, tapping away on a laptop computer. He looked like he was in his mid-thirties. His hair was cropped short. He had an expensive navy blue suit, a brilliant white shirt, and a narrow blue tie with a faint camouflage pattern.

"Mr. McNaught?" The guy stood up. He had a pronounced French accent. "Mr. Carrick's expecting you. Please, go straight through." He indicated the door to his right.

Carrick was sitting behind a brown leather desk. It looked like it was made out of ancient, beaten-up steamer trunks. He closed the lid of his slim silver laptop and emerged, holding out his hand. He was around five-feet-six tall, but stocky. I guessed he'd have been a powerful man when he was younger despite his lack of height. Now he was in his early sixties. His hair was thin and gray, but his face was hard and determined. His eyes were dark and piercing. His black suit was well tailored, and he wore his plain white shirt with no tie.

We shook hands, then he dropped onto a couch in front of his desk like the one in reception. He gestured for me to sit on an identical one on the other side of a low coffee table. The table had a glass top that covered a deep cavity full of more models of buildings.

Carrick held up both hands, palms out. "Before we even start, let's get all the cards on the table. Who are you working for? Vidic? Shevchenko? Ibrahimovic?"

"None of the above." I settled back on the couch. "I'm not working for anyone. I'm here on my own behalf. And I have a very simple proposition for you. I recently came into some money. A lot of it. I want to use some of it to buy your building. I'm prepared to be generous. Like I told you on the phone, the place has sentimental value. So please, name your price."

"I don't believe you." Carrick glared across the table. "You came into money? Bullshit. You're working for the Russians."

"Why do you think that? I've never even heard of those guys you mentioned."

"I don't *think*." Carrick smiled, but without a hint of warmth. "I know. Because the Russians have been plaguing me for two years to sell to them. Have you seen the area recently? It's hot. Everyone wants a piece. But I'm not interested in selling. It's not just a building we're talking about. It's people's homes. Have you seen the places the Russians build? They're all empty. All the time. It's the same as London. It's just a way for those guys and their fat-ass buddies to move their money around. To hide it. And to park their other assets, like paintings and wine collections. They're sucking the soul out of the city, and I won't be part of that. I love this place too much. So go back to your bosses and tell them, when George Carrick says no, he means no."

"Let's cut the crap, Mr. Carrick. I have no bosses. I want the building for myself."

"Even if that were true, it's not for sale."

"We haven't even discussed the price."

"That would be a waste of time. The building's fate is sealed. I'm knocking it down."

Carrick went to his desk, took a file from a drawer, and dropped it onto the coffee table.

"See for yourself. It's all in there."

I looked through the file. There were quotes from movers for transporting furniture and possessions. Quotes from demolition specialists. A timeline for permit applications. And the draft of a legal document gifting the land to the city for use as a park.

"Is this for real?"

"Every word."

"The deed's not executed."

"Not yet, no." Carrick bounced up on the balls of his feet, making himself momentarily a couple of inches taller. "I'm still negotiating with the city. I need a watertight deal that ensures the land can only ever be used as a park. I don't want those sneaky Russian bastards getting it through the back door."

"If you don't mind me saying, you seem pretty obsessed by these Russians."

"I am. And I have good reasons. Those guys will go to any lengths to get what they want. They started with a lowball offer. It was insulting. I refused. Then the tricks started. They tried to drive my tenants out of the building, to hurt me in the pocket. They sabotaged the place. Burst the pipes. Made holes in the roof. And when I sent contractors round to do the repairs, they attacked them. Then they brought a bunch of rats and let them loose. But I didn't budge. I was hoping to ride it out. I thought they'd find something shinier, and lose interest. Then they attacked a tenant.

A nice old lady. They put her in the hospital. That was the final straw. I thought, screw you! If I can't have the place, no one can. I'll flatten it, and make it impossible for anyone to build anything new there. In the meantime, I've brought in security to protect my tenants. And I'm making plans to find new accommodations for them in other buildings I own."

"Are you getting some kind of tax break for donating this land?"

"No."

"But you will end up making more on the rent."

"Wrong again."

"How so? At least two of the apartments are rent controlled. If the tenants move, they'll lose that protection."

"Correct. Technically. But I'm prepared to honor our current terms. I won't charge them a penny more."

"That all sounds great, George. But if you'll forgive me, it doesn't tally with what I've been hearing from the tenants. They say you're impossible to reach. That you refuse to do any repairs."

Carrick bowed his head for a moment. "It's like I told you. I tried to get the repairs done, but the Russians scared off my contractors. And I have to lay low, for my own safety. You should see the threats I've had. These guys don't mess around. And I can't help my tenants if I'm in the hospital. Or the cemetery."

"Maybe. But I have one other problem. When I talked to Jonny, he said Norman Davies—the guy who attacked your nice old lady tenant—worked for you."

"He did." Carrick bounced on the balls of his feet. "Davies *worked* for me. As in, past tense. I fired him when I found out what he did. Scratch that—what the Russians obviously paid him to do to make me look bad."

"Jonny said you were behind the attack."

"He's a lying asshole. You believed him? How would a slug like

Jonny know anything about my business? And were you there when he talked to Norman? How do you know what he really said?"

"Those are fair points, but here's something else I don't understand. If you're so innocent, and so determined not to sell, why did you agree to meet me?"

"I figured it was another Russian trick. I thought maybe they were trying to get Norman to lie. If he accused me, and I got convicted, I couldn't run my business. I'd be out of the way. And even if I wasn't convicted, the mud would stick and the tenants would likely leave. Either way, there'd be more pressure to sell. Which I won't do. I'm just trying to get that message across."

"How about this, then. If I can convince you I'm not working for the Russians, will you sell to me? I'll guarantee to fix the place up. Make it a fit home for the tenants again. I'll sign legal papers committing to it."

"No dice. I'm sorry. You just don't understand these guys. If I sell to you, they'll pressure you. They'll keep going after the tenants. Sooner or later someone will wind up dead. And that would be on me. This is the only way. But if you're really determined to buy a building, I have others. Good ones. I could show you what's available."

"Thanks, but no. I'm only interested in this specific building. It's a sentimental thing, like I said. Just promise me this. If you change your mind, call me. No one will beat my offer."

"I'll bear it in mind. But don't get your hopes up. I'm not going to sell."

"OK." I got to my feet. "I understand. And it was nice to meet you. There's just one last thing." I took Jonny's phone out of my pocket and set it on the table. "I'm sorry for that little subterfuge. It seemed like the only way to reach you. I hope Jonny's feathers aren't too ruffled. Please apologize to him for me."

Chapter **Eighteen**

FRANK CARRODUS WAS ALONE IN THE JANITORS' ROOM WHEN I got back from the Empire State. He was sitting on one of the couches, unpacking some books from a box.

"Anonymous delivery." He held one up. It was called *Small Pig*. "For the kids, I guess."

"I guess." I paused on my way to the locker room. "And it's a good idea, I'd say. I didn't see too many books when I was down there."

"I wonder who sent them?" He pulled out another one. *Little House on the Prairie.* "I hate this anonymous bullshit."

"What do you think? Maybe someone whose kid used to get looked after down there?"

"Who knows. That would be a nice gesture, I guess." He closed the box and moved it to the floor. "Hey, have you heard the latest? My sister got a real kick from that janitor story, so she put word out to her friends at other police precincts around the city in case he showed up again anywhere else. One of them called her this morning. She said two of their officers pulled a guy out of a hole at a construction site in Hell's Kitchen, Friday night. And get this. The guy said he'd been thrown in there by a dude calling himself The Janitor. Said he was on some kind of a mission to clean up the city's dirty streets. Or some shtick like that."

"That doesn't sound quite right." I shrugged. "Anyway, did they charge the guy?"

"I don't think so. They probably just locked him up overnight. He was most likely drunk or stoned or something. But hey, don't knock it. A story where a guy like you or me could be the hero for once? You've got to love that."

Carrodus left to take the box of books downstairs. I changed into my coveralls and restocked my cart as quickly as I could, then headed up to the third floor. I was making a late start, I had to leave early to get to another meeting, and I didn't want to lose momentum with my search for Pardew's file. But if I let my second plate drop—looking out for the Masons—people could lose their homes. Maybe even their lives. I'd spent most of my life believing that my father disapproved of the choices I made. That he resented me for turning my back on my family. But in this situation, for the first time, I figured there was a fighting chance he'd have thought I was doing the right thing.

I started by sweeping the hexagonal corridor. I worked fast. The rhythm was satisfying. I could see the progress I was making. And it was good for thinking. My conversation with Carrick was not what I'd been expecting. If he was telling the truth, it would be a big step forward. The tenants were getting rehoused. That was a massive item ticked off my list. *If* Carrick was telling the truth. I needed more information before I could relax, though. And I still had to come up with a way to flush out Norman Davies. And whoever trashed the evidence against him.

When I need the inside track on finance or real estate, there's only one person I go to. Ro Lebedow. I first met her years ago, during a particularly difficult case I was embroiled in. I'd been assigned to keep tabs on a guy who was trying to portray himself in certain circles as a kind of revolutionary messiah. The vision he was peddling involved the humbling of the United States through a set of simultaneous, devastating attacks on seven major cities, each carried out by a terror cell from a different enemy nation. It was a sound plan in many ways, not least because it required us to apprehend seven separate groups, in diverse locations, each with different methods and practices, all at the same time. In the end we figured that if we could locate the safe houses he was using to accommodate the various groups, we could coordinate raids across the country, swoop in, and sweep up the terrorists before they could do any harm. The key would be to trace the relevant property transactions. All of them. If we missed even one, people would wind up dead. Ro helped us, making sure that every place was correctly identified, and in the process she uncovered a massive stock fraud that the guy was trying to pull off under cover of the attacks. She's helped me a couple times since then, on an informal basis, and we've kept in touch.

With Ro you don't just benefit from her knowledge and insight. There's also an advantage in how fast she moves. Other people, if you called them for help one morning, they might have something for you the next day. If you were lucky. Ro asked if I was free after lunch.

I arrived at her office at 2:30 as agreed and found Ro on an exercise bike in the corner by the window, overlooking Bryant Park. She was wearing a sky blue tracksuit, her long silver hair was tied up in a ponytail, and she had a towel from The Peninsula hotel spa wrapped around her neck. She grabbed the remote when she saw my reflection in the glass, turned down the '70s rock music that was pounding out of a CD player on her bookcase, and kept on pedaling.

"Paul, hi!" She eased off the pace very slightly. "Are you well? Good. So, let's get started. First, the facts. The demolition permit Carrick showed you? It's for real. Unless it's part of an elaborate bluff, which you can never totally rule out with this guy, the building's toast. Is that going to be a problem?"

"Not for me." I crossed to the window. "Maybe for the tenants. Why's he doing it?"

"I have no idea. He hasn't filed any replacement permits. There's nothing on the grapevine about new projects or developments. I'm sure something's going on, but he must be playing some kind of extremely long game."

"Could he be doing it to take a tax loss? That was my first thought."

"You don't know much about tax avoidance, do you, Paul?" Ro shook her head. "But this guy does. You can bet your ass he's got every angle covered. Every loophole jumped through. Every cent of every allowance taken. This year, the big thing's low-cost housing, because of the governor. There's a huge incentive for investors. And Carrick's invested big. Right up to the limit."

"OK. But something else must be going on. I really need to figure out what he's up to with this building."

"Good luck with that. The guy's about as straight as a corkscrew."

"What do you know about him?"

"You know me. I'm all about character. The way I understand

the guy, it's like this. Imagine you were determined to make it as an actor. Hollywood is your dream. You work your ass off. Establish yourself. Make a certain kind of role your own. Would you feel good?"

"I guess."

"OK. But what if the only role you could make your own was the ugly loser who everyone laughs at, and who never gets to sleep with the leading lady?"

"I guess I wouldn't feel quite so good. But how is that relevant to real estate?"

"George Carrick had a tough start. He was born in '58, in Alphabet City. So he was in his teens during the seventies. That was a terrible time to be on the fringes of New York City, specially if you had no money. He fell in with a bad crowd. Got busted for some protection racket thing, and wound up in jail. He came out again in the Reagan years. Suddenly greed was good and rules weren't so important. He got a job as a rental agent. He was great at it. There were some mutterings about race issues, but he turned in the best figures at the company he worked for so no one cared. He made a name for himself, borrowed big, bought property, built a portfolio. Then he tried to make the move into development."

"He got his fingers burned?"

"Not at all. The odd one of his deals went south, sure, but overall his record was outstanding."

"So what was his problem?"

"Property development is a world of its own. Immense amounts of cash are involved. Carrick has a lot by regular standards, but he's no Saudi prince. He knew he had to bring something else to the table. So he made his name as a fixer. If there was a permit problem? A zoning issue? Yuppies protesting because they didn't want some new skyscraper so close to their condo? Carrick knew who to talk to. He got so good that nothing big happened without him. But then he could never break out of that role. He could never call the shots, because despite trying—and getting mighty close—he could never control the money. He wanted so desperately to be a mover and a shaker. To be part of the big-time Manhattan set. He worked for them. He worked with them. He greased their wheels. They couldn't succeed without him. But he always felt like a servant. Never one of them."

"If you can't join them, beat them. Or something like that." I stepped back and leaned against Ro's desk. "Were there ever any rumors about Carrick using strong-arm tactics?"

"Back in the eighties, maybe." Ro increased speed. "But nothing for a long time."

"How about the Russians? Any special resentment over them moving in? They've been putting serious money into some high-profile projects, from what I hear."

"That's true. They have. But Carrick's been helping them, from what I've been told. And making a lot of money in the process. No. The word online is that if he resents anyone, it's still the old-school Manhattan guys. He'll work with anyone and do anything, doesn't matter how shady or how risky, as long as it turns a dollar and brings him a step closer to crashing their party. It's probably his biggest weakness."

"So how does that factor into demolishing this building?"

"I have no idea. It makes no sense. Unless he's discovered oil under there? Or gold?"

"He told me he's giving the lot to the city. To use as a park."

"A lot that size is a bit small for a park. It's possible, I guess. Maybe one of those micro–bird sanctuary type deals? But whatever it is, a guy like Carrick, he's doing it for a reason. He's getting something in return, I guarantee."

Ro had given me plenty of food for thought, but I felt like I still needed a better handle on Carrick. Was he really an outsider, like me, doing his best in an inhospitable world? Or was he an untrustworthy asshole, ready to trample on anyone who stood between him and his next dollar? It was a tough question and I needed an answer fast, because his word was the only thing that was keeping a roof over the Masons' heads. And their neighbors'.

I decided to head back to the courthouse. There was time to search a couple more chambers that afternoon, and I was starting to rely on the mopping and sweeping to bring a little clarity. I left Ro's building and was heading for the subway when my phone rang. But it wasn't my regular one. It was the clone I'd made of Jonny's, over the weekend. I hit the answer key and it was like being added to a three-way call, except on listen only. I heard Jonny grunt a greeting, and then the voice of the person who'd called him. It was a voice I recognized. George Carrick's. He was summoning Jonny to a meeting. That night. At an address on 75th Avenue, in Brooklyn.

If I were Jonny, that would be the last place in the world I'd go. You wouldn't find me in the same county as anywhere proposed by George Carrick. But luckily for me, Jonny didn't have my sense of self-preservation. He agreed to be there. Which meant, much as the realization killed me, returning to the courthouse would have to wait. I had preparations to make, and not long to make them. Not if I was going to be ready on time.

Chapter **Nineteen**

THE GUY JONNY WAS SUPPOSED TO MEET ARRIVED TEN MINUTES late. I watched him pull into the small lot next to the designated building in Brooklyn. He was driving a white van. It had no windows at the back, and no markings of any kind. The guy swung it around wide, then reversed and stopped on a patch of weeds near the door.

He climbed out, and I recognized his narrow, pointy face right away. It was Norman Davies. I'd seen his photograph in the court file.

The building only had one story. It was maybe twenty feet tall and was built of brick, with peeling cream exterior paintwork. A straggly creeper was growing up its far corner near the wall separating it from the lot on the next street. There were cleaner patches where signs might once have been, but now there was nothing to identify the place. Or its owner. Davies walked back toward the street, grabbed hold of a rickety wire mesh gate, and started to pull. The gate was also twenty feet high, and half the width of the lot. It was suspended on a girder by three pairs of rusty wheels set into a narrow groove. They squealed in protest, but Davies put his back into it and finally got the thing closed. He secured it with a padlock and crossed to the door of the building. It was metal. Painted yellow. The finish had dulled with time, but it still stood out against the crumbling brickwork. Someone had welded a panel over the letter slot. Davies pulled a handle next to it and disappeared inside.

I dealt with the padlock on the gate—that was quicker and safer than climbing over—crossed to the van, and made sure no one was inside. Then I opened the yellow door as softly as possible and slipped into the building.

The air was heavy with the stink of rusty metal and gasoline. The floor was made of cement. It had been poured in sections, and years of detritus had got caught in the gaps. The surface was covered with dark stains. Some were oil. Some, maybe other things. Yellow lines, now faded, marked out where pieces of unidentified equipment had been. You could see the holes where the anchor bolts had secured them. Steel pillars, painted white, rose up to meet the roof beams. Bright red fire extinguishers were still attached to every other one. The underside of the ceiling had been pulled off at some stage, exposing joists and pipes and cable trays.

There was a roll-up metal vehicle door in the center of the wall that joined the street. It looked new. A control panel was mounted next to it, with red and green buttons on its front and shiny metal conduits running up to its mechanism and down to the ground. Someone had dropped off a bunch of pallets just inside the entrance. There were seven. Each was still stacked with large cardboard boxes, but no markings were visible despite the loads having been shrink-wrapped in clear plastic.

High in the opposite wall there was a round ventilation port, where a fan's jammed blades stood firm against the gentle breeze.

Below that were rows of metal shelves. There were two sections. One was blue. The other green. Both were empty. Their paint was chipped, and the remains of yellow labels clung to their edges. I couldn't read what was written on them.

The whole width of the wall opposite the door was taken up with windows. All of them were boarded up except one, in the center of the row. There was a metal stool in front of it, in a pool of yellow light that was spilling inside from a nearby streetlamp. A guy was sitting on it. He was wearing dirty sneakers, mud-stained jeans, and a Mets hoodie. The hood was pulled up, hiding the guy's face. His arms were crossed defensively.

Norman Davies was standing in the center of the space, looking around. His face was pinched and spiteful. Movement in the far corner caught his eye. He spun around and pulled his gun, searching for a target. As he watched, a rat scampered back under one of the shelves.

"Don't panic, Norm." It was Jonny's voice, and he sounded nervous. "It was just one of your cousins."

Davies shook his head and stepped toward the figure on the stool.

"That's close enough." The nerves in Jonny's voice were spiraling toward outright panic. "I don't know what's going on. Why are you here? Why have you got a gun? George Carrick told me he was coming. He said he had a job for me."

"Well, there is a job to be done." Davies stopped ten feet away from the stool. "And you know Carrick doesn't do these things himself. So that's why I'm here." He raised the gun and lined it up on Jonny's chest.

"No!" Jonny screamed and spun around sideways on the stool. "Norm, don't! Please!"

"Jonny, you're an idiot." Davies lowered the gun. "You always were an idiot. I hated working with you. I only brought you in to do the simple stuff I was bored with, but you couldn't even do that right." He raised the gun again, this time to Jonny's head level. "I've wanted to do this so many times. Carrick kept saying no. But now you've been shooting your mouth off about me and that old bitch in the hospital? That was your final mistake."

"No!" Jonny swiveled back the opposite way.

Davies tracked his movement and pulled the trigger, hitting Jonny in the shoulder. The noise was deafening in the enclosed space. Davies reached down to retrieve his shell case, then stepped closer to Jonny's fallen body. He lined up on Jonny's head. Then he lowered the gun.

"What the?" Davies nudged the body with his foot. The hood slipped down, and waves of long blond hair spilled out across the floor.

"Who's the idiot now, Norman?" Jonny appeared from inside the stack of cardboard boxes with his walkie-talkie still in his hand. "I thought you'd notice you were talking to another dummy—specially given it was a woman—but that was all we could get on such short notice."

Davies stepped toward him, the gun raised again in a two-handed grip. "Get on the floor, asshole."

"Don't do anything hasty, Norman." I flicked on the lights, stepped forward, and pointed to four tripods set up around the room. "See the cameras? They're very special. They have awesome low-light performance. And wireless networking. Which means they picked up everything you did here and sent the footage to a secure server. The only person who has access to it, aside from me, is my lawyer. If anything happens to Jonny or me, the film goes to the police. And if that happens, you go to jail. For twenty-five to life. There'll be no snafus at the courthouse this time. You can trust me on that."

Davies lowered the gun. "But Jonny moved." He looked puzzled. "Or the dummy did."

"We used fishing line." I smiled at him. "It's too thin to see in the dim light. But don't worry. It's an old trick. It always works. A little bit of movement makes the deception seem so much more convincing. So don't go beating yourself up for being a total moron, or anything like that."

Davies suddenly perked up, and his eyes narrowed. "Wait a minute. You said you'd send the tape to the police *if* anything happened. But you're both OK. So . . ."

"So you have a decision to make." I looked him in the eye. "You have two ways to go. You can tell us about George Carrick. Specifically, what he ordered you to do at the apartment building where the old lady was hurt. Then you can walk away. Or I'll edit the end of the tape. Jonny will lie low. And you'll go to jail."

"Bullshit." The hint of a mocking smile started to play around the sides of his mouth. "The tape's bogus, and there's no other evidence."

"Actually, there's plenty of other evidence." I smiled at him. "Or there will be, if you choose that path. For example, there'll be you, unconscious after crashing your van on the way back from dumping Jonny's body. His blood will be found in the back. You have GSR on your hands. Jonny's blood will also be found here, on the floor, exactly where the tape shows you shooting him. Your prints are all over the gun. And the police have a hard-on for you like you wouldn't believe after you got that undeserved walk."

Davies's mouth sagged open, but he didn't speak.

"That's an interesting gun." I pointed to it, still in Davies's hand. "It looks old. Well used. When the crime lab runs ballistics, will they find links to any other crimes, do you think?"

"Hold on, stop." Davies took a step back. "Your plan's no good. If I roll on Carrick for the apartment building thing, I'd be incriminating myself, too."

"No." I shook my head. "You wouldn't be. That's the beauty

of the US criminal justice system. If you tell us specifically about Carrick's instructions regarding the Masons, you're safe. Because you've already been into court for that. You walked. And you can't be tried for the same crime twice. As long as you keep to that one area, you're bulletproof."

"Are you sure?"

"I'm certain. Google it, if you don't believe me. Search for the definition of *double jeopardy*."

Davies tucked the gun into the back of his jeans and took out his phone. He typed a few words and scrolled down the screen a little way. His mouth moved silently as he read, then he nodded. "OK. I'll tell you. But only about the Masons."

"Good decision. Let's get that on tape, then we can all go home."

"Norman? Just one last thing." I zipped the final camera into its case after we finished recording. "I need you to stick around for a while, in case any more questions crop up."

"No way." Davies shook his head. "When Carrick realizes I didn't obey him, and Jonny's still alive . . ."

"That's no problem. I've arranged a hotel. You can stay there a couple of days."

"Forget it." Davies crossed his arms. "I'm leaving town. You can call me if you need me."

"That doesn't work. There's another problem." I pointed to the corner of the room. "See that camera?"

Davies turned to look and I slipped my thumb behind his right ear, squeezing his lobe hard against my finger for five seconds. He squealed and wriggled, and jumped back as soon as I let go.

"Hey!" He felt behind his ear. "What did you stick to me?"

"It's a tracker chip." I kept my voice matter-of-fact. "It's the kind the FBI usually uses on cars and trucks, but I didn't have time to get a personal one. It means they can find you anywhere in the world, via GPS. You can't get it off. You need a special solvent that's not available to civilians. My friend at the New York field office promised to remove it when Carrick's in jail. We won't need you then. The only way for you to do it yourself is to cut your ear off. So if you run, we either track the chip or look for an idiot doing a bad impression of Vincent van Gogh."

"Who?"

"Just go to the hotel, Norman. Order room service. And stay there."

It could be that I'm getting softhearted, but I gave Norman a ride to the hotel. Or it could be because I decided to keep his truck. I left him on the sidewalk, anxiously touching his ear, then continued toward the bus station.

"Take this." I handed Jonny a bunch of twenties as we were getting close. "Go wherever you want. And don't come back. Not unless you want George Carrick to send someone else to finish Norman's job."

"Is it true?" Jonny took the money. "What you told Norman? About not going to jail for the thing with Mrs. Mason?"

"It's absolutely true."

"I don't believe you. I think you tricked him."

"What if I did? He's an asshole. He was going to kill you."

"But he didn't. And now he'll end up in jail because of your lies."

"If he ends up in jail it'll be because of his crimes. Jail's the best place for him. He deserves it. And what do you want from me, anyway? I'm a janitor, not a saint."

Chapter *Twenty*

GEORGE CARRICK STOOD UP AND SMILED WHEN I WALKED INTO his office the next morning.

He emerged from behind his desk, bounced on the balls of his feet, then gestured to the couches. We took the same places as before. Today, he was wearing a gray suit with a tie, and his laptop was open on the coffee table.

"It's good to see you again, Mr. McNaught." Carrick smiled. "I'm glad you've come to your senses. I have plenty of buildings, like I told you. I'm sure I can find one you like, and that makes sense to your wallet as well." He leaned forward and hit a key on his laptop, and then took a moment to check that a webpage was loading properly. "Here's what I currently have on the market. This is a private site. I can give you the link, but please don't share it with anyone else, OK? Good. Now, do you want to start with a particular budget, or shall we just dive in and see what grabs you?"

"Let's dive in." I picked up the computer and scrolled through the first couple of listings. "These are nice, George. Much better than the place the Masons are living in. Well, where Mr. Mason's living. Mrs. Mason's still in the hospital, I believe."

"Of course they're better. The Masons' building is due to be torn down. All of these, they're good for years to come."

"How about from the tenants' point of view? Do you think they'd be safe in these kind of places?"

"They'd absolutely be safe." Carrick shrugged. "Well, as safe as you can be in New York City."

"That's good." I nodded. "That means a lot, coming from you. Because let's face it, you should know."

Carrick's eyes narrowed. "What do you mean?"

"I mean that you sent Norman Davies to attack Mrs. Mason. You did that. Not the Russians."

"That's crazy." Carrick stood up. "You can't come into my office and make bullshit accusations about me. You need to leave. Now."

Carrick reached for the laptop, but I pulled it away, out of his reach, and slid a thumb drive into a slot on its side. I held him at bay until the right menu popped up, then hit Play and put the computer back down on the table, where we could both see the screen. Norman Davies's ratlike face appeared. He looked flushed and nervous, but his squeaky voice was clearly audible as he stated his name and the date of the recording. He went on to confirm that Carrick sent him to his building in Hell's Kitchen to intimidate Mrs. Mason. Davies held up a key to the building and swore that Carrick had given it to him. He also talked about the wrench. He said it was Carrick's idea to use it, because he knew from experience that they're scarier-looking than bats or clubs. The problem was, Davies claimed, the wrench was heavier than he'd expected, never having used one before, and that was why his "warning" blows had hurt the woman much more than he'd intended them to.

Carrick was still on his feet. Veins were bulging in his temples. His fists were clenched and he was leaning in toward me like he was suspended by an invisible rope. He reminded me of a pit bull straining to break its leash. "This is total bullshit! It's made up. From beginning to end. Davies was paid to say all that stuff. He was just saving his own skin. Where is he? The little asshole. I'll kill him."

"His statement's not made up." I stayed on the couch. "And I'm going to the cops with the video unless we can reach an understanding. Right here. Right now."

"Forget it." Carrick stomped across to the window and gazed out down Fifth Avenue. "The building's still not for sale. I'm still knocking it down."

"You'd go to jail, rather than sell it?"

Carrick shrugged. "I've been to jail before. It's no biggie. And I have better lawyers now. I'd never get convicted. Not with what you've got."

"Maybe we can find a way to avoid testing that theory. Let's talk about the demolition. You're really going through with that?"

Carrick nodded.

"I don't understand. Why do you want to? How do you benefit?"

"I don't want to!" Carrick raised his voice. "The whole thing's ridiculous. It's not my idea!"

"So why do it?"

"Because I've been told to. *Ordered* to."

"By whom?"

"It was Walcott's fault, the idiot. It was his mistake. But it's Madatov's order."

"Walcott? Madatov? Who are these guys?"

"Walcott's a finance guy. We do business sometimes. I help him out with development deals. He has cash—or he knows people who have it—but nothing else. I provide the expertise. Madatov—he's a whole different story."

"How so?"

"I'd never have gotten dragged in if I'd known Madatov was involved. The guy's a psycho. And not a Hollywood-style one, who does weird things to a few people because his dad was mean or a talking dog told him to. Madatov's from Azerbaijan. It's an old Soviet republic, but he's been here for years. They're trying to rival the Russians and the Ukrainians. No one had heard of their country when they arrived, so they built a reputation all on their own. Madatov's the worst of them. He'll do anything—and I mean *anything*—to get what he wants, and to keep his people in line."

"How did the money guy get involved with him?"

"Walcott worked in Azerbaijan for years. He was tight with the rulers after the USSR collapsed. There were heaps of money, from a ton of oil and gas. The politicians basically stole it all. They needed help to clean it. Hide it. Move it around. And also to spin their 'elections' to avoid there being a revolution. The regime finally collapsed last year. Walcott came back to the States and started introducing himself to the Azerbaijanis who were already here. He's basically trying to carry on like it's business as usual. Which is asking for trouble."

"So he screwed something up?"

"Right. Walcott came to me saying he had funding for a development. A major project, up on Central Park South. They're breaking ground next year. Anyway, as usual, he had the money but needed help making things work. Which I gave. But which I wouldn't have given if I'd known one cent was coming from Madatov."

"How did Walcott screw up, if the project's proceeding? Is it over budget? Massively late?"

"No." Carrick threw up his hands. "The project's in perfect

shape. The problem was that Walcott got his wires crossed. Mada-tov apparently just wanted to give some cash a quick rinse. Major developments like the one we're talking about make huge profits, but that takes years to happen. So that got Madatov mad, and he started dealing out punishments."

"Your punishment is to demolish your building?"

"Right."

"Why? Isn't that a little random?"

"No, actually. It's all about the view. Madatov has a place nearby. Mine blocks his view of the river."

"So this Madatov guy wants you to demolish a perfectly good building and throw a bunch of tenants out on the street to improve his view?"

Carrick shrugged. "Look, it's a pain in everyone's ass. But from my point of view, really, I got off light. Listen. A year or so ago, Madatov got in a beef with some guy about a painting he bought. It turned out to be a fake. No one was suggesting the guy deliber-ately ripped him off. It was just one of those misunderstandings. Swiss bankers were involved, Nazis, whatever. Anyway, Madatov did this thing to the guy that's some kind of ritual from his home country. They take starving rats, a fire . . . let's just say it's not pretty."

"What about Walcott? What was his penalty?"

"His is easy. He just has to pay a fine. That shouldn't be hard. The guy's made a gazillion dollars over the years, or so he claims. Although I guess he can't actually be that great with money, be-cause he came to me, asking for a loan. Can you believe that? After what he did? I told him, the second word's *off*. Pick the first for yourself."

"Where could I find this Madatov guy? Does he hang out at this place near yours?"

"He does. But you should stay away. First of all, you don't

want to find him. Word has it he caught a guy snooping around a house he owns in Connecticut one time, so he stripped him naked and tied him to a tree near a wasps' nest and watched while he got stung to death. And second, Madatov's become super paranoid. No one's seen him for months."

"How does he communicate, then?"

"Through his lawyer. A guy named Roberto di Matteo. He's the only one who's allowed access anymore. Apart from his security guards—trusted guys from home—and his mistresses. He has two of them. He must come out sometimes, though, even if it's just to kill people. He's still racking up the bodies as fast as ever."

"And where's Walcott?"

"In hiding somewhere. While he raises the money, I guess. He has an office on Wall Street. His assistant keeps it open and takes messages. I don't know if he gets them. He and I aren't exactly speaking."

"OK. Just one more question before we talk about a solution to your video problem. After Davies got arrested for hurting Mrs. Mason, you fixed the evidence so he'd be released. How did you do that?"

"That wasn't me." Carrick sat back on the couch opposite me. He seemed smaller somehow, like some air had been let out of his chest. "I wasn't expecting the idiot to get arrested. When he did, I panicked. I reached out to Madatov, through his lawyer. The message I got back just said, 'It's handled.' I didn't know what they were planning." Carrick paused for a moment. "Honestly, after I reached out, I was worried. I was expecting them to have him killed in the jail."

"All right, George, so here's where we are. I see two problems. One's moral. One's practical. Morally, you broke the law. You got a woman hurt. And you sent Davies to kill Jonny Evans. You should go to jail. Good lawyers or not."

Carrick leaned forward with his elbows on his knees. "What's it called? Extenuating circumstances? Think about Madatov. I wouldn't have done any of those things if it wasn't for him. And Walcott's stupid mistake."

"Maybe. And Davies didn't kill Evans, so we can let that go. No harm, no foul. And if you went to jail, that would make our practical problem worse. Your tenants. They need a place to live. A decent place."

"I already promised to rehouse them."

"I know you did. But you also lied about sending Davies to hurt Mrs. Mason, and then you tried to set up a murder. So call me cynical, but I don't believe you."

"You can trust me. I swear. Listen. I'll get my lawyer to write it up. We'll make it a legal contract. I'll guarantee that everyone will be looked after."

"They can all go together to the same building, if they want?"

"Of course."

"They can stay in the same neighborhood?"

"If they want to."

"They'll pay the same rent as now. And that'll be frozen."

"Not frozen. I'll give them the same terms as rent control. That's what they have now. Most people in New York would kill for that."

"OK. But the point is—no monster rent increases. Now, Mrs. Mason. She'll either need a first-floor apartment or a building with an elevator."

"No problem."

"And she'll need help with her medical bills. There's a possible new treatment, which might get her out of her wheelchair."

"No way." Carrick crossed his arms. "How much would that cost?"

"I don't know. How much is it worth to stay out jail?"

Carrick stood up, crossed to the window, and bounced on the balls of his feet as he stared out over the city. "All right." Carrick turned back around. "I'll help with her bills. Within reason."

"And if she is permanently in a wheelchair, you'll pay for her to have a helper."

"Are you out of your mind?"

"What? You're happy to pay assholes like Davies to hurt people, but not to help them?"

"OK. A helper. If she stays in the chair. But not twenty-four/seven. Only when she needs to go out. To the store, say once a week, or to the doctor."

"To the doctor whenever necessary. And three trips out every week, wherever she wants to go."

Carrick rolled his eyes, then nodded.

"Good." I smiled at him. "Seems like we have a deal, then."

"Not quite. I need the tape of Davies's *confession*, plus all the copies you made."

"There's no need. The point is, I'm keeping you out of jail so you can provide for the tenants."

"I understand that. But humor me. Please."

"OK. I'll give you the tapes once the agreement's signed. Have the papers sent to my hotel. The Brincliffe."

"Give me a day."

"No problem. But one thing. At the hotel, have your messenger leave the papers addressed to Paul *McKenzie*. There was a snafu with my name when I registered, and I've been too busy to sort it out."

Chapter *Twenty-one*

I STOPPED AT THE BRINCLIFFE HOTEL TO COLLECT SOME THINGS on my way to the courthouse, then went on to the Grosvenor to make myself another reservation. It was a nuisance having to rent two rooms until Carrick had the legal papers delivered, but I was back to battling my old habits. I couldn't have anyone knowing where I was staying. And it was a small price to pay to solve an immediate problem. It was good to know that Carrick's tenants would be properly looked after. And hopefully the new treatment would help Mrs. Mason. I would have liked to see Carrick behind bars, though. It left a bad taste in my mouth, allowing scum like him to stay on the streets, but I couldn't see a way around it. I had to settle for the lesser of two evils. As for the others, I had more decisions to make. With Carrick staying out of jail, it would seem harsh to get Davies locked up. He couldn't just walk away from the attack on Mrs. Mason, though. Could he volunteer for something? Do some kind of community service? I could talk to Carrodus, before or after my shift. He seemed to have his finger on that kind of pulse. Then there was the Azerbaijani dude, Madatov. I had to do something about him. We can't have ex–Soviet gangsters throwing Americans out of their homes so they can improve their view. I wanted to root out his contact in the NYPD, as well. And Walcott? I wasn't sure. Money laundering wasn't something I knew too much about. Which meant I needed to make one more call before heading to the courthouse.

Ro's availability was limited that day, so I had to swallow my frustration and cut my shift a little short. I cleaned what was absolutely necessary, but that only left me enough time to search two extra rooms. I had to wait for people to leave each of them. A small group came out of the first one, bubbling with elation. More people were involved in the second. They were dressed smartly for the occasion, but their mood seemed somber and disappointed. Almost depressed. I wondered how I'd have felt if I'd been at Pardew's trial. And I wondered if I'd ever get the chance to find out.

Ro was at her standing desk when I arrived. She had a sharply tailored black suit on with silver sneakers, and her heels were waiting by the door with her snakeskin briefcase. Her laptop was open, but I couldn't help wonder how it could compete with the view. She seemed to be watching it out of one eye, like she couldn't be completely disconnected from the pulse of the city. She seemed to feed off its energy.

"You really do pick 'em, Paul." She half turned and shook her head at me. "If Carrick's iffy, Walcott's an absolute sleaze. He was, anyway, before he left the United States. He was a campaign consultant. And a lobbyist. Only with a difference. If his client had a rival who was too strong? If a politician was reluctant to vote the right way? Or wanted too big of a bribe? Walcott had ways of making that kind of problem go away. Shady ways. Actually, he was beyond shady. He was in total darkness. The FBI was watching him. He knew they were closing in. So he went to Armenia, when it looked like they had the upper hand in the Caucasus. Then he flipped to Azerbaijan when the balance of power changed. It's one of the ex–Soviet republics."

"I've heard of it." In fact, I'd more than heard of the place. I'd been fully briefed on it, years ago, ready for an assignment. I didn't go, though, due to a last-minute change of allocation. I heard that the guy who replaced me got on the wrong end of a bad conduct discharge. The rumor was he landed in the pocket of a local sleaze merchant. An American expat who was high up in the government, but I hadn't heard a name before. "Were there any other Americans over there, doing what he did? Or just Walcott?"

"No others." Ro paused to watch a fire truck barge its way through the traffic. "The place was an utter cesspool of corruption. So, naturally, Walcott fit right in. He had skills. He had no morals. Which was the perfect formula for worming his way in with the elite. All the way up to the president. There was a rumor that he had his own suite in the palace."

"In return for doing what?"

"First, you've got to understand the economic situation over there. It's all about oil and gas. The country's awash with the stuff. When the USSR fell, those industries were privatized. Which is a fancy way of saying *stolen*. The inner circle amassed outrageous wealth. The president had a private zoo, believe it or not, and he stocked it with some of the rarest animals in the world. The defense secretary built a collection of flightworthy vintage MiG fighter planes, which he kept at his own personal airfield. The commerce and industry secretary liked cars, so he bought dozens of them on the taxpayers' dime. And nothing cheap. We're talking Ferraris. Lamborghinis. Aston Martins. Maseratis. All this time thousands were starving in the streets. And against that backdrop, Walcott did two things. He ran the spin machine, holding off a revolution by making people think things were getting better and that the elections were real. And he helped his buddies get the bulk of their wealth out of the country. Even they knew that times were too good—for themselves—to last. Then eventually the regime did fall, and the fat cats all had to flee."

"To the United States?"

"No, actually. Walcott's buddies all went to Moscow. I guess they stuck him with the blame for the worst of their excesses, and the Russians bought it. They made it clear that Walcott wasn't welcome. He came back to New York on his own. And he's having trouble getting on his feet, I hear. FBI agents are like elephants. They never forget. Apparently they're still all over his finances. Rumor has it he was too greedy. He kept his cash in Baku for too long. He didn't want to lose any. Even money shrinks in the wash, you know. Now he can't bring it here without opening a giant can of federal worms. No one knows where the money he has is coming from, but reading between the lines, I bet he's back to his old tricks."

"Which lines are you reading between?"

"Well, he seems to be spending most of his time in property development. That makes sense—he has the foreign contacts, and they have the cash. And nearly every deal he touches falls apart."

"Perhaps he's lost his touch?"

"On the contrary. I think he wanted them to fail."

"Why? To hurt people?"

"No. To help them. A failed deal is not the best way to launder large amounts of cash, but it's quick and easy. Think about it. Here's what you do. You start by forming an investment consortium, which is a bona fide legal entity. It's new, but clean. All the partners deposit their shares. A project comes up. They make their proposal. And lose, on purpose. Then they dissolve the consortium and retrieve their cash. Now they can take it to the bank, because they received it from a legitimate organization and have the paper trail to prove it. I think Walcott arranges everything, then takes a cut at the end. In cash. It's lucrative, and invisible."

"It's downright devious."

"Not as devious as the Cayman double dip. If you want a twofer, you do this as well: Set up a consultancy in the Caymans. It's capitalized at, say, twenty million. On paper that's split fifty-fifty between you and a partner. Except actually all the cash is yours. Your consultancy advises on the development deal, which of course fails. Then you sue your partner, saying it was his fault. You win, because it's the Caymans and you get what you pay for. You're awarded ten million in damages. The company collapses, and the receiver pays you back your supposed original stake—the remaining ten million. So you get the whole twenty, less costs, now clean."

"OK. I see the mechanics. But what about Walcott himself? Can you help me get a feel for the guy? I know he facilitates crooked deals. But are his hands dirty? Are Americans getting hurt by the things he does?"

"I'd say yes, and yes. Guys like him are unlikely to be choosy. It's a dime to a dollar that if he's laundering money for the Azerbaijanis, he's also doing it for drug dealers, mob bosses, you name it. Plus, the Azerbaijanis who are here are bad, bad guys from what I hear. Hiding their money makes it harder for the police to arrest them. So you end up with more drugs on the street. More women being trafficked. And so on. People think money laundering is victimless, but it's not. And even when Walcott and his buddies bankroll developments that do go ahead—what are they? Expensive. And mostly vacant. They're stopping regular folks from buying homes in the city."

"OK. So how do you take a guy like Walcott down? And what kind of time would he get?" I thought of Pardew's case. "I've heard that white-collar crimes can be hard for juries to understand."

"You're right. They can be. So I'd do this. Associate Walcott with a bad guy whose money he cleaned. Show that the money came from a criminal enterprise. If anyone died during the commission of any of the crimes, it becomes an automatic felony homicide. And if you get an aggressive enough ADA—I know a couple if you need names and numbers—she could argue for accessory after the fact."

Chapter Twenty-two

BEFORE TALKING WITH RO, I'D BEEN FLIRTING WITH THE IDEA OF giving Walcott a pass. I'd thought, maybe he wasn't as bad as a guy like Madatov. Now I wondered if he was worse, skulking around in the shadows, enabling other people's crimes, and growing fat in the process.

After the conversation I googled Walcott, so I'd seen his jowly face. That made him a tangible target. But there was nothing online about Madatov. No biography. No photograph. That made him a mystery. So that evening as I sat outside his house in Hell's Kitchen in the van I'd stolen from Norman Davies, I willed him to come out. I wanted to put a face to a name, as if that would somehow make it easier to size the guy up.

I'd been watching for half an hour when a car pulled up outside the house. It was a late-model town car, the rounded version, in obligatory black. I reached for my camera. The front door opened, and a security guard came out. He looked up and down the street, then ushered someone out. A man. But not Madatov. It was his lawyer. Roberto di Matteo. I'd googled him, too.

After another ten minutes the only light in any of the upstairs windows went out. Then the same procedure played out with a town car arriving and a security guard checking the street. Only this time two women left the house. Madatov's mistresses. They were both tall and blond with short mink jackets and shorter leather skirts. Their legs were long and their heels were high, and they moved with a practiced elegance.

Another hour went by, and there was still no sign of Madatov. He must have been there earlier, to meet with the lawyer. But now the house was dark. He could still be home, but asleep. Or he could have slipped out unnoticed to take care of some private business. Heads or tails . . .

In training at Fort Huachuca we were taught never to go into a building cold. To always wait for intel. For plans. Blueprints. Eyewitness accounts. Anything to give us an edge. But in the field, we soon discovered that intel was often wrong. Plans could be out-of-date. Blueprints, inaccurate. Accounts, false. So we learned to read buildings, and their circumstances and surroundings. Then decide for ourselves whether to go in.

This building was designed to discourage intruders. It had six stories, the same as the Masons' building, which was the historic limit for the area. So there were no taller neighboring buildings to drop down from. The front door was modern. It didn't match the rest of the façade. That was deliberate. It was to draw attention to the giant lock. The door glass was laminated and I'd guarantee it was real, not like at the courthouse. The first- and second-floor windows were barred. They used a subtle decorative pattern, but they looked strong. There were no downpipes to climb. No trees with convenient limbs to give you a boost. Cameras were mounted on the wall, ostentatiously angled toward the steps. There was an oversized alarm box, complete with a monitoring company's warning signs. Inside, there were guards. Two were on duty, with maybe more stood down. The ones I could see were tall and wide. They moved like soldiers, and they were armed. They carried radios and constantly appeared busy, checking monitors and tapping away at keyboards. Their workstation was brightly lit and it was huge, like it had been taken from a major corporate headquarters.

I took in all the detail, and I was encouraged. The alarm system might alert the security guards but there was no way it would make a sound or link to a monitoring station. If Madatov was the heavyweight he was reputed to be, the last thing he'd want would be noise, attracting attention and maybe prompting someone to call the cops. Likewise, he'd want to avoid any scenario that could bring overeager rent-a-cops snooping around his premises. It would be a similar story with the cameras. The external ones would be linked to the guards' monitors, but if there were any at all inside they wouldn't go any higher than the first floor. Madatov wouldn't want anyone seeing—or recording—what he was up to and who was with him. Carrick had mentioned that Madatov was the only resident, so there was no risk of bumping into a neighbor carrying a basket of clothes back from the laundry. The window bars were pointless. You'd never break in at the front, where passersby could see. You'd go for the roof. Which was no higher than the neighbors', due to the historic limit. It was only separated by a four-foot gap. And it had a boiler house on top, which meant there was definite access to the rest of the building.

I grabbed my pack, checked my equipment, and eased out of the van onto the sidewalk. I didn't go to the next building, because if I was handling security for Madatov I'd put a discreet camera there, too, just in case. I went to the one after that. And I went to the right, because for some reason most people default to the left.

The building was simple to get into. The door clicked open

after I tried just one buzzer. I didn't even need to make up an excuse. No one saw me on my way up the main stairs, and I quickly found the small service flight that led to the roof. Someone who lived there kept bees. There were two wooden hives, six feet high, with taps on the sides for harvesting the honey. That was a good idea. There's a world shortage of bees. It was nice to see New York doing its bit.

I stepped across to the next roof. There were two round tables folded up on this one, ten chairs, and a propane grill under a bespoke cover. Four wooden planters overflowed with bright flowers. There was a door to the stairs, an outdoor clock, and a thermometer. I crouched near the wall and checked Madatov's roof. It was empty. The surface wasn't finished, just sprinkled with gravel to help distribute rainwater. I took my time, using my flashlight to methodically quarter the area and look for the glint of a tripwire or the raised profile of a pressure pad. When I was satisfied it was clear, I stepped across.

I moved slowly to avoid disrupting any gravel and made it safely to the door. It was locked. It took two minutes to pick, then I slipped inside and crept down one flight of stairs to the top corridor. There were doors to two apartments. I listened at the first one. There was silence, so I picked that lock, too. I guessed the place had been rehabbed sometime in the last five years, but I'm no expert. The fittings—the kitchen, the bathrooms, the door furniture, the windows—all felt expensive. And unused. There was no furniture. No appliances. No possessions. I wondered, was it an investment in property, or privacy? Or both?

It was the same story in the other apartment on sixth, and both of them on fifth. But when I reached the fourth, I could see that something was different. The lock on the front apartment's door caught my attention. It stood out from the others because it was huge. Serious-looking. And solid. It took three minutes to get it open, mainly because I was being so careful not to scratch its shiny gold surface.

The door opened into the living/dining room. It had a tall, wide window and I saw that one thing was true—Carrick's building did block the view of the Hudson. There was a giant chrome telescope on a matching tripod. A dark wood floor. A pair of white leather couches, with a plaid throw on each. A wooden coffee table with a book lying open on it. A biography of Baryshnikov. There was a TV on a stand with a Blu-ray player, but no additional sound system. A stack of discs. Some books, mainly about ballet and World War II. A couple of novels. And a laptop.

I took out a black, featureless box from my bag and plugged it into one of the laptop's USB ports. It was the same kind of machine as I'd used to clone the ISIS commander's computer in Afghanistan back in March, so I was confident it would give me an accurate snapshot of Madatov's data. I figured I'd have to pull some favors to read it, though, because even without password and encryption issues, any documents he created would probably use the language from his homeland. Which I didn't know.

I left the machine to do its work and checked the kitchen. It was a clean, simple space. There was a table with three chairs. A plant. A Bluetooth speaker. A stack of freshly washed plates and pots on the countertop. And enough food in the fridge to last the better part of a week. I started to wonder who'd bought it and where, then pushed the thought aside. I don't know why, but the idea of criminals and terrorists doing their grocery shopping like regular folk always makes my skin crawl.

The apartment had three bedrooms. The first was obviously Madatov's. His bed was made. He had a dozen suits hanging in the closet. The size labels would put him at around six feet tall. He favored black with black shirts, and no ties. He only had black shoes. They were all a little dusty, but there was no telltale dirt on the soles.

The other two rooms belonged to the women. They each had a closet full of clothes, which looked expensive. Lots of shoes, mostly with dangerously high heels. Workout gear. Makeup, and other personal stuff. But nothing with their names on it, and only one photograph. It was in the second woman's room, in a simple wooden frame set on the nightstand and angled toward her pillows. I scanned the background, hoping I'd be able to figure out where it had been taken, but it was no good. The image was too faded. And its surface had been damaged from contact with some kind of liquid. I couldn't be sure what it was. But if I had to guess, I'd say it was someone's tears.

I heard a discreet tone from the other room telling me that the cloning process was complete. I collected my machine, took a couple of final pictures, and let myself out. I checked the apartment opposite, and found it was empty like the ones upstairs. I figured the apartments on the first floor, and possibly the second, would be used by the security guys, so I'd have to stay clear of those. That just left the third. Those apartments would most likely be vacant, too. I was tempted to get out of there and find someone to start work on the data I'd just stolen, but old habits. I had to go down and check, just to be thorough.

The front unit on third was empty, as expected. But when I opened the door to the rear one, I stopped dead in my tracks. It was like finding a portal to another realm. The first thing that hit me was the stink. I could smell bodies. Cheap perfume. Fried food. Vomit. Disinfectant. And maybe a couple of other bodily fluids.

I went into the living room. There were three large couches crammed in there. They were covered with cheap blue fabric, and all kinds of women's clothes—mainly skimpy ones—had been heaped up in precarious piles. A couple dozen shoes were strewn around, and five cheap carry-on suitcases were lined up against one wall.

I moved on to the bedrooms. There were two cots in each room. None of them had pillows or clean sheets. And next to each one was an IV stand. The fluid bags were empty, and the lines were blocked with dried, bloody residue. I'd come across scenes like this before. Once in Romania. And once in Belarus. In both cases local gangs would kidnap teenage girls. Drug them up. Get them addicted. Make them good and compliant. Then take them to their brothels and use them till they died.

I wondered where the girls who'd been in those cots were now. How long they'd been gone. How much time they had left. And I prayed there'd be a clue in the data I'd taken from Madatov's computer. Even if it was too late for these girls, this wouldn't be an isolated incident. It would be part of a production line. Others would be coming to take their places.

They might already be on their way.

Chapter *Twenty-three*

ATKINSON HAD MADE HIS FEELINGS ABOUT MY THEORIES VERY
clear the last time we spoke, so it came as a surprise when he called
and invited me to breakfast again.

It came as less of a surprise when he picked the Green Zebra.
He was there first, that morning. He picked the table we'd had for
our first meeting. He picked the same food. Eggplant Benedict. I
ordered the same kind of coffee. The place was as busy as usual,
but I found it even more aggravating. The snippets of people's
conversations that washed over me were nothing but trivial. The
arguments I overheard were petty. People kept bumping into one
another and cursing. Plates were crashing. Silverware was rattling.
I felt like I was crawling out of my skin. I kept picturing the bedrooms in the apartment in Madatov's building. Imagining the
women on those cots. Sick. Vomiting. Homesick. Scared. Thinking
their lives had already been destroyed. Having no idea they were
about to get so much worse.

"Anything on Pardew?" There was a sarcastic note in Atkinson's voice.

"Not yet."

"I can't say I'm surprised. I knew that was a long shot. But that's not why I asked you to come here. I've got an update on another case you were interested in." He slid an envelope to me across the table. "Have a look at these. But don't let anyone else see."

There were five eight-by-ten color photographs in the envelope. They were all of Norman Davies. One showed his body, covered from the waist down with a plain white sheet, lying on a stainless-steel mortuary table. One was a close-up of his head, taken from the left side so you could see where the bullet had smashed through his skull. The rest showed his torso. Specifically the parts of it that had been burned by the tip of a soldering iron.

"Recognize him?"

I said nothing.

"I think you do. He was the suspect in the Mason assault. The one who walked."

I shrugged. "Live by the sword . . ."

"You were very bothered by that case, McGrath. Don't deny it. Just tell me what you know about Norman Davies turning up DOA."

I shook my head. "I don't know anything about that. When did it happen?"

"Take another look at the picture. He died from a .22 to the head. There's an entry wound, but no exit. Meaning the slug bounced around the inside of his skull, pulping what little brain he had to start off with. It was a professional hit. But it happened after he was tortured. Somebody wanted information from him. I want to know who. And what."

"Those are reasonable questions." A server dropped off my coffee, and I took a long sip. "It's a shame you didn't act when I told you about the problem. If you had, you could have asked him yourself. Except that you wouldn't have to, because he wouldn't be dead."

"I'm acting now." Atkinson drummed his fingers on the table.

"*Now?* That's more than a little late."

"It wasn't my case before. It is now. That's how it works. The point is, I'm going to find the guy who killed Davies. If you know anything about that, now's the time to speak."

"I don't know anything about it."

"Where were you last night?"

"At what time?"

"Between eight and midnight."

"I was at my hotel."

"You weren't. I checked. You weren't there all day, and you didn't come back all night."

"Which hotel did you check?"

"The Brincliffe." There was a note of triumph in Atkinson's voice. "Under your fake name."

I shook my head. "Well, that explains it. A simple misunder-standing. I moved to a different hotel, and forgot to cancel the old room. I'm at the Grosvenor now. Room 346. I had room service last night. Pizza with extra anchovies and a bottle of Prosecco. Give them a call. Check my account."

It's an old trick. Order something that's not on the menu while you're out. Have it left outside your room. Call for the tray to be removed when you're back. And be generous with the tip. You never know when you might need an alibi.

"I'll check. You can count on it." Atkinson drummed his fin-gers, then looked up at the ceiling for a moment. "There's one other weird thing about Davies." He took out his cellphone and called up a photograph. "Look at the back of his ear."

The chip I'd stuck on him was still there.

"It's from a cellphone." Atkinson put his own phone back in his pocket. "But why was it on his ear? Have you seen anything like that before?"

I shook my head. "Beats me."

Atkinson tipped his head slightly and looked away, as if trying to make a decision about something.

"OK." He finally nodded. "Call me if there's any news about Pardew."

"Of course."

"Good. Now, is there anything else? Or has your well dried up?"

"Nothing else." I stood up to leave. "Nothing I can't handle myself, anyway."

Chapter Twenty-four

Norman Davies. He was an asshole. That was taken as read. But was he an idiot? Or was he unlucky? And how badly had he screwed up my plan?

I left the Green Zebra, took a cab to Bowery and Canal, and walked the final two blocks to the Brincliffe. No one obvious was watching the exterior so I went inside and asked the clerk whether a package had been left for me. While she checked with the concierge I casually scanned the lobby. It took fifteen seconds to spot them. Two guys, sitting in armchairs midway between the exit and the bar, pretending to read the newspaper.

There wasn't a package for me so I left the hotel and strolled west on Broome, timing it so that I just reached the next intersection as the light changed. I watched the reflection in the window of an Italian restaurant across the street and saw the two guys from the hotel lumbering after me. It would have been easy to lose them, but that would have defeated my purpose. I let them follow for another two blocks, then took a sharp left into an alley. I checked for security cameras, chefs on cigarette breaks, or anything else that could give me a headache. There was nothing to worry about so I turned and waited.

The two guys stepped into the alley side by side. One of them adjusted his coat the way an amateur does to make sure you know he has a gun, because he doesn't realize you'll already have spotted the bulge.

"Where are we going, fellas?" I kept my voice calm and my hands down by my sides. My argument wasn't with them. They were just doing their jobs—albeit not very well—so it was only fair to give them the chance to walk away.

The guy with the gun stepped forward and reached out to grab me.

I stepped back and held up my hand. "Use your words. Do not touch me."

He kept coming and tried to take hold of my arm. I waited until his fingertips brushed my sleeve, then planted my thumb on the back of his hand. I dug my fingers into his palm and twisted up and around, locking his wrist. Then I pushed back and down. The guy dropped to the ground, squealing, and ended up with one knee planted squarely in the middle of a rancid, discarded pizza.

I waited for his whimpering to die down. "OK. I'll let you go. But if you touch me again, I'll break your arm."

I released the guy and he struggled to his feet, staggered back a yard, then went for his gun. I let him get it free from his waistband, then grabbed his wrist with my left hand. I jabbed him in the solar plexus to knock the wind out of him. Then I tapped him under the chin to disorient him and expose his throat. If he'd been a threat I'd have smashed his larynx. As it was, I just lifted his arm and pulled it back down sharply against mine, breaking his elbow joint. The gun clattered to the ground. I lifted his arm again and slid my shoulder under his armpit. Then I straightened up, throwing my shoulder forward and hips back. The guy windmilled around, landing on his back and knocking the rest of the wind out of himself. I was still holding his right wrist, and I didn't let it go until I'd punched him in the face with the heel of my free hand. Then I picked up the gun, slipped it into my pocket, and turned to face the guy's buddy.

He hadn't moved.

"Your turn." I took a step toward him. "Where are we going?"

Carrick was wearing a dark gray suit with a chalk stripe, a vest, and a bow tie. He glared at me as I walked into his office, and then raised his eyebrows at his goon as if to say, *Where's your buddy?* The goon shrugged and looked away. Carrick told him to wait outside, then sent his receptionist out to buy flowers.

"They're for a funeral. But don't get anything too fancy." He sneered. "The deceased and I weren't that close."

As soon as we were alone, Carrick gestured for me to sit on my usual couch. He picked up the laptop from his desk, plugged in a memory stick, set it on the coffee table, and hit Play.

Norman Davies's face once again filled the screen. He spoke more slowly than last time. He sounded scared, and he kept glancing down to his right as if he was reading from something. He confirmed his name and the previous day's date, then claimed that he was making the recording of his own free will. He said he wanted to clarify for the record that his previous statement accusing George Carrick of being complicit in the assault on Mrs. Mason was false. He said he'd committed that crime entirely of his own volition, and had been coerced into making the false accusation by Paul McNaught, who was acting purely out of malice. Further, Paul McNaught had assaulted him, kidnapped him, held him against his will, and had attached an illegal tracking device to his person without his permission.

The only person I'd used the name McNaught with was Carrick . . .

I closed the lid of the computer so that I wouldn't have to look at the frozen image of his face. "Mr. Davies did have a troubled relationship with the truth, I guess."

"Enough to prove reasonable doubt." Carrick was smirking at me.

"How did you find him?"

"A little bird told me where to look."

I thought for a moment. "Jonny Evans?"

Carrick shrugged, but he couldn't hide his gloating smile.

"Where's Evans now?" I couldn't believe how stupid the guy was. Even earthworms have some sense of self-preservation.

"Somewhere you'll never find him." Carrick's smile grew wider.

"We'll see about that." I shook my head. "And Davies?"

"Who do you think the flowers are for?"

"OK, Carrick, cut the crap." I crossed my arms. "The deal for you to take care of your tenants. What's the status?"

"Off, obviously." He shook his head.

"That's a bad idea. You should rethink your position."

"You should rethink your position about screwing yourself. Those people are nothing but a pain in the ass. If you're so worried, you help them. Buy them their own building with all the cash you inherited. If that was even true."

A similar thought had crossed my mind. My father had a house in their area. I didn't need it. And it was the thing that had brought Pardew's fraud to light. Maybe even caused my father's death. I'd wondered if this could be a way to put it to good use. But I'd rejected the idea. Carrick was to blame. Which meant he was the one who had to pay.

"I'll make sure they're OK." I looked at Carrick across the table "One way or another."

"Do what you want." Carrick bounced on the balls of his feet. "Now go. Get lost. And don't cross me again. I'm only cutting you a break because I have bigger fish to fry right now."

Chapter *Twenty-five*

NORMAN DAVIES. HE WAS AN ASSHOLE. AND I GUESS HE WAS UN-lucky. Because I was an idiot for not anticipating that Jonny Evans would put himself back in play the way he did.

Evans's reappearance was the proximate cause of Davies's en-counter with the fatal .22. I would have preferred things not to have worked out that way, but I wasn't going to lose any sleep over it. What did trouble me, though, was the collateral damage. The deal to see that the Masons and their neighbors were taken care of. That was dead in the water now, too. I was going to have to come up with a new plan. They needed somewhere decent to live. And Carrick needed to go to jail. It was his own fault. He'd brought it on himself by setting fire to the lifeline I'd thrown him. It was no good blaming Madatov and Walcott now. Carrick was going down with them. Hard. I would see to that. The only ques-tions were when and how.

I left Carrick's office and walked south on Fifth until I came to Madison Square Park, where I'd come to meet Bob Mason after

Detective Atkinson refused to get involved with his wife's case. On a whim I followed the path toward the fountain and saw that the bench Bob and I had used was vacant. I figured I'd sit there for a minute, on my own. It would be a good place to think. To plan my next move. I closed my eyes and leaned back. The sun was warm on my face. The city sounds were soothing and familiar. I could feel my mind clearing. Beginning to focus. Ideas starting to form. And just as they were taking shape, my phone rang.

"Paul?" The voice on the other end of the line sounded a little ragged around the edges. "It's Harry. I think I've got something."

Harry Hamilton was the army Intel buddy I'd drafted to take a crack at the clone of Madatov's computer.

"Harry, you're a star. Fire away."

"Listen, I don't have a complete picture yet. This guy uses security protocols like you wouldn't believe. But I've made a good start. It looks like there's some stuff about drugs and guns that could buy our boy some righteous jail time. I did what you said, though, and tried to focus on the trafficking. Here's what I found. First, the bad news. I couldn't dig anything up about those women whose stuff you saw. There's no clue as to where they might have gone. I'll keep trying, but right now it's like they never existed. So now the good news. If you can call it that? I don't know. Anyway. Look, sorry, I was up all night and now I'm stupidly jazzed on caffeine. But here's the thing. I think I've figured out when the next batch of women is being brought in."

"Great work. When?"

"In six days' time. On a ship named the *Caucasus Queen,* out of Sevastopol. It's due at dock 7B."

"Harry, that's wonderful. You could have saved lives, here, not to mention sparing people a world of misery."

"I'm happy to help, Paul. I'll keep digging. And I'll be back in touch if I find anything else useful."

Harry hung up, and I practically jumped off the bench. The adrenaline was starting to flow, and I could feel the pendulum of fate swinging back my way after the morning's shit storm.

It was time to step things up a gear, so I called Frank Carrodus and told him I needed some personal time. Then I collected Davies's van from the open-air lot on Warren Street where I'd been keeping it and set off to pick up some supplies. I needed some clothes. Some tools. And two pieces of specialized equipment. I had to try four stores to find those. That was frustrating, but on the other hand it's debatable whether they should be sold to civilians at all.

I parked in the service bay at Walcott's office building and changed clothes in the back of the van. I got my tools together and made my way in through the rear entrance. Signed in at the Receiving Room. Then headed down to the basement. The walls, floor, and ceiling in the service corridor were all painted gray. There was no carpet, so the area was chilly and echoey. I passed an exercise room, which no one was using. A maintenance store, which was locked. And then I found what I was looking for—the telecom room. I picked the lock and crossed to the Main Distribution Frame, which connects the internal cables to the ones coming in from the public network. The thing was like a tall, twelve-foot-wide metal-framed wardrobe with no doors or sides, crammed full of multicolored spaghetti. Fortunately it had been installed at the far end of the room so it would provide good cover if anyone came in, and its engineers' log was kept up-to-date, so I could easily identify the cables that served Walcott's office suite. I quickly disconnected them. Then I locked the room behind me and took the elevator up to Walcott's floor.

A small, highly polished brass plaque on the door to the office suite read simply, *Rigel Walcott & Associates*. There was no business description or supporting information. I paused outside to activate the cell signal jammer I'd just purchased—I didn't want any overzealous employees calling the phone company to check my credentials—then knocked and went in.

The carpet in the reception area was royal blue and densely woven, with gold shields and griffins inlaid at regular intervals. The walls were paneled with mahogany. The smell of polished leather was coming from somewhere. On the right, two wingback chairs stood at either side of a low table. A Lewis chess set was laid out on a marble board. One pawn of each color had been moved as if a match had just begun, and a biography of Garry Kasparov was lying open on the white side of the board. Black-and-white photographs were lined up in narrow frames on the wall. Most showed Walcott in a hard hat and coveralls at various construction sites around the world, smiling and shaking hands with mayors and businessmen and assorted dignitaries. The largest one, in the center, showed Walcott in a dark suit, deep in thought, playing chess with Kasparov himself.

The reception desk was on the other side of the room. It held a computer, a diary, a stand for a fountain pen, and a china cup and saucer. There was no receptionist. Ahead, there were two doors. The one on the right had a plaque that read *Conference Room.* The other door was blank. It opened and a curly-haired woman emerged. She was maybe in her fifties and was wearing a gray pantsuit and flat black shoes.

"Can I help you?" She let her glasses slide a little way down her nose and peered at me over them.

I wiped my palm on my coveralls and held out my hand. "Paul. From the phone company. What's the problem? Was it you who called it in?"

"We don't have a problem." The woman ignored my hand. She crossed to the desk, lifted her handset, and listened for a moment. "Oh dear. Apparently we do."

"If it wasn't you who called, I must be in the wrong suite. Sorry to disturb you. I'll get out of your way."

"Wait." She was still holding the handset. "You're already here, and we have phones that don't work. Couldn't you just fix them?"

"I shouldn't. I'm supposed to find who originally reported the fault and help them first. Why don't you call it in right away, get a ticket number, and maybe Dispatch will allocate it to me, if no other jobs come in before I'm done."

"Call it in how? Our phones don't work!"

I shrugged.

"Look, wouldn't it be more efficient just to fix our phones first? That would save you coming back, or someone else coming out when you're already here."

"I guess." I shrugged again, but with less conviction. "Well, OK. I'll take a look. But you've got to promise not to tell anybody, or you'll get me in trouble."

"That sounds about right. Getting in trouble for helping your customers."

"Hey. I don't make the rules."

"I'm sorry—I'm sorry. I won't tell anyone."

"Thanks. By the way, any chance of a coffee while I'm here?"

"I would, only it's just me in the office and I'm not supposed to leave . . ."

"No problem. I get it. And anyway, my wife's always telling me, Paul—cut out that caffeine. So she'd be happy, at least. OK, let's get started. Can you point me to your phone system's CPU?"

"Sure. It's through here."

I picked up my tools and followed the woman into the conference room. It had the same carpet and wood paneling as reception. Similar photos. A shiny oval table. Six Eames office chairs, in apple green. And a wide window, with its blinds pulled all the way down.

The woman continued to the rear of the room and pressed the edge of one of the wall panels. A section about a yard square swung open, giving access to the suite's breaker box and phone system.

"Here you go." The woman pointed to the equipment, then turned and started back to the door. "I'll be at my desk. Call me if you need anything."

I unscrewed the phone system's plastic shell and set it down on the table in case the woman came back in to check on me. I waited six minutes. Then replaced the cover. Closed the panel. And went back out to reception.

"That all looks fine." I scratched my chin. "I ran a diagnostic on the CPU which came up green, but I reset it anyway to be on the safe side. I need to check the terminals now. Is there one in here?" I nodded to the other door and went in without waiting for her to respond. This room had a plain carpet. It was still blue, but a darker shade, which clashed with the desk's burgundy leather top. The thing was gigantic. I wanted to take it to pieces. It reminded me of one I came across in Budapest once, which turned out to have fourteen separate secret compartments. I resisted the temptation to dismantle it and continued to search in all the usual places. There was nothing of interest, though. And worse, no computer. I'd hoped to get a cloned copy and drop it off with Harry on the way to my hotel. There was only a charging cable protruding from beneath a bust of Nero. That suggested Walcott used a laptop, and had probably taken it home with him, or to wherever he was hiding.

There were a couple of dozen books inside a glass-fronted bookcase. Most of them were about chess. A couple were about antiques. One was about classic English sports cars. I checked inside all of them. None had any documents concealed between their pages, or hollowed-out hiding places. A pair of photographs in heavy silver frames were perched on the top shelf. They'd been taken abroad, judging by the style of the buildings. One showed Walcott with the president of Azerbaijan. I recognized him from the briefing I'd had before my aborted posting. In the other picture Walcott was shaking hands with another guy I'd been briefed about: Ramil Balayev. He'd been the Azerbaijani justice minister. In theory. In practice his main job was repressing the opposition. There were rumors of beatings. Electrocution. Amputations. No wonder Walcott kept that picture away from the public area of the office. It was strange that he kept it at all.

I went back to the desk and checked the phone in case there were any interesting entries in the memory or the call log. Nothing jumped out, so I picked up my toolbox from its position in front of the door and stepped out into reception.

The handle on the outer door began to turn.

"OK. I'm just about done." I slipped back into the conference room. "Just one last thing to check in here . . ."

I peeked out and saw Walcott in a navy blue suit standing by the reception desk, flanked by two goons. They were big, bulky guys with pseudo-military haircuts and large fancy weapons. In other words, amateurs. They were all show. Reassuring to have around, if you didn't know the business. But they'd be useless in a fight. Unless one of them sat on you. Or both did.

"What's going on?" Walcott glared down at the receptionist. "I couldn't get your cell. Or the office landline. The Feds—I thought we must have been raided again."

"No." The woman's voice was calm, bordering on patronizing. "The phones are just down. The guy's here fixing them now."

"The cellphones, too?"

The woman looked momentarily puzzled, then took her phone from her purse and checked its screen. "Oh. I guess so. That's weird, both kinds being down."

"Are you sure there's an actual fault?" Walcott's eyes narrowed.

"All I know is that the phones went down. A guy turned up to fix them with a bunch of tools and he seems to know what he's doing."

Walcott scowled. "We'll wait in my office. Let me know when the phone guy's gone."

I didn't move until I heard Walcott's office door slam shut.

"Nailed it!" I smiled at the woman and headed for the outer door. "There's one last thing to do in the comms room downstairs, and then your service'll be back right away. I guarantee."

"Wait." The woman stood up. "All our cellphones are down, too!"

"Sorry." I shrugged. "Different provider. Nothing I can do about that."

"But both kinds of phone service going down at once?" She put her hands on her hips. "Isn't that a bit suspicious?"

"Not at all." I shook my head. "It's not even surprising. The cell circuits will be overloaded because of all the extra people using them while the landlines are down. I bet you they come back as soon as the landlines are fixed. Give it ten minutes. Maybe less. It'll be fine."

I hit the Down button, then reached into my toolbox and deactivated the cell blocker. The elevator took forever to come. I could feel the hairs bristling on the back of my neck, waiting for the outer door to open and Walcott to emerge. Not that it would have been the end of the world if he'd seen me. He'd probably only focus on the coveralls, anyway. Big shots like him don't generally notice the little guy. People they think are only there to serve them. But old habits. It could be a tactical advantage for Walcott to have no way of recognizing me. Who knew how things were going to pan out?

Walcott was still in his suite when the elevator arrived. I rode down to the basement alone. Made my way along the gray corridor to the telecom room. Picked the lock. Went inside. Crossed to the MDF cabinet. Located the cables that served Walcott's office. Reconnected them. And took the wireless repeater I'd bought that afternoon out of my toolbox. I knew it was a long shot, hoping that Walcott would be stupid enough to have a compromising conversation on an unsecured landline, but I figured it wasn't impossible. There was nothing to lose by trying, so I readied the connectors. Offered them up to the terminals on the frame. Was about to press the first one into place, and stopped dead. I'd heard a sound, to my left. Something I'd recognize anywhere. A shell being racked into the chamber of a pistol.

I turned, very slowly. The pistol was a Glock 17. A very serviceable weapon. It was known around the world for its reliability. It had a misfire rate in the region of one in ten thousand, from what I could recall. Not good odds, from my end of the barrel. And the hands that were holding it, leveled on my center mass, were rock steady. The person they belonged to was definitely alive this time. He was standing up. All six feet eight of him. His eyes were open. And his breathing was slow and calm.

The guy was no amateur. I knew that for a fact. I wasn't inferring it from his lack of nerves or his choice of weapon. I recognized him. I'd seen him before, years ago. At Fort Huachuca, Arizona. When we were both there to take a bunch of specialist courses at the US Army Intelligence School. His name was John Robson. He was the agent who was sent to Azerbaijan instead of me. The agent who was thrown out of the service after getting too close to Rigel Walcott.

I guessed Walcott's security detail wasn't as superficial as the two guys upstairs had made it seem, and silently cursed myself for not seeing something like this coming. Although the specific permutation brought an additional problem with it. Robson had disgraced the uniform. I wasn't in the army any longer. I had no jurisdiction. No obligation. No authority. But old habits die hard. Finding him in the employ of a known criminal wasn't something I could turn a blind eye to.

There was a solid wall a foot or so behind me. Another, two feet to my left. Neither had any windows. The MDF was a foot to my right. Leaving only one way out of the narrow space. Through Robson. He was facing me, six feet away, well out of reach. He was armed. He'd received the same training as me. And he'd no doubt supplemented that with a career's worth of dirty tricks.

We were in the basement, so if Robson fired there was a chance the shot wouldn't be heard. Although unless he missed, remaining undetected would be the least of my worries. And I knew he wouldn't miss.

Another concern was the MDF. Its perforated steel framework was horribly flimsy and the bundles of spindly multicolored wires that sprouted from its thousands of connectors were brittle and delicate. If something impacted any part of it—like, say, Robson's body—half the building's phones and Internet connections could be cut and it wouldn't be long before someone came running to investigate.

"John?" I raised my hands. "It's me. Paul. Paul McGrath. From the 66th. You know me. So stay calm. I'm not going to do anything stupid. I'm just going to put this down . . ." I gestured to the repeater that was still in my hand, then slowly crouched, moving back slightly to jam my right foot against the wall. "Then we can talk. I'm sure we can—" I launched myself forward, staying low and aiming for his knees. I wrapped my arms around his legs and the momentum caused him to jackknife over me, flailing wildly but still landing a blow on my back before stretching out to cushion his landing. He caught me between my spine and my right shoulder blade. I guess he used the butt of his gun, but it felt like I'd been hit by a lightning bolt. Torrents of pain ran up to the base of my skull and down into my pelvis, loosening my arms and allowing Robson to wriggle free.

We both rolled clear. No shots had been fired. The MDF was unscathed. Our positions were reversed, with Robson now penned in. Only he still had the gun. And it was still pointing straight at me.

"You need to walk away, Paul." Robson sounded slightly winded. "Walk away now, before you screw things up altogether."

"Why?" I got slowly to my feet. "So you can put a bullet in my back? No thanks."

"I'm not going to shoot you." Robson took a deep breath. "Not unless you make me. But you've got to understand something. Walcott? He's mine. The army's not having him. Not after all this time. Not after what they did to me. So do us both a favor and walk the fuck away."

"What happened to you, John?" I cautiously rotated my shoulder to see how badly it was hurt. "Walcott's scum. He's a piece of trash. Why are you still helping him? Is it money? Because—"

Robson lunged at me, his elbow scything toward the side of my head in a vicious arc. I twisted to block the blow with my upper arm, then continued past him, jabbing for his kidney as I went. My fist connected and I heard him gasp, but I knew the punch was too weak to do serious damage. My shoulder still wasn't working right and I'd likely done more harm to myself than him. Plus our positions were reversed again. I was penned back in. And Robson still had the gun.

"You think I'm helping Walcott?" Robson raised his Glock. "Why in hell would you think that?"

"Everyone thought that, John." I eased toward my toolbox. There were plenty of possible weapons in there. If I could just get the chance to grab one. Something I could use left-handed. "The word was, you swapped sides. Which is why you took a Big Chicken Dinner. And after you were kicked out, you went to work for him full time."

"I got discharged, all right." Robson lowered the gun. "Nailed for bad conduct. That much is true. But not for swapping sides. Because my CO caught me on my way to shoot Walcott in the head."

"You were going to eighty-six the guy? How come?"

"You have no idea what it was like over there, Paul. You so dodged a bullet. The corruption? The injustice? It made you ashamed to be human. And the way Walcott pimped himself out to those crooked asshole politicians who were basically raping their own country? It was disgusting. And all we could do was watch. Fill in forms. Put them in files. Anyway, one day I came across this scam Walcott was running. People over there, the regular Azerbaijanis, they were desperate to get out. To start new lives in Europe, America, wherever they could. I don't know how they got in contact, but Walcott was telling people he could get them US visas. For their whole families. All they had to do was bring one of their daughters to his compound. She could be sixteen. Fourteen. Younger. He didn't care. He'd keep the girl for a weekend. Maybe some of his government buddies would come over. And afterward, guess what? No one was getting visas. So I reported what I'd found out, and nothing happened. I pushed, and I was told nothing could be done, due to *diplomatic considerations*. Walcott was basically untouchable. I came up with six different ways to snatch the guy without harming any locals, and every time I was told no. In the end, I just snapped. I decided to deal with him my own way. But I could never get close to him in Baku, even after I became a civilian. So when the government collapsed and all his buddies abandoned him, I followed him back here. I was waiting for the right moment to take him down, but I must have spooked him somehow, 'cause all of a sudden he hired a bunch of guards and dropped out of sight."

"If that's true, I can't say I blame you for going after him."

"It is true. But the army did blame me. And now it wants Walcott all of a sudden? Which makes me want to know why. What's changed?"

"This has nothing to do with the army." I held my hands out, palms first. "I'm just a janitor now. A civilian, like you."

"Then why are you fucking with Walcott's phones?" Robson took a step closer to me. "Why are you here at all?"

"For the same reason you are, I guess. My path crossed with Walcott's. I didn't like what I saw. The authorities weren't interested. So I decided to do something about it myself."

"What did Walcott do?"

"Nothing, to me personally. But he's mixed up with two other assholes I took a dislike to. One's an Azerbaijani mobster who traffics young girls. The other's a landlord who had an old woman beaten so bad she's in a wheelchair for the rest of her life."

Robson smiled, but with no trace of humor. "Sounds like Walcott's kind of people."

"There's one other thing, though, that might be important. You didn't spook Walcott. He dropped out of sight because he owes the Azerbaijani guy money. A lot. And he doesn't have it. Which means you may not have to worry about him much longer. If Walcott can't pay, your problem will be taken care of for you."

Robson turned and slammed his palm against the wall. "No! That's no good. My life was ruined because of Walcott. I have to take him down myself. And I will, if it's the last thing I do."

A phone rang from somewhere on the floor, behind Robson's back.

"That's mine." I patted my empty pocket. "Must have fallen out."

Robson stepped back and glanced down at its screen. "Some guy called Jonny Evans."

"Outstanding." I held out my hand. "This could be important. Do you mind?"

Robson waggled the gun as a silent reminder to watch what I said, then slid the phone toward me with his foot.

I talked for a minute, then hung up.

"John, what if bringing Walcott down wasn't the last thing you did?" I slipped the phone back into my pocket. "What if we could work together? Join forces, and nail all three of the assholes I mentioned?"

"Working together could be good." Robson jammed the gun in the waistband of his jeans. "But not if it drags things out even longer. If you're serious, prove it. Come to his office with me, right now. You take the guards. I'll take Walcott. Show him exactly how untouchable he really is."

"I'm serious, all right." I paused until Robson met my eye. "But we're not going to do it like that. We're not going to act like a couple of low-rent button men. We're going to hit these guys where it hurts them the most. That phone call? It put the last piece in place. Almost. We just need to do a little more groundwork, then we'll be good to go. It'll be beautiful. Just like old times. As long as you're still up for some shenanigans . . ."

I

Thirty Years Ago

Roberto di Matteo could be described as many things, but he certainly was never one of life's deep thinkers. If anything, he was always a binary type of guy. To him, things were either OK, or they were not OK. If they were OK, he was happy to go with the flow. If they were not OK, he tried to change his course.

During his time at Columbia Grammar School, things were predominantly OK. The work wasn't too hard. He never stood out as a student, but he was never in danger of being asked to leave. There was plenty of time for the kinds of activities most suited to his abilities. Sleeping late. Playing cards. Drinking. Chasing girls. Playing video games, which had seemed super advanced back then but were laughably dated now.

Despite all the distractions, Roberto did just enough good work to get into Vassar. That was the version of history he liked, anyway. The rumor spread by some of his classmates said his admission had more to do with his mother being an alum, and a generous donation from his father, than his grades. But even if that was true, Roberto was OK with it.

At college, Roberto followed essentially the same path. Only there was more time for sleeping. More girls to chase. More beer to drink. Lots of other substances to experiment with. And video games that improved by the month. As long as you could foot the bill, which Roberto was able to do. Thanks to his father. And that was OK.

Roberto didn't get down to any serious work until it was time to think about law school. He must have raised his game sufficiently, though, because he ended up getting admitted to Yale. There were more pesky rumors about his father's donations, of course, but Roberto didn't care. By now, his eyes were firmly on the prize. He was ready to knuckle down. To tick all the necessary boxes—his degree, the bar (albeit not the kind he was previously familiar with)—and grab his future with both hands. Because there was a place waiting for him at his father's firm, in New York. It was a very prestigious firm: Suggett, Lyons, and Darracott.

At first, Roberto was OK with following in his father's footsteps. He liked the firm's fancy office on Lexington. The daily bagel delivery from H&H. The three- (or in his case, four- or five-) martini lunches with clients he was sometimes invited to sit in on. But when the initial gloss wore off, he found the going a lot more difficult than he'd expected. It turned out that his father being a partner made settling in harder, not easier. The other associates resented him. The other partners had high expectations, which left them frequently disappointed in him. He limped his way through one boring research assignment after another and made the occasional lackluster second chair appearance, hoping that if he could survive his first year, his prospects would somehow improve. He was wrong. His performance review on the anniversary of his hiring was harsh. And Roberto was not OK with that.

So he quit.

There were advantages to life as a solo operator, as Roberto soon found out. Sure, the office space he wound up with wasn't quite as upmarket as the big firm's. But what it lacked in polish and prestige, it gained in other ways. Like not having anyone in it who kept tabs on what time he arrived in the morning. What time he came back from lunch. *If* he came back. And when it came to hiring secretaries, he could apply his own set of criteria to the selection process. Criteria that weren't exclusively related to administrative ability. Or to any kind of ability, for that matter.

The first couple of cases Roberto tried after hanging up his own shingle worked out surprisingly well. They didn't draw him into deep legal waters, so they weren't too hard for him to navigate. They didn't take too long for him to wrap up, or require too much effort along the way. Those aspects were definitely OK. Less OK was the paltry amount of money they brought with them, but Roberto felt he shouldn't complain. The cases had really just been bones that his father and his friends had been kind enough to throw, and Roberto didn't want the source of such easy work to dry up. But regardless of his wishes, after a few months the flow of referrals had slowed to a trickle. Soon a full-on drought had set in. Faced with the prospect of having to slink back to his old man with his tail between his legs, Roberto was forced into an unpalatable realization. He was going to have to make his own rain, as they say in the legal profession. And that was not OK. He didn't mind snow, as long as he was in Klosters or Cortina for the skiing. He enjoyed the sun, provided he was on the beach in Bora Bora or the Maldives. But as far as he could see, rain had no redeeming features. All it did was leave you damp and soggy. He'd never liked it. Not even the metaphorical kind.

Roberto had often heard it said that you could make your own luck. He'd always thought that sounded tedious, so was amazed to discover that all you had to do was postpone any thought of rainmaking until you'd completed the final level of The Legend of Zelda. He achieved that feat one Monday around lunchtime and had been about to head out for a quick slice of pizza and maybe a couple of Peronis when Samantha, his latest assistant, announced that he had a visitor. Before Roberto could respond with a suitable excuse to dodge the meeting, a guy came into his office. He was around six feet tall with gray hair buzzed so short his stubble looked sharp, like hundreds of minuscule daggers. He moved with no apparent effort and folded himself into Roberto's visitor's chair without waiting for an invitation.

The spiky-looking guy spoke with a pronounced foreign accent. At first Roberto thought it must be Russian, though it turned out to be Azerbaijani. After the guy left Roberto had to look the place up on a map. He didn't have to think too long about the case the guy had offered him, though. It was to represent a friend of his. The guy made no bones about it, his friend was guilty. He wasn't looking for an acquittal. Just reasonable bail, so that he could be present at his daughter's wedding. That sounded straightforward enough. And the guy was paying cash, which was definitely OK.

As luck would have it, the ADA prosecuting the case was a friend of Roberto's from law school. Roberto had a word in the ADA's ear over a long, well-lubricated lunch. The ADA agreed to do Roberto a solid. Everyone was happy. Until the client skipped bail. He didn't even show up to see his daughter walk down the aisle. Roberto was having a hard time deciding whether he was OK with that when the guy who'd hired him showed back up. He brought more cash with him. A lot more cash. It was a retainer, he said, for a new client. The kind who, if nurtured correctly—and Roberto wasn't too naïve to understand what that meant—would leave Roberto never having to worry about making rain again.

And Roberto was most definitely OK with that.

II

THIRTY YEARS AGO

THE DICTIONARIES HAVE IT ALL WRONG. SO DO THE HISTORY
books.

They say that mines go down, under the ground. And that all
the gold in America was to be found out west. Neither of which
can be so, George Carrick thought to himself. Because he'd just
found his very own gold mine, right there in Queens. And there
was nothing subterranean about it, except for maybe the basement, which he wasn't interested in anyway because there was
no rentable space down there. He was focused on the twenty-
two floors that rose up above the sidewalk. The eight apartments that shared each of those floors. The fact that he'd just
secured the job of rental agent for the entire building. And
based on the quick and dirty door-to-door survey he'd just
done, it was high time for some of the units to change hands.
For new tenants to come in. Tenants with a lot more cash to
spend on their rent. Oh, yes. The building's turnover rate was

about to skyrocket. And as a result, truckloads of commission were about to come his way.

Carrick stepped out into the street and the pleasant visions of giant stacks of cash instantly vanished. They hadn't gone permanently, though. Nothing was going to rob him of his dream. They'd just been chased temporarily to a safer place by his sixth sense. Because he was looking at his car. It was parked diagonally across the street. Close enough to the building to be convenient, but far enough away for a casual observer not to necessarily peg it as his. There was no specific reason for him to pick his spot like that. It's just the way your instincts lead you to behave when you grow up in a place like Alphabet City. And it was the same kind of instincts that had attracted two kids to his car. It wasn't a nice car, by any means. It would be an embarrassment in most parts of the city. But it was a little too nice for that neighborhood. Which made it a problem. The only question in George Carrick's mind as he crossed the street was how big of a problem was it going to be?

Carrick reached into his briefcase, grasped his wrench, and stopped ten feet short of his car. He was ready to fight if necessary. The kids hardly looked formidable. There was a time when he would have welcomed the chance to deal out such a straightforward ass-kicking. But the months he'd spent in Sing Sing had altered his perspective. They'd given him a more strategic outlook. He now knew that violence is best avoided. Unless you can get someone else to do it for you, which didn't seem like an option in this particular situation.

"Five bucks." The first kid stepped up closer. He looked around eighteen. He seemed reasonably lively, but was so scrawny Carrick figured he'd snap if someone stared at him hard enough.

"How much?" Carrick bounced up on the balls of his feet. He didn't know what to do with a demand like that. It was a similar type of half-assed racket that had landed him behind bars. The experience hadn't been pleasant. He was older and wiser now. Part of him felt he should encourage the kids to take a different course. But five bucks? He was shocked at their lack of ambition.

"You heard." The kid took another step and behind him his buddy straightened up, ready to weigh in if necessary. "Give me the dough, asshole. Right now."

Before he could respond, another solution occurred to Carrick. He was going to be in the neighborhood a lot over the next few months. Mining every last vein of new tenancies in the building would take time. It could be useful to have his car looked after while he worked. To have some eyes on the street. But five bucks? Could he trust anyone who set their sights so low? He decided to test the water.

"I could give you *ten* bucks." Carrick tightened his grip on the wrench. "Or I could break your legs. Tell me why I should go with option A."

"Is there a problem?" It was a man's voice. Coming from behind him. And it wasn't friendly. Carrick should have anticipated that such green kids wouldn't be allowed out on their own. He should have been more aware of his surroundings. His instincts had gotten rusty. He'd been spending too much time in libraries, researching real estate opportunities, and going to job interviews. But this was no time for self-recrimination. So Carrick spun around, pulling the wrench out of his case as he moved.

The man he now faced was holding a length of lead pipe in one hand. He had a bicycle chain in the other. He was broad. Powerful. The black leather of his boots was torn at the toes, revealing the glint of the steel caps beneath. His jeans were ripped at the knees. He wore a leather vest over a stained

denim jacket. Several buttons were missing and an approximation of a Maltese cross had been clumsily embroidered on the
left side of the chest.

The guy was taller than Carrick by about six inches. That
gave him an advantage when it came to reach. He gained even
more through his choice of weapons. Carrick automatically
stepped back, even as it dawned on him that he recognized the
guy's face. From Sing Sing. He was named Donny. They'd never
shared a cell, but had been in the same block in the jail. It was
well known in there—don't get on the wrong side of Donny, or
you'll end your sentence in the prison infirmary. Donny lunged
forward. Carrick braced himself, thinking, *I don't know the
neighborhood yet! Where's the nearest ER?* Then Donny's face,
usually a snarling mask of pure hate, suddenly softened. His
arms shot out, but the pipe didn't connect with flesh or bone.
Neither did the chain. Instead, Donny pulled Carrick in close
for a hug.

"Georgey? Man, am I glad to see you." Donny uncoiled his
arms after fifteen suffocating seconds. "You wouldn't believe
the kind of schmucks I've had to deal with since getting out of
the joint."

Ten minutes later, Carrick and Donny were in a bar two blocks
away. Its scarred wooden floor hadn't seen varnish in a decade,
but it was safe to assume it had seen other fluids—like blood—
much more recently. The mirror behind the line of grimy
second-tier spirit bottles was cracked. The half-dozen tall stools
looked like invitations for back surgery. The smell lingering in
the air was part abattoir, part chemicals from an industrial laundry. And Steppenwolf was on the jukebox, on a seemingly endless loop.

Donny led the way to a table with two chairs in the back corner. A giant photograph of a crying, naked kid after a napalm attack in Vietnam was on the wall near it. Carrick couldn't tell whether it was there as a protest or a celebration. He was still trying to figure that out when the bartender brought them some drinks without waiting to be asked. He left a beer for Carrick, and a beer plus two generous shots of whiskey for Donny. The guy quickly deposited the glasses then hurried away. He avoided making eye contact with Donny but couldn't help taking a curious glance at the newcomer.

"So." Donny downed one of the whiskeys. "What's new?"

"Not much." Carrick tried a sip of his beer. It was watery with no discernible beer taste, but he wasn't worried about that. He was straining to pick up traces of other flavors. He didn't want to give offense. But he didn't want botulism, either. "Just making a living. Or trying to."

"How's that working out?" Donny started on his own beer with much more enthusiasm. "Got anything going?"

"There's a couple of irons in the fire. I'm optimistic." Carrick didn't want to deliberately mislead anyone, but sharing wasn't part of his plan. "You?"

Donny shrugged. "Things are getting back to normal, I guess. It's better than being in the joint. But I've got to tell you, the place went downhill fast when I was away. None of the old crew is still around. I've got to start again, train up the kids. And man, talk about scraping the barrel. You saw those cretins out on the street. That's the level I'm dealing with. It's depressing."

"You need to work with good people. That's true." Carrick took a larger swig. He figured he needed to finish his glass before he could safely get away. "No one can argue with that."

"That's why I was so happy to see you." Donny reached

across the table and slammed his fist into Carrick's shoulder. "Old times' sake aside, I like you, Georgey. You're a good man. A safe pair of hands. And you know what? I have a couple of things going on that are right down your street. Your business was protection, right? So you could help me out. School these stupid kids. Free me up for other things."

Carrick took another sip of beer, but this time as cover so he could scan the room. Although, even as he was doing that, he was asking himself why. There could be no one between him and the door, or an army of a hundred. Either way, he wasn't escaping the table if Donny didn't want him to. He knew the ice beneath his feet was thin, and he could feel the cracks beginning to form. "I appreciate the offer. Really. But here's the problem. I'm not as strong as you, Donny. I only just survived the last stretch. I can't risk going back again. I just can't."

Donny downed his second whiskey and Carrick saw that the regular, dangerous sneer was returning to his face.

"But I do like the idea of working together." Carrick nodded with as much sincerity as he could muster. "And I have an idea. That building you saw me leave? Pretty soon, some tenants are going to be vacating their units. It's going to be in their best interests. Only some of them don't know it yet. They need someone to explain it to them. You mentioned schooling people. Do you think that's the kind of lesson you could teach?"

"Is there money in it?"

"Oh, yes." Carrick smiled. "Plenty."

"Then I'm in." Donny crashed his empty glass onto the table. "But I have one more question. These people. Any of them black? Or Mexican?"

"Some of them." Carrick hesitated. "Why?"

"Because them I'll *teach* for free."

III

GUBERNATORIAL. Was it inappropriate to think that was a stupid word, even after you've started your run for the governor's mansion? Pete Aldis closed his hotel room door and burst into a fit of giggles. But it wasn't just the word that was tickling him. It was the reality of the whole situation. *He was running for governor.* How crazy was that?

Aldis crossed to the window and looked out over the parking lot. It was still three-quarters full. Most of the people who owned those cars had come to see him. To hear him. To listen to his ideas. So actually, scratch that. It wasn't crazy at all. Just because he hadn't known his ultimate destination when he'd started his journey, that didn't devalue his reason to continue. He'd started because of what he believed in. Education. Opportunity. Law. Order. Access to decent health care. And others believed in him. Only a couple, to begin with. His wife, Paula, who'd encouraged him to speak up at a local town hall meeting. Looking back, that was the starting point. And then his brother,

Dave, had gotten on board, happily shouldering the extra load of running the family business while Pete was away campaigning. Soon the activists in his local party added their support, as they grew sick of the old order's empty rhetoric. The audiences at rallies grew larger, and the applause louder. And now, that day, he truly believed in himself. Not because of the reception at the two speeches he'd just given, gratifying as that had been. But because of his rival for the nomination, Eddie Colman. They'd had a deal—a gentleman's agreement—not to politicize the recent murder of a twelve-year-old schoolgirl, allegedly by an undocumented immigrant. Colman had waited until Aldis had come offstage after his second speech, then released a statement. A very inflammatory statement, pandering to their party's most vocal extremists. When he heard about it, Aldis was furious. But the feeling didn't last long. It was soon replaced by a surge of confidence, because it had caused his late father's voice to sound in his head. Once again he heard the words his father had hammered home from his earliest days of playing sports: *Son, they only foul you if they're afraid of you.*

Aldis ordered steak from room service. He asked for it to be cooked so rare that if a vet was in the hotel, it could be brought back to life. Then he called his wife while he waited for his dinner to be delivered. Paula was in the early stages of her second pregnancy and couldn't travel because of the morning sickness. Pete didn't like being apart from her, but supposed he had better get used to it. Unless that was counting chickens. He didn't want to invite bad luck.

When the food came, the meat was woefully overcooked, but Aldis ate it anyway. He would have liked to wash it down with a glass or two of red wine, but had been warned by his campaign manager: Appearance is everything. Don't allow any photographs to appear of empties on a trolley outside your room. So he made do with a Coke. Took a shower. And was getting ready for an early night when he heard a knock on his door.

"Who is it?" Aldis looked through the peephole and saw a guy in his mid-thirties wearing a black suit and a tie with the hotel logo on it. He was carrying a wooden clipboard.

"Mr. Aldis?" The guy looked at the clipboard as if double-checking the room number. "My name's John Berry. I'm the hotel's celebrity liaison manager. This is just a routine call. We want to make sure everything's going great with your stay with us."

"I'm hardly a celebrity, Mr. Berry. Are you sure you've picked the right guest?"

"You're running for governor, aren't you?" Berry smiled. "That's celebrity enough for me. And I've got to tell you. Calling on you makes a nice change from the idiots I usually have to deal with. Pop singers. Movie stars. Sports people. Those guys are all assholes. If you'll excuse my French."

"Consider it excused."

"Thank you." Berry paused for a moment. "So, Mr. Aldis, would it be OK if I come in rather than talk to you through the door?"

This was awkward. Aldis was tired and didn't want to deal with some hotel PR bullshit, but he didn't want to become known as a prima donna, either. His campaign manager had warned him: Bad reputations start easy and spread fast. "Sure." Aldis sighed quietly to himself. "Give me a moment to throw on some clothes. I just jumped out of the shower, so I only have on one of your fluffy robes."

"Don't put yourself out, Mr. Aldis, please. This will only take a minute or two. I just have a short questionnaire to run through to get your valued feedback, then I'll need a quick signature and I'll be out of your hair. And believe me, after some of the things I've seen around here, one of our robes counts as Sunday best."

Aldis didn't like the idea of letting a stranger into his room when he wasn't properly dressed, but he didn't want to appear precious, either. For a second he thought of calling his campaign manager for advice. Then he looked through the peephole again, peering as far up and down the corridor as the fish-eye lens would allow. He could just see the one guy. It wasn't like there was a bunch of paparazzi lurking around, so he decided to get the encounter over with. He opened the door, Berry stepped into the room, and from out of nowhere a woman followed him inside. She looked to be in her early twenties with coils of bottle-blond hair piled up on top of her head and lots of makeup on her face. She was also wearing a black suit, only hers was much shorter and a great deal tighter.

"Who's this?" Aldis tried to keep the surprise out of his voice.

"Her name's Ms. Pritchard." Berry gestured with his free hand as if presenting a loyal subject to an ancient monarch. "She's my new assistant. She's still learning the ropes. Is it OK if she sits in? We won't be here long."

Aldis and Berry took the low armchairs either side of the coffee table near the window, and Pritchard turned the desk chair around to make an elongated triangle.

"OK." Berry waited for his colleague to settle. "Let's get the ball rolling. On a scale of one to ten, with ten being the best, how would you rate the privacy of your check-in experience?"

Aldis didn't really understand the question, but he had no desire to drag the process out by asking for clarification. "Eight."

"Hmm." Berry's face clouded over a little as he ticked a box on his clipboard. "A little lower than I'd hoped, but it's important we know where to focus our efforts to improve, I guess. Now, next up, using the same scale, how would you rate the discretion of our bell staff?"

"Ten."

"OK." Berry put his pencil to work. "Thank you. And how—"

"I'm sorry to interrupt." Pritchard was fidgeting awkwardly in her chair. "This is so embarrassing, but I really need to use the bathroom. Do you mind?"

She was up and halfway across the room before Aldis had managed to answer.

"And how—" This time Berry was interrupted by the room phone.

Aldis answered the call, listened for a moment, then gestured for Berry to take the handset. "It's Reception. For you."

Berry listened for ten seconds before replying to the caller. "Really? No. This is a very bad time. I'm with Mr. Aldis. He's a very important guest. Can't someone else handle it?"

There was a shorter pause before Berry spoke again. "Well, I guess I'll have to. If there really isn't anyone else. But I'm not happy about it. Tell security I'll be there in two minutes."

Berry hung up and started moving toward the door. "I'm so sorry, Mr. Aldis. There's a problem with some of our other guests. A rock band, from England. They're in the presidential suite and there are reports of a small fire, and something about dead rodents. The police are already on their way, so I need to get up there and contain the damage. I'll be back soon as I can. If it gets too late, put the *Do Not Disturb* sign out and I'll catch up with you tomorrow."

"Hold on." Aldis put his hands on his hips. "What about your assistant? Miss Pritchard?"

"The woman's a pain in my ass." Berry reached the door and

pulled it open. "She spends half her life in the bathroom. I don't have time to wait for her. Tell her to come upstairs as soon as she's done, would you?"

Berry stepped into the corridor and let the door slam behind him. Aldis tightened his robe. He thought about calling his campaign manager again. Then the bathroom door opened. Ms. Pritchard appeared. Her hair was down. Her suit was gone. She was just wearing black stockings, a lacy black and silver garter belt, panties, and bra. The garments were tiny. Especially the bra. She leaned back against the doorframe and raised her arms above her head, and Aldis couldn't help wondering how much longer the flimsy material could hold out.

"Oh no." Aldis held up his hands, palms out. "Stop that. Go back inside. Put your clothes back on. Nothing like that's going to happen here."

Pritchard levered herself away from the doorframe and started walking slowly toward him. Her hips were swinging. Her breasts were swaying. And she had a smile on her face that said she didn't believe him. "Come on, darling, don't be like that. It's just you and me now. Let's have some fun while we're alone. No one will ever know . . ."

"Put your clothes back on. I mean it." Aldis turned back to the table and reached for the room phone. "I'm calling security."

"You're new to this, aren't you?" Pritchard moved closer. "You need to loosen up. The campaign trail's a stressful place. You need to unwind. All politicians do it, you know."

Aldis picked up the handset. There was no dial tone. He rattled the cradle and tried again. The line was still dead. He turned instead to the desk, where his briefcase was lying open. Pritchard was already there, standing in front of it. As Aldis watched, she reached behind her back and unhooked her bra.

She shrugged it off her shoulders. Dropped it into the briefcase. And scooped up the cellphone that had been plugged into its charger.

"Is this what you're looking for?" She winked at him. "Come and get it." Then she slid the phone down the front of her panties.

Aldis took one step forward, then stopped. He couldn't take the phone away from her. Not now. Not without touching her in some compromising way. His only play was to cut and run. So he turned toward the door, but she quickly moved across to block his path. She stepped toward him. He moved back, toward the bed. She took one more step, then slipped the phone out of her underwear.

"I didn't know you'd be so shy." Pritchard pouted. "I thought that would be a fun game, but I guess I was wrong. So let's try this instead." She held up the phone for a moment and then threw it past him, onto the bed.

Aldis turned and dived after the phone, but Pritchard was already moving and she landed first, winding up on her back underneath him. He tried to roll away but she wrapped her legs around him and held on tight. He struggled harder. She let go and he flipped onto his back. She rolled after him. Got on top. Straightened up. Shuffled forward until her knees were pinning his forearms. Reached down and tore off her panties. Pushed her crotch down into his face. Then she raised her arms above her head, closed her eyes, and writhed around as if in absolute ecstasy.

For a moment Aldis was too shocked to move, then he wriggled free and shoved Pritchard so hard in the chest that she flew off him and landed on the floor to the side of the bed. She got straight up and ran to the bathroom. He sat and straightened his robe, which had come undone in the struggle. Two minutes later Pritchard reemerged, back in her suit. Aldis registered the thought that she must have nothing on underneath it. Then he shook the image from his head. Walked to the door. Opened it, and stood to one side.

"I'll be talking to Mr. Berry about this incident, when he comes back for his clipboard."

"If you must." Pritchard paused in the doorway. "In the meantime, goodbye, darling. No hard feelings?" She reached out to Aldis's crotch and squeezed. "Oh. I was wrong about that, too!" Then she stepped out into corridor, headed for the elevators, and didn't look back.

Aldis crossed to the bed, flopped down, and covered his face with his hands. He could smell Pritchard's perfume on his skin. It wasn't altogether unpleasant. Nor was the next thought that crossed his mind: Eddie Colman must be absolutely terrified, to be trying to foul him at this extreme level . . .

Forty-five minutes later Aldis heard another knock at his door. He was expecting Berry, back to apologize. To limit some more damage. But when he looked through the peephole he saw a man he didn't recognize. This guy was older. He'd be in his late thirties, minimum. Possibly his early forties. His dark hair was neatly combed, and his suit was an amazingly bright shade of azure. Either he was required to wear it as some kind of uniform—like if he was the hotel manager, maybe—or he was out to deliberately attract attention.

No longer caring about his robe, Aldis opened the door.

"Good evening." The guy held out his hand. "My name's Rigel Walcott. I'm here to help. Is it OK if I come in?"

"Help with what?"

"Your career. I'm a political consultant."

"I don't need a consultant. My campaign manager handles my political career, and I'm very happy with the job he's doing."

"Well, consulting's not all I do. I'm also a speechwriter. And I thought you might need a hand drafting your announcement."

"What announcement?"

"That you're withdrawing from the race for governor."

Aldis laughed. "I'm not withdrawing. I'm winning."

"Maybe you were." Walcott nodded thoughtfully. "But in politics, the winds of fortune can change direction very fast. And if you don't react quickly enough, you can very easily sink."

"I don't know what you're talking about."

"Well, they say a picture's worth a thousand words." Walcott took a six-by-four photograph from his jacket pocket—still tacky from the developers—and handed it to Aldis. It showed him on the bed, his robe gaping open, grappling with a seminaked Ms. Pritchard.

Aldis felt his stomach slowly fill with lead. "How did you get this?"

"How do you think?" Walcott shook his head. "This is what you get for hiring an idiot for a campaign manager, instead of someone like me. I'd never let a client of mine accept the first hotel suite he's offered. Anyway, this picture's just to give you an impression. I have guys working on lots of others. Enlarging. Cropping. You get the idea. Some will be perfect for the newspapers. Others—the more R-rated ones—I'm saving for your wife. I hear she's expecting, by the way. Pregnant women can be very emotional, can't they? How do you think she'll react when she finds out what you get up to when her back's turned?"

Aldis crumpled the picture into a jagged ball and reached around with his other hand to grab the back of Walcott's neck. "Open your mouth. I'm going to stick this down your throat till you choke."

"You could do that, I'm sure." Walcott made no attempt to free himself. "You seem very . . . beefy. As the pictures show. But if you do that, you won't solve your immediate problem. Which is, tomorrow's paper is going to carry one of two things. Your photo, or your withdrawal from the race. And in addition, if you assault me you'll go to jail. In which case you'll no doubt wind up with other body parts getting shoved in your face. And it's unlikely you'll find them as attractive as these." Walcott pulled out another picture. This one showed Pritchard straddling Aldis. "How did my colleague taste, by the way? She's new to the team and I haven't had the pleasure yet."

Aldis let go of Walcott and stepped back. "You're a sick bastard."

"Sticks and stones, my naïve friend." The mocking smile faded from Walcott's face. "Now. It's decision time."

IV

Twenty Years Ago

The three guys filed down the basement steps and took their allotted places in the horseshoe of wooden chairs. They were precisely on time as their boss, Javid Madatov, always demanded of them. The strange thing was, Madatov himself hadn't arrived yet. They'd never known him to be late for anything before, whether here in New York or at home in Baku.

Counting Madatov's, which faced the horseshoe, there were three empty seats. Which was another mystery. They all knew why Kamran's was unoccupied. Kamran was dead. He'd been shot in the face the night before, when their stickup of a back-street bookmaking operation went pear-shaped. But where was Maksim? Why wasn't he there?

They'd all known times could get tough, especially at first. Madatov had warned them. He'd been very clear about that. And he'd also been clear that if they stuck together and rode out the inevitable storms, the move to America would pay off in spades. Surely the boss and his most trusted lieutenant hadn't cut and run at the first sign of trouble?

None of the guys spoke. They knew from experience, when the black clouds are gathering, it's best to keep your doubts to yourself. If the worst happens, bitching about it doesn't help. And if the clouds pass, you don't want to look like you lacked faith. That can be bad for your health.

After ten minutes of silence the door at the top of the staircase scraped open. Madatov appeared. He stood silhouetted against the brighter light for a moment, then strode down the creaky steps with the swagger of a rock star on his way to the stage. He was wearing a black suit and shirt, as usual, but had a large Band-Aid over his right eye and he was carrying an Adidas sports bag that none of them had seen before.

"Gentlemen, I apologize for keeping you waiting. I had some business to attend to that took longer than expected." Madatov lowered himself onto his seat. "Then I had to change my clothes."

"Boss, have you heard from Maksim?" Pavlo, the guy on the right-hand side of the horseshoe, fidgeted anxiously in his seat. He was separated from the others by the two remaining empty chairs, and it seemed as if the isolation was bothering him. "I tried to call him earlier. I got no answer, and one knows where he is."

"I'll get to Maksim later." Madatov's nose wrinkled as if he'd smelled something putrid. "First, we have some business left over from last night." He took an envelope from his jacket pocket and handed it to the guy at the opposite end of the horseshoe. "Urfan, this is for you."

Urfan opened the envelope and took out its contents—a thousand dollars in cash—and looked up at Madatov with wide, surprised eyes. *"Mən başa düşmürəm."*

"In English, Urfan." A note of frustration had crept into Madatov's voice. "For them to obey us, the Americans must understand us. How many times must I tell you this?"

"Sorry, boss." Urfan looked down at the floor. "I try to say, I not understand. Last night, we fail. We took no money. Nothing. How can it be so you pay me?"

"Was it your fault we failed?" Madatov's voice was calm and reasonable now. "Was it you who sold us out to those pigs who ambushed us? Who cost Kamran his life?"

"No, boss!" Urfan looked up, his eyes even wider. "You I never betray! And Kamran I love like my brother."

"Then why should you be punished?" Madatov raised his eyebrows. "No. You are loyal. You do your work. You get your reward. That's how it has been, and how it will always be. And it's the same for everyone." Madatov took out another envelope and threw it to the next guy in line. "Anar, there's yours."

Anar checked inside the envelope, folded it, and slipped it into the back pocket of his jeans. "Thank you, boss."

"Now, Pavlo." Madatov picked up the sports bag and tossed it onto Pavlo's lap. "You were asking about Maksim earlier. Why he's missing. I know the answer. So let's clear that up."

Pavlo was completely still, like he'd been turned to stone.

"You see, the first three jobs we do after coming here, they were perfect. We go in. We come out. No one even breaks his fingernail. Then, last night, disaster. Pavlo, you were outside in the car, so you didn't see all of what went down. So I will explain it to you. Me, I cut myself on some idiot's face." Madatov pointed to his forehead and rolled his eyes. "Urfan, your arm got slashed. Anar, you were knocked unconscious. We had to drag you out. Kamran, well, may he rest in peace. And Maksim? He walked out without a scratch. I lie awake all night, and I get to thinking, why was that? Was Maksim a better fighter than all of us? Did he know some new way to defend himself we could all learn from? So I go to see him. I ask him. And you know what he tells me?"

The room was completely silent.

"Maksim tells me, we fail because he told the Russians we plan to come. He told them every detail. And in return, he took big money from them."

"*Donuz!*" Urfan sprang to his feet, sending his chair clattering against the back wall. "*Haramzade!* Sorry. The English words I do not know."

"It's OK. Sit." Madatov waited for Urfan to retrieve his chair. "But that wasn't all Maksim told me. Pavlo, why don't you open the bag now?"

Pavlo didn't move.

"Pavlo." Madatov's voice had dropped an octave. "Open. The. Bag."

Pavlo's hand was shaking almost too much to take hold of the zipper, but eventually he managed to get the bag unfastened.

"Look inside."

Pavlo pulled the sides apart, peered through the opening, and vomited onto the floor.

"Don't keep it to yourself." Madatov laced his fingers together and stretched out his arms, causing each knuckle to crack in turn. "Show your friends your presents."

Pavlo's face was pale. His whole body was quaking. Very slowly he slid his hand through the gap and pulled out a Ziploc bag. Inside was a pair of human ears.

"Keep going."

The next bag Pavlo produced contained four fingers. The next, most of a nose. The last, an eyeball with a section of optic nerve still attached, like a sea creature's slimy tendrils.

"The eye, that was when Maksim gave up his other piece of news." Madatov stared at Pavlo. "He told me he wasn't working alone. He said it wasn't even his idea. He said it was yours."

"No!" Pavlo jumped up, sending bags of body parts cascading onto the floor. "That's not true. He was lying. Trying to save his own skin."

"No, Pavlo." Madatov just looked sad now. "Maksim's skin was well beyond saving, and he knew it. He was telling the truth. Which means you have a decision to make. You can die right now, right here in this room. Or you can help us settle the score."

"I'll help." Pavlo's eyes were bulging. "Just tell me what you want me to do."

"Nothing difficult." Madatov took a piece of folded paper from his pocket and passed it to Urfan. "Go to a pay phone. Urfan and Anar will go with you. Call your contact, and tell him exactly what's written on that paper. Remember, Urfan speaks Russian, so if you try anything stupid, he'll know. And then you'll get the same as Maksim. Only I'll start with your balls. I'll freeze them. Take them to Baku. And make your kids eat them. Are we clear?"

"Yes, boss." There was a tremor in Pavlo's voice.

"Good. Now. One more thing. Anar—when you're done with the Russians, call Dimitrij. Tell him, that lawyer he said he'd lined up? The Italian-sounding guy? It's time for him to start earning his money."

V

George Carrick was looking fine in his Brioni tuxedo, he imagined—the same kind that James Bond wore. The ballroom carpet felt soft and plush beneath the leather soles of his mirror-polished Church's shoes. He took his time on the way to the stage, casually strolling from his table—front and center, of course—and basking in the rapturous applause from the appreciative audience. He paused modestly in front of the podium before accepting the Waterford crystal trophy from his grateful boss. He stood for a moment, savoring its weight and substance. It must have been expensive. It *should have been* expensive, to be a fair reflection of his value over the decade he'd spent as the #1 rental agent in the company. Probably the whole city. The whole country, even.

Then it was time for his speech.

Except that he didn't give a speech. He wasn't wearing a tuxedo—just a slightly stretched black suit a dry cleaner had given his old friend Donny in lieu of protection money the previous month. His shoes were from China, not England. They weren't shiny. The carpet was as thin as toilet paper. There wasn't a stage or a podium. And there was only one table, crammed in the corner of the cheapest function room at a hotel where the only kind of *balling* that took place was in bedrooms that were rented by the hour. The boss had at least given him a trophy, though. A four-inch-high hunk of plastic, crudely molded to look something like a guy striding along, holding a briefcase by his side. It was exactly like the ones he'd won for each of the nine previous years. Had the boss bought them in bulk? Probably. He was cheap enough. And he must have stored them somewhere without air-conditioning, because this one had started to melt. Its legs were bowed slightly, like it had rickets. Receiving it was demeaning. He should stick it up the boss's ass. But he knew he wouldn't. The sad truth was, he'd take it home and put it on the shelf in the living room with the others. Only maybe at the back, to hide its deformity.

At the nine previous award ceremonies, Carrick had split once his dominance had been recognized and he'd noted which of his colleagues had failed to look sufficiently supportive. This year things were different. He was happy to sit for a while. Finish the rubbery chicken in its tasteless, wine-free sauce. Enjoy the boss's discomfort as he tried to wriggle out of ordering another bottle of the hotel's cheapest Asti Spumante. Or *nasty* spumante, as he'd heard the waitstaff call it. That really summed the boss up. He had a new Rolls-Royce outside—which he always left on the street because he would never spring for valet parking even when it was available—but he wouldn't stump up for drinkable wine, even on his company's one big event of the year. He claimed that was because only German wine was worth paying restaurant prices for, since his father was from the Rhineland, and there was none on the list. But everyone there knew the truth.

Carrick drained his final glass and decided it would be wise to hit the bathroom one last time before leaving. When he came out, a coworker named Amber Mitchell was lying in wait for him. Carrick was always wary of Amber. As the only woman on the team, he suspected that she had access to closing techniques that he and the other guys couldn't offer. Not without subcontracting, which would eat into his commission and was therefore unacceptable. Carrick tried to step around her, but she moved, blocking his path. She reached out, placed her palm on his chest, and started to slide her fingers under his jacket. Carrick was taken aback. He hadn't seen that coming. Then he realized she wasn't being amorous. She was going for the trophy in his pocket. He'd had to take it to the bathroom, because with this mob, you can't even leave a ten-cent trinket unattended.

"Give it to me!" Amber's words were slightly slurred.

Carrick grabbed her wrist and pushed her away. "If you want the prize, work harder, you lazy bitch."

"Give it to me." Amber lunged at him. "You don't deserve it."

"The hell I don't." Carrick stepped back. "The numbers don't lie. I'm number one. I always have been. And I always will be. Although I could coach you, if you think there's a way to make it worth my while . . ."

"You disgust me."

"Suit yourself." Carrick turned to go.

Amber grabbed his arm. "It's not your results I have a problem with. It's how you get them."

Carrick shrugged. "I don't know what you mean. Every deal I do is fair and square."

"You're a liar." Amber crossed her arms. "How many ethnic minority tenants are there in the buildings you manage?"

"I have no idea. I don't keep track."

"Well, I do. There are none. Zero. Zip. And if you ask me, that's no accident."

"Are you suggesting I drive ethnic tenants out of my buildings? Because that's total crap. I've never pressured any tenant—of any color or creed—to get out. I swear on the Bible. And I challenge you to prove otherwise."

"Bullshit." Amber was swaying a little. "What you do is deliberate. You dog whistle, then you charge racist assholes like yourself extra to live in whites-only buildings."

"That's pure fantasy." Carrick shook his head. "Just some kind of nonsense you dreamed up to smear me with because you're a bad loser."

"It's not nonsense." Amber wagged her finger. "I have proof. I've been watching you. Keeping records. So either you stop, or I'll turn you in to the city."

"How can I stop something I'm not doing? That doesn't make sense. You're drunk. Go home. Sleep it off."

"No. I'm serious. I have a friend, a lawyer, and she's going to help."

Carrick took a moment to think. He didn't like where the conversation was heading, all of a sudden. "OK, Amber. Maybe you do have a point. Maybe I do need to make some changes. Some improvements. But I'm sure we can find a more constructive way forward than arguments and threats and lawsuits. Let's get together. You, me, and your lawyer friend. We can talk. What do you say?"

Amber's arms dropped to her sides. "Talk. Sure. We could do that."

"Excellent. Now, listen. I have a showing at one of my buildings tomorrow, first thing. So how about we meet afterward? There's a bar I know in Queens. It's a nice place. Out of the way. Informal. Say 10:00 A.M.?"

Carrick watched Amber totter back to the table, then he went in search of a pay phone. He did have a cell, but he figured that with some calls it was better if there was no record. Especially those involving Donny. It was good to have someone like him to rely on, but help comes at a price. The thought of the extra cost he was about to incur killed Carrick's last remnant of enthusiasm for the party, so right after he hung up he headed for the exit. He was almost outside when he heard a man's booming voice rumbling down the corridor after him, like a peal of thunder.

"Good night, George." It was the boss, cutting and running before any more drinks could be ordered. "Congratulations on another win. Same again next year?"

"Actually, no." Carrick decided that was as good a moment as any to break his news. "I quit."

"What?" The boss grabbed Carrick's elbow. "Why? Where are you going? Is this about money? Because if it is, don't be hasty. The grass is not always greener, you know. So let's sit down in the morning. Come over to the office. I'm positive we can work something out. I sure as hell don't want to lose my number one guy!"

"It's not about money." Carrick bounced on the balls of his feet. "And I'm not coming to the office. There's no point wasting your time. Or mine."

"So what is it?" The boss leaned in close. "Come on. Tell me. You owe me that much, after ten years."

Carrick had promised himself he wouldn't say any more. It

would be better to just drop out of sight. The boss would soon forget about him. Then, in two years—or three, or five at the outside—he'd reintroduce himself. When he bought the company. And closed it down.

The temptation was too great. Carrick couldn't hold back. "See, I have money now. And I've been putting it to work. I've been building my own portfolio. It's time for me to get serious. For me to be taken seriously. So this is it. I'm crossing the river."

A huge smile engulfed the boss's face, broader even than when Carrick had announced that the rent at his largest building had gone up by forty percent. "The Manhattan set? The movers and shakers? Really? You think those guys will ever accept *you*?"

The sound of laughter was still ringing in Carrick's ears long after the boss had crossed the street and climbed into his dusty six-figure behemoth.

VI

TEN YEARS AGO

THE WINDOWS RATTLED BEHIND HIM, AND RIGEL WALCOTT
turned from his desk just in time to catch sight of the little gray
dart as it disappeared from view. It was the defense secretary's
latest plaything, no doubt. Some decrepit old Soviet contraption
that had no business still being in the sky. Walcott couldn't
identify the model—he had no interest whatsoever in planes—
but he figured it was a safe enough bet. After all, no one else
was allowed to fly over the government compound. And the defense secretary was no fool. A few thousand feet in the air was
the place to be if you wanted a little uninterrupted away time.
God knew it wasn't safe on the streets of Baku anymore. Or
pleasant, even if you took a few bodyguards along, with all the
homeless people lying around. Walcott felt fortunate to prefer
the kind of activities you can indulge in without leaving the
house.

Walcott turned his attention back to his visitor. The guy was
an executive from a gas distribution outfit and he was droning

on about some tedious proposal to increase efficiency through consolidation, which was code for wanting to take a sizable chunk of business away from a rival operation. Such a move would require the approval of the president. And access to the president was controlled exclusively by Walcott.

"I think this chart sums the position up perfectly." The executive pointed to the final slide on the iPad he'd perched on the edge of Walcott's desk. "As you can clearly see, if our recommendation is implemented without delay, the country will benefit to the tune of five point seven billion manat over the next five years."

Walcott's face remained impassive. "So the country benefits. I take it your company benefits. But who else benefits from your scheme?"

"It's funny you should ask that." An oily smile spread across the guy's face. "You see, in the course of testing the feasibility of the technological aspects of our proposal, we happened to carry out several field studies in a remote part of Uganda, in Africa. While we were there, we stumbled across a small colony of Rothschild's giraffes. Now, these animals are very rare, as you may know. They're critically endangered, in fact. As responsible citizens, we would like to help them. If we're awarded this contract, we'll be able to generate sufficient funds to bring a breeding pair to a safer country. Say, here. Although we'd still need to find suitable accommodation for the animals, so I was wondering if the president, given his particular experience in these matters, could perhaps suggest somewhere? Maybe I could put the question to him, if we have the opportunity to take the project forward?"

"Maybe you could." Walcott leaned back and steepled his fingers. "If you have the opportunity. However, you'd be surprised how many proposals have crossed my desk recently. All of them offering to flood the country's coffers. And all of their sponsors having coincidentally come across an exotic animal in need of relocation. So. What else do you have to offer?"

"Well, I truly believe our package is the most well rounded, if considered in its entirety." The guy tipped his head to the side: "Perhaps if you had more time to assess it, you'd agree? If you were studying it in more conducive surroundings? Say, on our corporate yacht? It's currently moored off Santorini, Greece. There's a helipad on board. You could fly out tomorrow and go anywhere you want in the Mediterranean. Or the Aegean. And you could stay as long as you want. I mean, you could take as long as you need to properly assess the benefits of the proposal for the country."

"I hope you're not trying to bribe me with a free vacation. My assessment is purely economic. As things stand, I can't recommend what you're proposing. You simply haven't provided enough detail. However, if I had access to all your figures and assumptions, and uninterrupted time to study them, perhaps that could change."

The guy smiled. "I can have all the information you need, here, first thing in the morning."

"Good." Walcott nodded. "Send the information. By close of business tomorrow will be fine. But don't bring it yourself."

"Why not?" The guy swallowed hard. "I put the proposal together. I'm the best placed to explain the intricacies."

"When you came to give your preliminary presentation last month, you brought two colleagues with you. Two young women."

"With respect, I don't think that's right. My boss and I presented last time."

"I'm not talking about the presenters."

"Oh. OK. Now I know who you mean. But those girls are just

interns. They have no detailed knowledge of our systems. No authority to make changes to our offer."

"I understand that. And I want them here tomorrow, or there'll be no deal."

"You're saying, if the girls come, we get access to the president?"

"Not necessarily. Whether matters progress depends on the girls' . . . demeanor. There's no guarantee. But I can tell you this. If they don't come, you definitely have no chance."

The guy was silent for a moment. "OK. I think I can make that happen. But the girls, they're very young. I wouldn't want to send them anywhere they might not be . . . safe."

"What do you mean?" Walcott leaned forward. "Why might they not be safe?"

"Well, there are rumors about things that might have happened on other occasions." The guy closed his eyes for a moment. "No one mentioned your name, of course, Mr. Walcott, but they're the kind of thing that makes me worried."

"I see. Who did you hear these rumors from?"

"I'm not trying to make trouble for anyone. I'm just looking out for my interns. As long as they'll be safe, I'm happy to send them along."

"Good. Tell them to be here at 5:00 P.M. They should be prepared to work late. Now, who's been spreading these rumors?"

"I don't like to say."

"Who?" Walcott banged his fist on the desk. "Look. Do you want the president to hear your proposal, or not?"

"It was Tarlan Huseynov."

"OK. Thank you. Now, tell your girls not to be late."

Walcott waited for ten seconds after the door closed, then hit a speed-dial key on his phone. His call was answered on the first ring.

"Connect me with Minister Balayev, right away. This is Mr. Walcott with the president's office."

The call was transferred and a man's voice came on the line.

"Rigel? This is Ramil. How's business?"

"You know. Can't complain. Now, Ramil, listen. I need your help. There's a guy, Tarlan Huseynov. Some energy company executive. I heard he's been spreading salacious rumors about me. There's a chance he's being set up by one of his rivals, I guess. But talk to him anyway, would you? See if there's anything to the story?"

VII

"*Bu lanet görünüşdən nifrət edirəm!*" The woman turned away from the window and stamped her foot, causing the giant shiny telescope to rattle on its stand.

"In English, Nataliya." Madatov looked up from his laptop and glared at her. "How many times do I have to tell you?"

"You know what I'm saying." Nataliya marched across to the couch and flung herself down in the corner opposite another woman, who could almost be her twin. "I hate this fucking view!"

"Tell me something new." Madatov closed the computer. "Anyway, the view's not that bad. Would you rather be in Baku?"

"I would, actually, yes." Nataliya crossed her arms tight across her chest. "If that meant we weren't living like we were in a jail."

"If I hadn't brought you here, you would be in a jail. Or in a graveyard. So shut up and stop complaining."

"Like you brought us here as a favor." Nataliya pulled her

throw around herself. "Why can't we at least move to the top floor? You can see the water from up there. A little bit."

"I've told you a thousand times." Madatov cracked his knuckles. "The center of the building is the safest. We shouldn't even be on the street side, so count your blessings."

"Couldn't we just—"

"No."

"But—"

Madatov's phone rang, and he held up his hand for silence before answering. "Yes. Good. I'm glad you could get here. You know the address? Good. My man will pick you up outside in ten minutes. Then I'll see you at the venue soon after that."

"Was that the poor guy?" Nataliya's voice had softened.

"It was." Madatov stood and slipped his phone into his pocket. "The deal's on. Go downstairs. Get the girl. The new one. Make sure she's ready. Then take her over and get her situated. Collect Mahir on the way. Check he's had his blue pill. And make sure you're not followed. I'll meet you there."

The sign above the double doors read *The Rose Garden* in handwriting-style script, with its letters boxed in by intertwined red and pink flowers. Madatov didn't like it. He didn't like the name, either. He'd inherited it along with the business when the previous operator took involuntary retirement. He'd planned to change it, but had never thought of anything better. It wasn't a high priority—it wasn't like he could advertise the place—but it still annoyed him every time he went there. He scowled, then worked the lock and went inside.

The air was heavy with the scent of artificial flowers. It was another thing Madatov didn't like, but he'd once tried switching off the machine that produced the fragrance and had found that the room's underlying odor was even less pleasing. He suppressed a sneeze, then turned to Nataliya, who was already inside, waiting. She'd come in through the staff entrance and was now sitting on one of the couches in the center of the room with her feet up on the coffee table. She was wearing red stilettos, mainly because she hated having her toes on display. The sight of all the old ballet scars always reminded her how different her life could have been without people like Madatov taking control of it.

"All set?" Madatov stopped in front of her.

Nataliya nodded.

"Which room are they in?"

She gestured over her left shoulder.

There was a full bar to the side of the main entrance. Two doors in the wall to the left. Three in the back wall. And two in the wall to the right. All had cutesy little nameplates covered with more pictures of roses, starting with Sundance on the door nearest to the bar. Then there was *Angel Face, The Fairy, Double Delight, China Doll*—the one Nataliya had indicated—*Sleeping Beauty*, and finally *Daddy's Little Girl*. That one was reserved for a particular clientele, and Nataliya did her best not to think about the kind of things they paid to do.

"OK, good." Madatov checked his watch. "We should still have a few minutes. Want a drink?" He crossed to the bar, took a bottle of Moët from the fridge, opened it, and grabbed two glasses.

"Do we have to do it this way?" Nataliya shifted her feet to the floor and leaned forward. "It's so fucking *qəddar*."

"Speak English!" Madatov handed her a glass. "And yes. We have to do it this way. There's more money in it. Unless you want to go back to work. Make up the difference on your back."

"I want to kill you, you bastard." Nataliya put her drink down, untouched.

Madatov laughed, but before he could reply his phone beeped. He checked the text, then drained his glass. "They're on their way up. Come on. Get ready. It's showtime."

The doors swung open and a guy hurried into the room, taking short urgent steps. He wasn't much under six feet tall, but he seemed far smaller because there was hardly any meat on him at all. His face was almost as gray as the cheap, shiny suit he was wearing. His chestnut hair was shaggy and unkempt. His eyes were wild, flickering around the room from Madatov to Nataliya to the sets of bawdy pictures on the walls without ever settling on anything in particular. All in all he had the look of a weak animal that knew it was about to become something else's prey. It didn't help that he was followed inside by Madatov's giant ape of a security guy.

"Mr. Garayev." Madatov stepped forward. "It's so nice to meet you in person. Can I offer you a drink? Champagne, perhaps, to celebrate your impending reunion with your wife?"

"Yuliya? Is she here?" Garayev's eyes were still dancing around the room. "Can I see her?"

"She's here." Madatov smiled reassuringly. "And you can see her very soon. Assuming we can work out the outstanding business arrangements. You brought the money?"

Garayev's eyes widened for a moment, then he unslung the duffel bag from his shoulder and held it out. "Here it is. Of course."

Madatov tipped the bag's contents onto the coffee table, gave them a cursory glance, then turned back with a puzzled expression creasing his face. "Mr. Garayev, what's going on? I thought you wanted to take your wife home today."

"I do! It's our little girl's birthday at the end of the week. She's back home with my mother, and I need to book flights and arrange our travel."

The lines bit deeper into Madatov's forehead.

"What?" Garayev gestured toward the table. "The money's all there. Count it! Please. It's what we agreed."

Madatov covered his eyes with his palms for a moment, then shook his head. "Oh, Mr. Garayev, didn't you listen? The amount we talked about, that was for travel and accommodation only. If you want to take her home, I'll need a matching contribution for the loss of future earnings. I'm not running a charity here, you know."

"I don't have any more." Garayev's breathing was becoming fast and shallow. "I've given you everything."

"OK, well, don't get upset." Madatov flashed a cheery smile. "It's not the end of the world. We've still made progress here. Yuliya can work off the rest, and then be with you in half the time. I'm sure she'll be grateful for that, at least. She has seemed a little homesick, to tell you the truth."

"No!" Garayev's hands balled themselves into fists. "Please. I'm desperate. Let me take her home today. I'll pay you whatever you want. I just need time."

"How much time?" Madatov tipped his head to the side.

"I don't know. Two months, maybe? I will pay you. I swear."

"Two months is a long time."

"OK. Six weeks. No. A month. Give me a month!"

"A month might be doable."

"Oh, thank you." Garayev closed his eyes for a moment. "Thank you. I'll get you the money, I promise. Now, please, can I see Yuliya?"

"You want to see her?" Madatov raised his eyebrows. "OK. Follow me."

Madatov led the way to the door marked *Double Delight*. He pushed it open, then stood aside to allow Garayev to go through first. The space was long and narrow, more like a generous closet than a room. Its walls were painted flat cream. The wooden floor had been recently polished. There was a pair of couches, back to back along the center, facing wide windows that were covered with closed venetian blinds. The couches looked solid and were finished with smooth gray upholstery beneath a protective layer of clear vinyl. There was a wooden table at either end, each holding a family-size box of Kleenex, and next to those, on the floor, was a plastic trash can with a swinging lid.

"I don't understand." Garayev turned back toward the door and almost tripped over his own feet. "What is this place? Where's Yuliya?"

"You'll see her in a minute." Madatov perched on the arm of one of the couches. "But before you do, there are some things it's important for you to be clear about. First, Yuliya's staying here till you pay me whatever amount we agree on. Second, if it takes you a month to come up with the money, Yuliya's working for that month. I'm not giving out free food and shelter. And third, this is what working looks like." He stood up and opened the blind on the right-hand side.

"Yuliya." Garayev almost whispered her name, then stretched out and touched the glass. "Oh my God."

Yuliya was lying on a bed. She was on her back. Her arms were above her head, handcuffed to a brass headboard. Her long black hair was fanned out across the pillow. Her face would have been pretty, if not for her vacant, stoned expression. She was wearing only a tiny pair of plain white panties, and there was a bite mark on her right breast. Madatov rapped on the window and a man came into view. He was naked, and his Viagra was clearly doing its job.

"No!" Garayev screamed and made as if to punch the glass, but the security guy wrapped his arms around Garayev's chest and pulled him back.

"I should maybe explain something. Your wife was a little unruly at first, so we allocated her to a certain subset of clients. Those, shall we say, who are particularly large. And who like it rough." Madatov rapped on the glass again and the guy climbed onto the bed.

"Stop him!" Garayev was struggling to break free from the security guy's monstrous arms. "Make him stop. I'll pay you anything."

"Anything?" Madatov turned to stare at Garayev. "How about double the outstanding amount?"

"Yes." Garayev nodded frantically. "Double. No problem."

"In one week?"

"OK. Yes. One week." Garayev nodded again. "I'll get the money. Somehow."

"Good boy." Madatov patted him on the shoulder. "I knew you'd see sense."

"But you've got to stop that guy." Garayev finally wriggled one arm free and pointed to the window. Right now. Before he touches Yuliya. And then don't make her do that anymore. Because I'll pay you. I swear."

"I believe you will pay me." Madatov cracked his knuckles. "But here's the thing. If you want me to bench her for a whole week, that'll cost you more. Say, triple the outstanding amount."

Garayev's eyes widened and he was having trouble catching his breath.

Madatov rapped on the glass and the guy leaned down,

tore Yuliya's panties off her inert body, and threw them to the floor.

"OK!" Garayev was almost choking. "Triple. I can do it. Just make him stop."

Nataliya didn't speak when she got back to the apartment after dealing with Yuliya, and she wouldn't set foot in the lounge where Madatov was stretched out on one of the couches. She pointedly ignored him, and stormed straight into the kitchen. Madatov thought she was sulking, maybe thinking back to the time he'd bought her freedom. Though that would be pretty ungrateful, given that they weren't even married and he'd also freed Nataliya's friend—and now flatmate—Mariya when she'd asked him to. But Madatov was satisfied with the extra profit he'd just made, so he decided not to pick a fight. He opened up his laptop and focused instead on the delivery service menus. Successful business always made him hungry, and he was still debating whether to order Thai or pizza when Nataliya slipped out of the kitchen, headed down the corridor, and ducked into Mariya's room.

"We have a problem." Nataliya couldn't stand still. "The girl we just sold back to her husband? Yuliya? She had a kid."

Mariya sat up in bed. "Are you sure?"

"I heard the husband say so. He said their little girl's birthday is this week."

"The bastard. Madatov promised. He said he wouldn't take another girl with a kid. He swore he wouldn't. What are we going to do?"

Nataliya stopped dead in the center of the room. "You know what we have to do. It's what we should have done a long time ago."

VIII

ONE YEAR AGO

GEORGE CARRICK LOOKED GOOD IN HIS BRIONI TUXEDO—THE same kind that James Bond wore. He knew he did. And so he should. He'd spent a small fortune having it altered to fit him properly. A second small fortune, when you consider how much the thing cost to start off with. And he'd spent an hour in front of the mirror before leaving his apartment to make sure every last detail was right. He'd tried on four different bow ties before making his final choice. Real ones, not the ready-tied kind, and fixing the knot neatly with fingers as wide and stubby as his was no easy feat. He'd switched back and forth between alternative cummerbunds a dozen times before abandoning them both in favor of a vest, figuring that avoiding horizontal stripes was a smarter move for a guy with a figure like his.

A martini, shaken not stirred? Or a glass of vintage Bollinger? That was the question in Carrick's mind as he approached the unmarked door to The Aviary's private dining room. Or maybe he should start with one of their legendary signature cocktails? He'd need an appropriate drink in his hand, given that he was finally about to look down on the city that for so long had looked down on him. He was still mulling over his beverage options when he reached for the door handle and a guy suddenly appeared from a concealed alcove. He was tall. Broad. His expression was so vacant he could have been a zombie, if he hadn't moved so fast. And he barely fitted into his tux, but not for the same reason that Carrick's tailor had struggled with.

The guy said nothing. He just stood there, blocking the door.

"I'm George Carrick." He said it as though it was obvious.

The guy didn't respond.

"I'm here for the party tonight."

Carrick wondered why the guy remained like a statue, then the penny dropped. He may have gone up in the social stratosphere, but he was still physically in New York. He reached for his wallet and took out a hundred-dollar bill. The guy didn't make the slightest move to take it.

A subdued *ping* behind Carrick's back announced the arrival of the elevator. Its door slid open and two guys stepped out. Carrick recognized them. They were investors in the project he was there to celebrate. From the Middle East. They were princes, Carrick had heard, but they never wore crowns. Just regular suits. Not even very nice ones, in Carrick's opinion.

The princely investors approached but showed no sign of knowing Carrick. In some unnaturally fluid move the big guy swept him aside and opened the door to let the Arabs go inside. Carrick stepped forward to follow them and found his path implacably blocked again.

"I'm with them, numb-nuts!" Carrick's voice came out louder than he'd intended it to. "I need to get inside. Will you move out of my way?"

"I can't do that, sir." The guy could have been a robot for all the empathy he was displaying.

"Why not?" Carrick was struggling to bring his voice back under control.

"You're not on the list."

"There's a list? What list?"

"It would be best if you step back now, sir."

The elevator door opened again and a man emerged. He was on his own, wearing a striking peacock blue suit. It could only be Rigel Walcott. The guy who'd contacted Carrick and brought him into the project in the first place.

"Rigel." Carrick stretched out his hand. "Thank goodness you're here. Will you please tell this jackass to move so I can join you inside?"

"George." A flash of recognition crossed Walcott's face, mixed with a moment of surprise. Then he took Carrick's hand and gave it a cursory shake. "How nice to see you. Let's sit for a minute. Over here." He took Carrick's elbow and guided him across to a curved bench covered in burgundy velvet in an alcove to the side of the bar's regular entrance.

"What's the story here, Rigel?" Carrick hissed.

"Well, you know how it is." Walcott shrugged. "It's a small room. There are important people. You have to get the right balance."

"The right balance? What, do you think the building's going to tip over?"

"Well, no."

"No. You just mean, not me."

"It's not my decision, obviously, George. I'd have invited you, but that's not how these things work."

"That's total bullshit. You said the party's for important peo-

ple. So tell me. Who's more important to this project than I am?
The answer's no one. It never would have gotten off the ground
without me."

"No, George. It never would have got off the ground without
money. The bottom line? Nothing's more important than that."

"Bullshit. You can get money anywhere. No one else can
bring what I do to the table."

"We're talking billions of dollars."

"We're talking unique expertise. When you came to me this
scheme was DOA. If the military was involved, they'd be calling
it *project fiasco*. Project disaster. Project incompetent bunch of
spoiled rich assholes."

"That's a bit harsh, George."

"Harsh? No. I don't think so. Why were none of your rich
buddies aware that the ban on demolishing single-occupant
residences was coming in? That was public knowledge. It had
been for two years. When you came to me, there were forty-
eight hours left. Do you know how many strings I had to pull to
get all the contractors on-site that fast? The risks I had to run?
There was no time to get permits. I could have gone to jail.
There wasn't even time to get the gas supply switched off. We
could have blown up half the city."

"But we didn't, George, did we? It all worked out. There were
no explosions. The contractors took the rap for the permit
thing. The fine was peanuts, only a couple of million, and we
paid it for them, anyway. And you got paid, too. Considerably
more than peanuts. And that has to be worth more than hanging out at a boring party with people you don't even seem to
like."

"So that's it? I'm just an employee? A servant? Not fit to be
in the same room as the money men?"

"No." Walcott put his hand on Carrick's shoulder. "That's not it at all. You're a trusted partner. A highly valued member of the team."

"So, I can come to the party?"

"Like I said. That's not my call."

"Then fuck you, Rigel." Carrick pushed Walcott's hand away, stood up, and started toward the elevator. "Fuck you very much. For everything you haven't done."

"Wait." Walcott was on his feet, too.

Carrick stopped and turned back. "I can come in?"

"Well, no. But there's something else I want to talk about. A new project."

Carrick started toward the elevator again.

"There's money in it."

Carrick reached for the Call button.

"A lot of money. And remember, money's the only language these guys speak."

Carrick pulled his hand back. "All right. What's the project? Who's the client? And what do you need from me this time?"

"The project's whatever we want it to be. The client's a contact of mine. A friend of a friend, from Azerbaijan. Where I used to live. I can vouch for him. And for the depth of his pockets."

IX

A Month Ago

Had Rigel Walcott allowed his standards to slip?

He had to admit, it was possible. It was probably hard to avoid when you spent a decade with a corrupt dictator in one corner and the head of his secret police in another. These things had been obvious advantages back in Azerbaijan. They probably wouldn't have hurt if he'd been able to relocate to Moscow along with the others. But in the United States these last few months, if he was honest, they'd hamstrung him. He hadn't noticed the full impact at first—he'd been too busy staying ahead of the leeches from the FBI—but his previously legendary attention to detail had been eroded. His sixth sense coated with a layer of rust. That's how the mistake had been made. How the miscommunication with Madatov had occurred, leading to the raving psychopath's money getting locked up long term—in what was still a damn good development project, Walcott swore—rather than taking a quick trip around the rinse cycle. And how Walcott had landed in his current predicament.

The signs could no longer be ignored. Walcott realized it was time to raise his game. Starting immediately. With the food. For the occasion he'd transformed the conference room at his office suite into the approximation of a dining room. The Eames chairs had been wheeled temporarily into his office, and a set of knockoff Louis Quatorze carvers he'd gotten cheap on the Internet put in their places. A blue velvet cloth had been laid over the table and the center of the space filled with cheese and cold cuts and seafood he'd ordered in from Eataly. And around the edge, he'd arranged the pièces de résistance: A vat of swallows' nest soup in honor of his first guest, Zheng Zhi. An ensemble of matsutake mushrooms, which he knew to be Makoto Yamaguchi's favorite delicacy. Five tins of Kolikof albino caviar, which he was sure everyone would eat but hoped would particularly impress Sergei Sinitsyn. And a generous platter of jamón Ibérico, which he'd heard Iago Asensio was particularly partial to. Looking over the spread before his guests arrived, Walcott was confident that he'd nailed it: Plenty of fillers, and something special for each of the guys who'd benefited the most from his last three money-laundering schemes. How could that level of consideration not lead to a cooperative atmosphere?

Walcott didn't bring up business for the first ninety minutes. He summoned the last of his patience and let his guests enjoy their food, plus a couple of magnums of Boërl & Kroff champagne. He allowed their conversation to roam free. Then, once the first round of Balvenie had been poured, he opened the left-hand panel in the back wall of the room and took out a stack of slim green leather binders.

"Here you go, gentlemen." Walcott passed one binder to each guest. "Some food—for thought, this time."

Silence descended as each man read Walcott's proposal.

Sinitsyn was the first to finish. "No" was all he said before tossing his copy on the floor.

"No?" Lines creased Walcott's forehead. "Why not? It should be a no-brainer. My enterprises have worked for you before, haven't they? You've each said you'd be happy to do business together again. All I'm asking is for an advance. One and a quarter million dollars each now, and in return you'll receive one and a half million dollars' worth of my services before the end of the year. From your points of view, it's money for nothing. A quarter of a million mailbox dollars each. How can you possibly decline? Unless that forty-year-old scotch has gone to your heads."

"It's a no from me, too." Asensio handed Walcott his binder. "Not because I think you're offering a bad deal. But because we know what you want the money for."

"What difference does it make what I want the money for?" Walcott set the binder on the table. "How I spend what I earn is no one's business but my own."

"Not so, my friend." Yamaguchi shook his head very slightly. "You want the money to settle your debt with the Azerbaijani, Madatov. The man's a savage. No one's going to put themselves in the middle of a dispute he initiated."

Walcott felt his cheeks begin to burn. The last thing he wanted was for his problems to become common knowledge. "That's ridiculous. I'm not saying I owe Madatov a penny. But even if I did, why would he care where I get the money from? And if he is indeed a savage, that somewhat argues against him being too scrupulous, yes?"

"You owe." Zheng frowned. "He cares. The word is out. You are not to be helped. You made the bed, you lie in it yourself."

"You're all together on this?" Walcott looked at each man in turn, and each one nodded. That was a shame. He'd hoped he wouldn't have to go the other route. Reluctantly he opened the next panel along in the back wall, took out a stack of red binders, and handed them around. "I'll save you the trouble of reading this time. Here are the details of the last project we worked on together. Minus my involvement, of course, since my proceeds were taken in cash and therefore are untraceable. I'll be passing a copy to the Feds unless the one point two five each is in my account by close of play tomorrow."

Yamaguchi sighed. "This saddens me, Rigel. You're like the sumo who stepped into the ring one time too many." He pulled a piece of paper from his pocket. "This is a copy of a wire transfer you made to a bank in the Cayman Islands. How long will it take the Feds to connect it to your case against your *partner* in the development consultancy that collapsed over there?"

For the first time in his life, Walcott didn't have an immediate retort.

"What you did today was lazy, Rigel." Sinitsyn got to his feet. "Word is, you have the money to pay Madatov. It's just not in the United States. Bringing it here might not be easy, but that's where you should focus your energy. Go to Azerbaijan and carry it home on your back if the banks won't help. Just don't try to stiff your friends again."

Walcott watched his *friends* file out of the room in silence, then felt a sudden pain shoot up his left arm. It subsided after a moment, so he reached for the whiskey and poured himself a generous measure. It was an exceptionally fine scotch. He let his mind drift for a moment as he savored the soft vanilla sweetness of its finish. The pleasure it brought him was pure and profound. But he'd have happily given up fine liquor for good in return for a call to Ramil Balayev. One phone call, and the knowledge that his enemies would be taken off the board, no questions asked. Just like the old days.

X

Javid Madatov was a sadly misunderstood man, Roberto di Matteo concluded.

OK, so there were two sides to his character. Roberto could see how people might take issue with one of those. He himself was more inclined to turn a blind eye to it. Partly because Madatov's dubious side had kept him lucratively employed for almost his entire career. And partly because he was inclined to chalk it up to the forces of nature. It was like with a spider. If a juicy fly was stupid enough to land in the center of its web, no one complained when it got eaten. And if another spider built its web too close? Well, that was tough. And anyway, Roberto preferred to focus on Madatov's other side. The good side. The neglected side. The side that led him to stand up for his friends, regardless of circumstances. To look after them. To see they were OK, as long as they were loyal. And to come up with the occasional surprise. Like with the video game store.

Madatov could easily have sold it after its previous owner

was no longer in a position to continue breathing. He could have made a tidy profit. But he didn't. He knew that playing video games was Roberto's hobby. So he gave the store to him instead. It offered Roberto early access to all the new releases. Plus a convenient way to get his hands on the classics, which he frankly preferred. And there were practical aspects to the arrangement, too. The store was a perfect cover for channeling payments to bent cops. It saved Roberto from having to attend tedious meetings in parks. Churches. Bars. And all the other bullshit places the less fortunate bagmen have to go. Not to mention that he actually enjoyed putting in a couple of hours, every other Friday. So that day he raised an imaginary toast to the guy he could have at least called half a friend. He hung his jacket on the back of the chair. Clipped his OWNER/ MANAGER badge onto his shirt pocket. And happily stepped from the office onto the shop floor.

During the first ten minutes of his shift, Roberto relieved an eager teenager of two hundred dollars. Lieutenant Ospina arrived halfway through the transaction. He pretended to browse the shoot-'em-up section until the kid was safely outside, then he approached the register.

"I bought this last week." Ospina produced a copy of Grand Theft Auto V from a shopping bag and placed it on the counter. "It didn't work. I think the DVD-ROM's scratched or something."

"I'm sorry to hear that. Thanks for giving us the opportunity to put it right." Roberto opened the game's case and looked inside. It was empty. "Yep. I can see the problem. I don't know how this happened, but the easiest thing is just to replace it." He turned to a shelf on the back wall and took down another box, which he'd previously packed with fifty-dollar bills.

"Thanks, man." Ospina reached across to pick the game up, but Roberto kept it pressed to the counter with his fingers.

"Any news?" Roberto had been scanning the store while they talked and was confident that they were alone, but he kept his voice low, just in case.

"Everything's the same." Ospina glanced over his shoulder. "There's a pair of detectives all over your guy Madatov. They've tied him to four murders in the last six months."

"What makes them so sure Madatov's behind these killings?"

"All four of the victims were known enemies of his. And there was no sign of forced entry at the crime scenes. Each of the dead guys had been around the block. They were no mugs. They knew the killer. That's the only way it plays. The only common factor is Madatov. And it's only a matter of time until the detectives get something on him. It just makes it a little harder, is all, with him not coming out on the streets anymore. Except to do the murders, obviously."

"Have they made any move for a warrant on Madatov's brownstone?"

"No. They can't be sure the murder weapons are there, and if something else comes up nobody wants to settle for a misdemeanor. And they won't move without proper paper, regardless. They don't want to risk Madatov getting a walk."

"OK. So what's next?"

"More of the same. They'll keep watching him. Working their snitches. Hoping for a break via electronics or cyber surveillance. I'll shield him the best I can, but he has an awful high profile with the brass. They're throwing a lot of resources at catching him. I can't promise to keep him free forever."

"Understood. Just do your best. And remember, as long as

the circumstances remain the same, the ATM stays open. You know what I mean?"

"Absolutely. And I appreciate that. Maintaining the status quo. That's what I'm all about."

Roberto let go of the game box. "There's one more thing to talk about. You're getting a little extra this week. Because you have an extra task. It's nothing major. A piece of evidence that needs to get tainted. It's connected to a perp named Davies. The case number and all the other details are inside. Make sure to let me know when it's taken care of."

XI

Two Weeks Ago

GEORGE CARRICK TUNED OUT THE SOUND OF THE VOICES FOR A moment. The whining. The worrying. The soul searching. It was driving him crazy.

He knew it would make sense to only work with professionals. Especially at his age. Amateur investors are a source of aggravation, and that was something he didn't want. But they're also a source of money, and money wasn't just something he wanted. It was the thing he needed. As much of it as possible. As quickly as possible. Because without it, he'd never earn the respect he was due. He'd never get even with the pompous assholes like Rigel Walcott, who thought they were better than him.

The couple had quieted down now. They were in their fifties, and had recently come to the city from Florida. They'd sold some company and wanted a way to make the money work for their retirement. Or maybe it was to help out their kids. He couldn't remember, and he didn't care.

"The way I look at it is this." Carrick managed to conjure up a brief smile. "The models, in the cases. They're impressive, right?"

The woman nodded tentatively.

"And the best thing about them?" Carrick paused. "Is something you can no longer see."

"What is it?" The woman glanced down at the set of miniature high-rises nestling in the cavity in the coffee table.

"The gross mess they were designed to replace." Carrick nodded sincerely. "You see, when you invest with me, you're also investing in the future. Your own. The city's. And America's. It's not just the smart financial thing to do. It's the patriotic thing to do."

"You're saying that other buildings had to be demolished to make room for all these developments?"

"Every project is different. Sometimes old decrepit tenement-type buildings have to be cleared away. Sometimes commercial premises have to be. And look, I understand. Change can be hard, in the moment. It's human nature to cling to what we've got. *Bird in the hand syndrome,* I like to call it. Plus some people aren't blessed with much imagination. They don't have the vision to see a better version of the future. Take this very building. It's pretty much the definition of iconic, right? It's famous around the world. An enduring symbol of American excellence. But you know what was here before it? Not an empty lot. No, ma'am. It was the original Waldorf Astoria. It was only thirty-six years old when they tore it down. Did people protest? You bet they did. But were they right?"

"Mr. Carrick, knocking down a hotel is one thing. Even a beautiful one. But people's houses? Their homes? Isn't that what we're talking about, to make our project happen?"

"You raise a good point. Homes are different. There's no denying it. And that's why you have to choose your partner very carefully. I hate to say it, but not all developers are the same. I shouldn't say it. We're supposed to stick together. To have one another's backs." Carrick pictured himself lobbing a grenade through the door at The Aviary, or whichever other fancy joint Walcott and his cronies would be hanging out at. "But the truth? With some groups, things happen that shouldn't. Profit gets put ahead of everything else. Some of the things I've heard about would shock you. They certainly disgust me. That's why I developed my own special approach to this type of situation. I can honestly say—and I've been doing this a long time—I have never personally forced anyone out of a building they didn't want to leave."

"But doesn't rent control come into play here?" The woman pulled a notebook from her purse. "Doesn't that give special protection? I've heard it can be more trouble than it's worth. Some people say it's better to walk away."

Carrick forced a smile. *God, how he hated rent control.* "Some developers do shy away from putting money into rent-controlled buildings, sure. Do you know what kind? Ones who want to screw their tenants. You see, rent control isn't some kind of magic. It's not the holy grail. It's just a type of contract that gives advantageous rent and other protections for certain types of tenants. There's no law that says it can't be matched, or even bettered. Which is why I've developed what I call my *enhanced relocation packages*. I have a team of specialists who work exclusively with me to implement them when circumstances call for particular attention. And I've never known a tenant to refuse once they've understood exactly what we're offering."

"So if we go ahead, no one will be taken advantage of?"

"Absolutely not." Carrick stood up and bounced on the balls

of his feet. "You have my personal guarantee. So, what do you say? Do we have a deal?"

The couple looked at each other, but neither of them spoke.

Carrick looked at his watch. "Guys, I don't want to pressure you, but opportunities like this don't come along every day. I'm in touch with two groups of Russian investors who are desperate to get on board. Now, I'm old-school. I'd prefer to be dealing in dollars than with roubles, if you know what I mean. But I also have bills to pay and contractors to keep busy, so I'm going to need an answer by the end of the day."

Carrick waited until his assistant buzzed through to confirm that the couple had left the office, then he took a prepaid cellphone from a box of them in his desk drawer.

"Donny, I'm giving the green light on another job. Have you replaced Davies yet? We need someone quick, but not someone who'll tread on his own johnson this time."

XII

A WEEK AGO

RIGEL WALCOTT HAD FLOWN ON HUNDREDS OF PRIVATE PLANES in his life, but he'd never been to an airport to meet one before. He'd always had people to do that for him. He was half wishing he'd sent someone else that morning, too, because aside from the travelers preparing to depart—he recognized the types, clustered around the lounge chairs and couches with their pre-flight cocktails, some watching the stock prices scroll silently across the large-screen TVs, others contemplating the flames in the oversized fireplace as they fought a losing battle with the air-conditioning—the only guys waiting there were chauffeurs. There were five of them standing in a tight group near the land-side exit for easy access to the smoking area.

Another inconvenience was that unlike at regular airports, there was no display screen to provide information about the planes that were due to arrive. Walcott could hear the occa-sional crackle from the radios behind the reception counter, but he couldn't make out any intelligible words. Sometimes the bursts of sound prompted no action. Other times a receptionist would glide across to the lounge and direct a group of passengers to the air-side door where a porter would be waiting to wheel their luggage out to one of the planes on the apron near the horseshoe of hangars.

Walcott kept watch out of the window, but still the plane he was so desperate to see did not appear. His fate was literally up in the air, and he had no way of checking on its status. Unable to stand still, and not wanting to draw attention to himself, he moved across to the far side of a trio of tall hotel-style baggage trolleys. The first held a couple of golf bags. The second, suitcases—Rimowas and Halliburtons in various rainbow shades of corrugated aluminum like some weird art installation. And the third, a single narrow wooden crate. The kind used to transport paintings. Valuable ones, usually. Walcott wondered what was inside. A Renoir? A Leonardo? Even a minor Richter or a Lichtenstein would be enough to get him off the hook. If he could somehow get the trolley outside, to his rented Escalade . . .

Movement on the runway caught Walcott's eye. It started as a smear of white and yellow dancing in the heat haze that was rising from the exposed asphalt. Then it solidified into the shape of a plane as it taxied along the shaded sections nearer the buildings. He checked its silhouette. There were three engines perched on the fuselage near the tail. That was good. It could be the type he'd chartered. A Dassault Falcon. It was more expensive, but he'd been told it was better than a Gulfstream and he couldn't afford to take chances. He waited anxiously as it crept closer. It turned slightly and its tail number came into view. Walcott read it. Twice. It was correct. Salvation was here at last.

The plane came to a stop ten yards from the terminal, with

its left-hand side facing the entrance for convenience. Ten seconds crawled past and its hatch didn't open. Another ten ticked away. And then the reason dawned on Walcott—it was an international flight so INS clearance was needed. Two minutes later a navy blue Crown Victoria with gold lettering rolled up slowly from somewhere between the hangars. Two officers stepped out. The plane's door swung down, its steps were lowered, and the officers climbed inside.

Walcott was glazed with sweat despite the chilly processed air of the terminal building. Why was INS taking so long? There should only be one passenger on board. How hard can it be to check one passport?

Five minutes later the officers were back in their car, driving away. Walcott hurried outside, his knees feeling like they'd been replaced with rubber. The noise of the jet's idling engines assaulted his ears and the smell of burnt fuel stung his nose. Then a man appeared at the top of the steps and Walcott's discomfort evaporated. The man waved and flashed a tired smile. He was the same kind of height as Walcott. The same kind of age. They'd been buddies in their campaign consultancy days. It had been tough for Walcott to track the guy down, but he didn't trust anyone else for a job like this.

The guy was halfway down the steps and Walcott was halfway between the terminal and the plane when a black Suburban raced into view. Its sound had been masked by the whine of the plane's engines. Another one followed, looping past the first and stopping near the plane's nose. A third vehicle trailed behind the SUVs—a red box van with FBI EVIDENCE RECOVERY TEAM in gold letters along its side—and it took up station near the tail.

Walcott stood as if he was frozen despite the sun beating down and the heat rising from the asphalt. An agent took Walcott's buddy by the elbow and led him to the first Suburban. Two more agents bustled up the plane's steps. The engines spooled down after a couple of minutes and the agents emerged escorting the pilots and the flight attendant. Once they were squared away in the second Suburban, an agent from the evidence van took a set of steps and climbed up to the cargo hatch. He opened it and then struggled to pass down two large beige nylon suitcases. His partner took one and hoisted it with both hands as if assessing its weight.

"Phew! This is heavy." The agent turned to Walcott. "There's more than beachwear in here, huh? Your buddy must be a world-class shopper. What kind of souvenirs was he bringing back?"

Walcott didn't answer.

"I didn't realize Baku was a destination for retail therapy." The agent lowered the case to the ground. "What do you know that we don't?"

Walcott remained silent.

"Or how about this. Maybe your buddy was bringing something else back for you? Like, say, maybe two and a half million dollars, cash? In each case?"

Walcott finally found his voice. "You think there's cash in the cases? Are you crazy?"

"I guess one of us is." The agent winked. "Let's open them up. Find out who's the goofball."

Walcott shrugged. "Go ahead. Be my guest."

The agent laid the case down, then paused. "Tell you what. You open it."

Walcott unzipped the case, then stood up without looking inside. The agent pulled back the flap. The case was crammed full of bundles that were held together with US Treasury bill wrappers. They were the exact size of banknotes. The agent took one of them out. He fanned through it. Then he threw it on the ground and walked quickly away, figuring that would cause less damage to his career than his preferred response, which was to punch Walcott in the face.

The bundle contained nothing but pieces of cut-up newspaper. Every other one in each of the cases was the same.

Walcott kept a smile fixed on his face until all the agents had left, but he knew he'd scored a hollow victory. The exercise was supposed to prove a concept. To provide a lifeline. Instead, the concept was shattered. The lifeline was in tatters. He'd burned through the last of his real cash. He was no closer to getting Madatov his money. And the pain in his left arm was back with a vengeance.

XIII

Over the years the ride became a little wilder, but it also became even more rewarding. It had gone through a really crazy patch this last year. Roberto di Matteo had thought about walking away. But then he'd more or less settled back into his old pattern. He liked the money he was making. And if anything, the work was a little easier. Which was OK . . .

That morning Roberto was playing golf on his computer, thinking vaguely about retirement, when his secretary buzzed through.

"Sir, I have a gentleman here who's asking to see you. He doesn't have an appointment, but he says Mr. Carrick sent him. Should I tell him to come back another day?"

Carrick. The guy was a weasel. That was for sure. But he did have a lot of useful contacts. "I have ten minutes, Gloria. Send him in if he thinks he can be quick."

The man who appeared in Roberto's office a minute later was

wearing a gray suit. He had neat hair. But later that day, when Roberto thought back on their meeting, he struggled to recall any other details of the guy's appearance.

"Hi. I'm Paul McDougall." The guy held out his hand. "Thanks for seeing me on such short notice. Mr. Carrick sent me over. He has a problem, and he thought it was better not to discuss it on the phone. I hope you can help."

"That depends. What kind of problem does Mr. Carrick have?"

"It's a little embarrassing, actually. One of his guys has been arrested. Another one. Jonny Evans this time. It's a similar situation to the Norman Davies case. A similar problem. And we're looking for a similar solution."

"Is it another assault?"

"It is. On another tenant, in the same building. A stabbing this time. Not fatal, fortunately. Evans was just supposed to scare some old guy. You know, wave his switchblade around, do a bit of yelling and screaming. But something went wrong. Evans got carried away, I guess. He did get out of there before the police and the paramedics arrived, but he panicked when he heard the sirens. He ditched the knife in a drain on the same block as the building, which wasn't the smartest thing to do. Mr. Carrick sent someone to get it back, but it was too late. The police had already found it. And that's a problem, because it's covered with the victim's blood and Evans's prints."

"It sounds like quite a mess. What are you looking for, exactly?"

"All we need is for the knife to disappear. There are no witnesses except the victim, and he's old, senile, and scared."

Roberto thought for a moment. He had the opportunity to charge a hefty premium here, he realized. He could argue that the risk was much greater, tampering with evidence so hard on the heels of the previous time. "OK, McDougall. I'll handle it. I'll just need the booking number from you. And you can tell Mr. Carrick, this has to be the last time."

"I understand. And don't worry. You can rest assured. You definitely won't be hearing from Mr. Carrick again."

XIV

PRESENT DAY

GEORGE CARRICK SETTLED BACK IN HIS CHAIR, SLIPPED OFF HIS shoes, and swung his feet up onto his desk. He was done for the day. Finally! Although he knew he shouldn't complain. Things were bearable. They were certainly better than they had been a week ago. The Davies problem had been solved. Permanently. The idiot McNaught had been sent packing, with his sanctimonious tail between his legs. The hassle and expense of rehousing those loser tenants in Hell's Kitchen had been avoided. So had the medical costs for that old Mason woman. Progress was definitely being made.

Carrick opened his top drawer and took out a cigar. It had been a gift from a grateful client. It was a good one. An expensive one. He held the tip in his teeth and reached for his lighter. Then put the lighter back. He couldn't smoke that cigar. Not yet. He still wasn't out of the woods. Jonny Evans wasn't returning his calls, for example. Which was a problem, because he needed those stragglers out of his building. Like, yesterday. It still rankled that he had to demolish it at all. It hadn't been bringing in a vast profit, but it had been steady. Carrick believed in maintaining a balanced portfolio, and if you want balance, you need a certain amount of steady. Now he wouldn't have enough. And the building was in a great area. Amazing things were happening there. His instinct told him there was a killing to be made, and he hated to miss out. Although, talking of killing, deep down he knew that getting away from Madatov with all his body parts still attached put him well ahead of the game. Losing the building still stung, though . . .

There was a sudden knock on the door. Carrick cursed himself for letting his receptionist go home before he left himself. Maybe if he kept quiet, whoever it was would go away? No. That wasn't his style. He swung his feet back down to the floor and slipped on his shoes. Then he paused. What if it was one of Madatov's guys? Coming to snatch him? No. It couldn't be. Madatov's guys wouldn't bother to knock.

"Yes?" He finished tying his shoelaces. "Who is it?"

The door opened and a guy stepped into the office. He was enormous. In terms of height, anyway. At least six feet eight. But the guy wasn't wide. He wasn't skinny, either. He was just in good shape. He had a nice suit, too. It was obviously bespoke. The tailoring was subtle, but Carrick had been around enough security-conscious guys to see that it was cut to accommodate a weapon. He opened another desk drawer with the pretext of returning his cigar. And then he left it open, his own gun conveniently within reach.

"I'm sorry to disturb you so late, Mr. Carrick." The tall guy came closer to the desk. "But it's urgent. Mr. Walcott sent me. I need your help."

"Walcott?" Carrick leaned back in his chair. "What does that one-armed Irish bastard think I can help you with?"

The tall guy smiled. "Nice try, Mr. Carrick. But Mr. Walcott's not Irish. He was born on Long Island. His father claims to be able to trace his family back to the *Mayflower*. His mother's German, from Hamburg. And he had both his arms when I saw him yesterday at his office on Wall Street."

Carrick nodded. "Very good. So really, how is the old bastard? I haven't seen him since he got back from Uzbekistan."

"It was Azerbaijan, where he was. And the two of you have done business in the last month."

"OK." Carrick held up his hands. "You know Rigel. But why did he send you to me? What kind of trouble are you in?"

"I need money."

"Well, I'm sorry, my friend. Rigel's wasted your time. And mine."

"You don't understand. I'm not looking for a loan. I'm trying to sell a building. Mr. Walcott had agreed to buy it. And at the last minute, he pulled out. He thought you might be interested in stepping into his shoes."

"What's wrong with the place, to make Rigel pull out?"

"Nothing's wrong with the building. The problem's with him. He wouldn't go into detail, but he said he has a cash-flow problem. He asked me to agree to a structured payment deal, with the first installment delayed for six months. Unfortunately I had to say no. I need the money now."

"Why?"

"Personal reasons."

"If Rigel pulled out, why don't you sue him? For breach of contract. I would, and I'm basically his partner."

"It was a handshake deal."

Carrick shook his head. "You're screwed, then, I guess. Unless . . . What kind of building is it?"

"Residential. A brownstone. It's a big, beautiful place. I had planned to live in it myself. You could sell it as a single-family home. Or convert it into apartments. There are lots of other conversions nearby. It has great revenue potential. I have all the projections. I'd be happy to share them with you."

"Where is the place?"

"Hell's Kitchen."

"How much are you looking for?"

"It was appraised for thirty-two mil. I'd take twenty-eight for a quick sale."

"Sorry." Carrick shrugged. "That's too rich for my blood. I can't help you."

"There's room for flexibility, if you'd be able to close fast."

"I don't know. Leave me whatever information you have. I'll think about it."

"Great." A broad smile spread across the tall guy's face. "And here's something else to chew over. I'm in a situation where I need to put my hands on some cash. It would be in both our interests for the sale price to appear low. So if you want the building, I'll knock off ten percent in return for a cash deposit, off the books."

"I could see that part working. But your asking price is still way too high."

"I could go to twenty-five."

"Twenty."

"Twenty-four."

"Twenty-two five."

"OK."

"But only if it checks out. And if I like it. I need to see it. Because no one has a better instinct for real estate than me."

XV

THE DOORMAN FLICKED THROUGH HIS MOLESKINE NOTEBOOK, nodded, secured the page he'd selected with the book's elastic strap, and laid it on the counter.

"See?" He pointed to the top line. "I wrote that down myself. 'RW, business trip, no return date.'" He dropped his voice to a whisper. "I put 'RW' because Mr. Walcott doesn't like anyone writing down his full name."

The visitor placed his attaché case on the counter. He opened it. Extracted a $100 note. And tucked it into the flap in the back cover of the notebook.

"I'm not lying!" The doorman crossed his arms.

"I'm sure you're not." The visitor closed his case and reset its combination lock. "What I've just given you is a fee, in return for a service I'd like you to perform. It's a very straightforward service. All I want is for you to call Walcott's number and leave him a message. What harm can there be in that?"

"I guess I could." The doorman didn't look convinced. "What do you want the message to say?"

"Pass me a pen. I'll write it down for you."

The visitor turned to a fresh page in the Moleskine and carefully printed *Paul McCann. Reception. First installment for Madatov.*

The doorman waited for the visitor to sit in the waiting area, then self-consciously read the message out loud to a cellphone voicemail box. Six minutes later one of the elevators' doors slid open. Two guys stepped out. They were tall and broad, dressed all in black, and had large chrome-plated pistols strapped to their belts. The visitor recognized them as the security guards who'd escorted Walcott to his office on the day the phones had failed. The security guards figured they were seeing the visitor for the first time.

"Mr. McCann?" One of the security guys took a step toward reception.

The visitor stood up. "That's me."

"Come with us, please, sir. Mr. Walcott will see you now."

There was a lot of white in Walcott's apartment. The floor, which was bleached wood. The walls. The Le Corbusier furniture. The inside of the blinds, which were drawn over every window, as if to guard against surveillance from drones or helicopters. The only relief from the overwhelming paleness came from the Steinway Grand in the living room, and a pair of Miró prints that were hanging in the hallway.

Walcott emerged from his bedroom wearing a royal blue

robe and slippers, and beckoned for the visitor to join him in the living room.

"So." Walcott wiped his glasses on the sleeve of his robe. "Are you going to tell me who you are?"

"My name's Paul McCann." The visitor balanced his case across his knees. "I'm a friend of a friend."

"This friend being Madatov?"

The visitor nodded. "He and I were talking—trying to solve a problem, in fact—and your name came up."

"How do you know my address?"

"Well, Madatov told me, obviously. When he suggested I get in touch with you."

Walcott's eyes widened and he slumped back on the couch, deflated. "Madatov knows I'm here?"

"Listen." The visitor leaned forward. "I think you've got the wrong idea. Mr. Madatov hasn't sent me here to hurt you. He's a smart guy. He sees that we both have, shall we say, geographically influenced liquidity issues right now. Granted, yours is a little more pressing, as you owe him a great deal of money and he's not famed for his patience. But he figured that if we put our heads together, we could both benefit."

"OK." Walcott sat up a little straighter. "How do we help each other?"

"It's like this." The visitor paused, as if he was marshaling his thoughts. "I'm a businessman. I own an import/export company. Right now I need to pay a supplier who's overseas. And the problem is, my money's here. For reasons I don't need to bore you with, the FBI is watching it. I can't transfer it. Not through the regular channels, anyway. So I asked Mr. Madatov if he could help. He still has resources in the old country. And contacts. Ramil Balayev is a mutual friend, for example. I believe you knew him, as well, from his time in the government? Anyway, Mr. Madatov agreed to assist me. But then he came up with an alternative idea. He said you have a similar problem, but in reverse. Your money's stuck abroad, and your creditors are here."

"That seems like a fair assessment. So what do you and Mr. Madatov suggest we do about it?"

"It's really simple. I give you cash, here. You transfer the equivalent amount in local currency from your foreign bank to my foreign bank. That way we both end up with our money where we need it. There are no records. And nothing touches the US banking system. It's an absolute no-brainer."

"So what's the catch?"

"There isn't one. As long as we trust each other. Which is why I brought this."

The visitor worked the combination locks and then passed the attaché case to Walcott.

"That's $100,000. Well, $99,900, actually, because I had to bribe your doorman to leave you the message. I'm going to walk out of here without it, and trust that you transfer the equivalent into my bank in Sofia. The routing information is in the case, as well as the cash."

"I can transfer that amount right away. So what's next?"

"When I see that the deposit's arrived, we can move on to dealing with the real money. Then I can pay my supplier, and you can pay Mr. Madatov."

"Are you sure you know the kind of numbers we're talking about here?"

"I believe so."

"Because I need five million dollars. That's a lot of cash to put your hands on. Can you handle it?"

"Actually, that is a problem. Five million's no good to me in

Bulgaria. I need seven point seven million. I can get the cash, no problem. The question is, are you happy to make the transfer?"

"Of course I am." A smile started to spread across Walcott's face. "Seven point seven's actually better for me. It'll leave me some spending money, once I've cleared my debt with Madatov. One question, though. What about the timescale? I'm under a little pressure to settle up."

"Doing it quickly suits me, too. I can get the cash together within the next couple of days. Give me your cell number and I'll text you to confirm."

"Will do."

"And in terms of logistics with the cash. Shall I bring it here?"

"That works for me."

"Excellent. Then I'll be in touch."

XVI

Roberto di Matteo nailed the one, final alien, then tried to catch his breath while the screen refreshed and the next extraterrestrial horde lined up to attack the earth. He was about to start blasting again when his office door burst open and a guy strode in. Roberto's secretary followed, gripping the intruder's arm as if being towed in his wake.

"I'm sorry, sir." The woman let go and folded her arms. "I couldn't stop him."

"It's OK, Gloria. I'll handle it." Di Matteo quit the game, scowled, and waited for her to leave.

The intruder sat down and placed his briefcase on the floor by his side.

"McDougall? What the hell do you think you're doing? I told you when you were here before that was the last time I was going to help!"

"You said it would be the last time you helped George Carrick. Today, I'm here on behalf of a different client."

"Really? Who?"

"Rigel Walcott."

Di Matteo paused. "What does he want?"

"He wants to propose a deal, so he needs you to set up a meeting."

"With Madatov?"

"Why else would I be here?"

"What kind of deal?"

"Walcott owes Madatov money. Five million dollars. Walcott's happy to settle his debt, but he proposes to pay with information. Or rather, suppression."

"You're making no sense."

The intruder took an envelope from his briefcase and tossed it onto the desk. Di Matteo cautiously opened it and looked inside. There were six photographs. He pulled them out. Each one showed a bedroom. Each bedroom contained a pair of filthy cots. Each cot was set up with an equally filthy IV stand.

"Should these mean something to me?"

"They were taken at Madatov's apartment, within the last week. They show that he's actively engaged in human trafficking."

Di Matteo shrugged and slid the pictures back into their envelope. "No, they don't. Even if the pictures were taken at his building, they prove nothing of the kind."

"Think of them as an anonymous tip. They certainly give probable cause for a search warrant. I imagine Madatov would prefer to keep the police out of his home and his business."

Di Matteo screwed his eyes closed for a moment. "Listen, burn the pictures. Tell Walcott trying to blackmail Madatov would be an epic mistake."

"You've got this all wrong. It isn't blackmail. It's trade. Knowledge is power, and power comes at a price."

"You really don't understand what a bad idea this is."

"Trust me, I know exactly what kind of an idea this is. And no one's changing their minds about it. So please, pass the message on. These are the only copies. You can keep them. Walcott will hand the phone they were taken with, and the memory card they were stored on, to Madatov himself. It has to be him, and it has to be in person. That's the only way the pictures won't see the inside of the police department."

"All right. I'll pass it on. But I can't promise what kind of response you're going to get." Di Matteo paused for a moment, wishing that life was as simple as a video game. "If Madatov agrees to it, when and where will the meeting be?"

"Central Manhattan. Tuesday. I'll text you the address with an hour's notice."

Chapter *Twenty-six*

THE PLACE WAS IMMACULATE.

That was my first surprise when I finally set foot inside the house in Hell's Kitchen that my father had owned. I'd pictured it having rooms full of moldering Victorian furniture shrouded with cobwebs, and walls crammed with creepy oil paintings of psychotic-looking ancestors. Or having been overrun by meth cooks. Or addicts. Or the homeless. I certainly hadn't expected it to have the scrubbed, antiseptic feel of a safe house. All it was missing was the standard selection of cheap beds and couches and a fridge full of bland, inoffensive food.

My second surprise was that the house was gorgeous. From the outside it was fairly anonymous. I'd walked past it on my way to and from the Masons' building and nothing about it had stood out. But inside, it was spectacular. The woodwork on show in the hallways and the staircases wouldn't have looked out of place in a stately English home. There was mahogany. Cherry. Bird's-eye maple. Stuff you can hardly find anywhere, anymore. And the tile in the bathrooms was equally magnificent. It was good enough to be in a museum. So was the marble in the entrance hall. The proportions of the rooms were perfectly balanced. And the top floor? The whole thing was a ballroom, complete with a sprung floor and an uninterrupted view of the Hudson.

The situation was a little disorienting. I'd never even owned a studio apartment before, and now I'd inherited a virtual palace. My father could have made a fortune stripping the place and selling the architraves and chandeliers and plaster moldings. It wasn't like him to have missed the opportunity, but I was suddenly very glad he'd left everything intact. Anything else would have been sheer vandalism. Although it did mean I felt obliged to be extra careful with the microphone I was there to install. And the wireless cameras. And the Sheetrock.

The second time I visited the house was only a day later. I let myself in, checked that all the cameras were working, then settled down to wait.

I knew within five seconds of John Robson escorting him inside that George Carrick would take the deal. I could see it on his face. He just couldn't conceal his excitement and greed. He still insisted on touring the whole house, though. I knew he'd want Robson to see his famous *instinct* at work. He stroked the banisters. Tested the grout with his thumbnail. Knocked on the pipework with his knuckles. Checked the dimensions of the principal rooms using a laser measure he produced from the pilot's case he was carrying. And he wound up in the kitchen, at the back of the house, as planned and on schedule.

"This is such a beautiful, spacious room, isn't it?" Robson crossed to the window. "And so bright. It would be great for parties. It has a separate pantry for storing food. A wine cellar. You could even create a dedicated space down there for your cigars. Unless you decide to flip the house, in which case all these features would make excellent selling points."

Carrick put his case on the floor and massaged his hand. "They might."

"Come on, George. You know they would. And whatever you decide, you're getting a steal." Robson gestured to the table, which was the only piece of furniture in the building. "What do you say? Time to put this baby to bed?"

Carrick was silent for a moment. He bounced on the balls of his feet. Then he lifted his case onto the table and pulled out a copy of the contract. "Here you go." He passed Robson a pen with his company logo on the side. "You can keep that, once you've signed. And the case. Everything's in it for the deposit."

Robson took the pen. "Five million, cash, as agreed?"

"Five million." Carrick nodded. "Right."

"Why am I not hearing the word *cash*?"

Carrick sighed. "It's not all cash, actually. Some of it's made up with other things. Deeds for other buildings. Like that."

"We agreed on cash." Robson gripped the pen so savagely, his knuckles shone white. "I need cash."

"Don't we all. But listen. The timescale was just too tight. I could only lay my hands on two hundred grand. The rest my lawyer pulled together. It's totally legit. He wasn't happy about the work, I can tell you, it was such a rush."

"And I would care about your lawyer's happiness because . . . ?" Robson's eyes narrowed.

"OK. Fair point. Screw my lawyer. He's a miserable bastard, anyway. But look. Let's just do this. It's still five million dollars. You won't regret taking it."

"I know I won't." Robson paused with the pen nib hovering above the signature line, and turned to look Carrick in the eye. "It's been a pleasure doing business with you, sir."

There was a crash of breaking glass from the front of the house. Almost immediately smoke started to billow through the doorway and into the kitchen. I watched Robson and Carrick trying not to rub their eyes as they started to itch. Then burn. Then water uncontrollably.

"George Carrick." The voice sounded harsh and metallic through the megaphone. "This is Detective Atkinson, NYPD. You're under arrest for the murder of Norman Davies. If you come out now with your hands above your head, you will not be hurt. If you make us come in and get you . . ."

"Quick." Robson grabbed Carrick's elbow and pulled. "This way. I can get you out. There's a way into the alley that no one else knows about. Come on! We have to hurry."

Carrick blundered after Robson and they both tumbled out of the back door. They helped each other to their feet, then staggered down the stone steps, clinging to each other, their eyes stinging and streaming. And waiting for them at the bottom, though they couldn't see, was Detective Kanchelskis and two uniformed officers.

Atkinson and two more uniformed officers slipped on protective masks and began a sweep from the front of the building, for thoroughness' sake. By the time they reached the kitchen, all that was left on the table was the crumpled, unsigned contract. There was no sign of Carrick's case. That—and the five million dollars' worth of paper it contained—was safely in the pantry with me, concealed behind my day-old temporary wall.

Chapter *Twenty-seven*

THE OPERATION WOUND UP WITH A LOT OF MOVING PARTS. A LOT of things that could go wrong . . .

Guys from the NYPD, the FBI, the DEA, and the INS were lying in wait for the *Caucasus Queen* down at the docks.

Guys from the NYPD and the FBI were set up at Walcott's building, waiting for Madatov to show up. John Robson was there, too, posing as the doorman. He'd volunteered for the job. All he had to do was sign Madatov in, then follow him up in the elevator. It was a small price to pay for the satisfaction of seeing Walcott, expecting an enormous delivery of cash, getting arrested with Madatov, who thought he was there to buy photos of the trafficked women's bedrooms.

My team had drawn the short straw. We had guys from the same agencies that were present at the docks, but all we had to do was watch Madatov's building. We were divided between an undercover van and a requisitioned apartment, partly as early warning, and partly as backstop. Neither role carried much weight. If we saw Madatov leaving, fine. But he could go to Walcott's building from elsewhere. Or the rumors of the hidden exit from his place could be true. On top of that, the new batch of women wouldn't get close to our location. They wouldn't even make it off the dock. We just had to wait, miles away from the action, in case someone slipped away or a new player emerged. Then, as a hollow consolation, we were supposed to bag Madatov's security guards at the very end of the operation. They're such small fish that I was surprised anyone would bother, but I guess the FBI casts a very fine net.

We waited, and waited, until something did go wrong.

My phone rang.

"Paul, we have a major problem." It was John Robson. "Walcott's dead. He had a heart attack. The asshole!"

"Wait one." I checked the app for my Bulgarian bank. "The transfer was made, so I guess he's not a total asshole. What do you guys want to do?"

"We're looking at two options. The first is to bust Madatov when he walks through the door. There are some warrants out for him, but they're old and the Feds don't think anything serious will stick. For the second option, I need to check something with you. As far as you know, did Madatov and Walcott ever meet? Or did they do all their business through Madatov's lawyer?"

"According to George Carrick, who worked with both of them, Madatov went reclusive before Walcott came back to the States. So they won't have met. Why?"

"Because if that's the case, Madatov doesn't know what Walcott looks like. Meaning I could sit in for Walcott. I could wear a wire. I know Azerbaijan just as well as he did, in case Madatov wants to shoot the breeze or set any traps. And I have the phone here, with the blackmail photos on it."

"What about the doorman? You're supposed to be him."

"I'll make a sign saying *Back in Five Minutes*. That's no problem. The Feds are on board, too. We just need the NYPD to sign off. And I'm told that has to come from Atkinson's captain."

I explained the situation to Atkinson. He put in the call, but his captain was reluctant to make the decision on the spot. He wanted to pass it further up the chain of command. Which for us meant more waiting. And waiting.

A black town car pulled up outside Madatov's building. One of his mistresses emerged from the doorway. She was wearing some designer's take on a motorcycle jacket, paired with a tiny black leather skirt. Despite the height of her heels she seemed to glide along the pathway rather than walk, and she folded herself into the passenger seat with effortless grace. The car pulled away with a squeal of its tires, then Madatov's garage opened. A shiny blue minivan nosed out and eased up the driveway. I could see Madatov's second mistress behind the wheel. She had on a tan trench coat and a pair of dark, oversized sunglasses.

Atkinson's phone rang six minutes later. It was his captain. He gave the green light for using a ringer in place of Walcott, so I relayed the news to Robson. And went back to waiting. For close to another hour. Until instead of plain wrong, something went weird.

Atkinson's phone rang again. He talked for a couple of minutes, then hung up.

"That was Kanchelskis, at the dock." Atkinson drummed his fingers on the steering wheel. "I don't get what's going on. The *Caucasus Queen* came in early because of the tide, or some nautical thing, so they got a jump on the search. They went all over the ship. Twice. There were no women, anywhere. They're positive.

Then a minivan—the one we just saw—showed up. And there were women in it. Six, plus the driver. They're all arrested, but none of them's talking. Except the driver, who asked for Madatov's lawyer."

The women had been taken to the dock. Not collected from it. Meaning they weren't being smuggled in. They were being smuggled out. And they hadn't been driven by Madatov. They'd been driven by one of his mistresses. The one who'd gone to take care of that piece of business right after the other had jumped into a town car and taken off. In a hurry. Like she had another burning matter to deal with . . .

I dialed Robson's number. There was no answer.

"Atkinson, start the engine. Move!"

"Why?" He reached for the key. "Where are we going?"

"Walcott's building."

"What about Madatov?"

"He's not in the equation anymore. His mistresses have taken over."

"What?" Atkinson pulled away fast, but without letting the tires squeal and draw attention. "Where's this coming from?"

"I'm just putting the pieces together. It's why no one's seen the guy recently. He hasn't become a recluse. He's dead. And his recent victims? The reason there were no break-ins? And no defensive wounds? It's not because they knew Madatov and let him in. It's because they didn't perceive the women as a threat. And now that they're in charge, they're not bringing new girls to the United States. They're taking the old ones home, to Azerbaijan. And they think Walcott is threatening their operation with the blackmail demand. They don't know it's bogus."

"And they don't know it's not Walcott who's at the rendezvous." Atkinson leaned harder on the gas. "It's Robson."

Chapter *Twenty-eight*

THE BLACK TOWN CAR WAS WAITING OUTSIDE WALCOTT'S BUILD-
ing when we arrived. It was sitting at the curb, its passenger door
lined up with the entrance and its engine running. That was a good
sign, I thought. The woman must still be on the premises. Maybe
there was still time . . .

Atkinson sent one cop to arrest the driver and the rest of us ran
inside to reception. The lobby was deserted so we went straight for
the elevators. I knew from my previous visit that riding up to Walcott's floor was a non-starter. The corridor was straight and narrow and it only had two doors: one to Walcott's apartment, and
one to his neighbor's, which had been commandeered for the day
for use as a command post by the NYPD and FBI. If the woman
was waiting for us with any kind of automatic weapon, things
could get very ugly, very fast.

There wasn't time for too much fancy planning—Robson, the
cop, and the agent were still not answering their phones—so Atkinson and I took the first elevator car that came. We rode to the

twenty-ninth floor, which was one below Walcott's. Then I went straight for the emergency staircase and crept up the last flight. Atkinson stayed and held the elevator for sixty seconds, then reached in and hit the button for thirty. I waited till I heard the muted *ting* as it arrived, then eased open the fire door and peered into the corridor.

Our attempt at a diversion hadn't been necessary. We were too late. The door to Walcott's neighbor's apartment was standing open and an arm in a dark blue sleeve, its hand slick with blood, was reaching out into the corridor. I ran forward and looked through the doorway. The police officer was lying on his side, one leg curled under his body, his eyes open but unfocused. A pool of blood the size of a dinner plate had formed under his abdomen. Beyond him, sprawled facedown beneath an archway leading to the living room, I could see another body. A woman's. I felt a tiny flicker of hope. Then I registered her height. Her shoes. Her clothes. Her hair color. Nothing corresponded with what I'd seen of Madatov's mistress. Meaning she had to be the federal agent. And she was completely motionless.

Atkinson caught up to me twenty seconds later. He grabbed hold of the doorframe and froze for a moment, then crouched down and checked the cop's neck for a pulse. I left him to figure out if there was any point in calling for the medics, and continued down the corridor.

I kicked Walcott's door just below the lock and dived through the gap as it flew open, rolling immediately to the side in case the woman was there waiting for me. My acrobatics were greeted by an ironic round of applause. It was coming from Robson, who was sitting on one of the couches in the living room.

"John?" I picked myself up and hurried along the hallway. "Are you OK?"

"Of course I am." He reached for a bottle of Heineken from the side table.

"Where's the woman? Madatov's mistress. Did she get here yet?"

Robson gestured toward Walcott's bedroom. I went in and saw a woman lying on the floor. She was definitely the same person I'd watched leaving Madatov's house, but now she was tied and gagged with strips of torn bedsheet. When she saw me she started struggling to free herself. When that didn't work she tried to wriggle closer and kick me, so I left her to her futile efforts and returned to the living room.

"You dodged a bullet there, John." I sat down on the couch next to Robson. "You resisted her. You might be the only one who ever has."

"I didn't resist her, Paul." He looked at me and winked. "I'm naturally immune."

Chapter *Twenty-nine*

I WAS TRYING TO REMEMBER THE LAST TIME I'D BEEN TO A BAR FOR no other reason than to get a beer with some friends.

To be precise, I didn't actually get a beer that day. I ordered a coffee, which drew some weird looks from the other patrons. When it arrived it was evident that the barman had taken it upon himself to add some whiskey, which I didn't complain about. And the people I was with weren't exactly my friends. I wasn't there to surveil any of them, though. I didn't have to squeeze any information out of anyone, or con anybody into trusting me. The situation wasn't unpleasant in that regard, but it was definitely unfamiliar. It left me feeling a little adrift, like I didn't have a good enough excuse for being there.

John Robson showed no signs of struggling to fit in. He was twenty feet away in the thick of a boisterous crowd of off-duty cops, a head or more taller than everyone around him, laughing and exchanging high fives as he recounted his afternoon's heroics for the twentieth time.

"So I open the door and this woman's standing there, OK? Well, no, that's not true. This *goddess* is standing there. She waits a moment, to make sure I've noticed how low the zipper on her cute little jacket has gotten. Then she stretches up and kisses me. She slides a hand down the front of my pants, and she says, 'Hey, big boy, this is your lucky day—' "

"She never said that!" One of the cops play-punched Robson in the shoulder.

"She just meant his height!" One of the others laughed.

"Oh, she said it." Robson grinned. "And fellas, trust me. She meant it. Anyway, she squeezes past, into the apartment. She turns to face me. Opens her jacket the rest of the way. Takes a step toward me. Kneels down. Makes like she's going to undo my pants. But what she actually whips out is . . . a nasty little switchblade from some secret pocket in her jacket. It was already crusted with someone else's blood. And she tried to stick it in my gut."

"What did you do?" The guy to Robson's right looked genuinely alarmed.

"Well, I wasn't really up for her idea, if you know what I mean." Robson winked at the guy. "So I kicked her in the head. Tied her up. And helped myself to Walcott's stash of beer."

I finished the last dregs of my coffee, put the cup down on the bar, and was about to slip past the crowd and head for my hotel when Detective Atkinson came up to me. His tie was loose, his top button was undone, and he had a half-finished pint of Guinness in his hand. I guessed it wasn't his first of the night.

"Good news, Paul." He slapped me on the shoulder. "I just heard from the hospital. The cop from Walcott's building? He's going to make it. So's the agent. They're both out of danger."

"That's great news." I closed my eyes for a moment. "I'm not going to lie. I was worried about them."

"I was, too." Atkinson planted himself on the stool next to mine. "So what do you think of McGinty's?"

I looked around and decided I liked the place. It was honest and unpretentious. The bar itself was made of polished mahogany, time served and bearing the scars of hard use. The furniture was solid. The floor, clean. The pictures on the walls—old scenes of Dublin and the Irish countryside—inoffensive enough. The prices, reasonable. By Manhattan standards, anyway. If you wanted somewhere to unwind after a stressful day's work, you could do a lot worse. As long as you didn't mind the crowd of cops. But then, that was probably the main appeal for most of the people in there. "It's a lot better than the Green Zebra. Do they serve breakfast?"

Atkinson grinned and took a swig of his beer. "I nearly said no. Did I tell you that? When you asked me to take your idea for that crazy plan to the lieutenant. There were too many agencies. Too much time on the phone, keeping me off the street. And you know what? I would have said no, if you hadn't handed me Carrick on a plate for the Davies homicide. I never said thank you for that. I should have. It put a major feather in my cap."

The barman brought another coffee without my having to ask. "My pleasure. I was happy to help."

"There's one thing I still don't understand. How did you put them together, Carrick and Jonny Evans? That wasn't even on our radar."

I shrugged. "Lucky break, I guess. Our paths happened to cross, and we got to talking. People like to confide in me, for some reason. Speaking of Jonny, is there anything you could do to help him? I heard he did well, helping to take down Madatov's guy inside the department. And I'd hate to see him end up like Norman Davies."

"I don't know." Atkinson drained his glass. "I guess I could try. But tell me this. How did you know Carrick would go for the brownstone deal? How did you know Walcott would fall for that cash swap idea?"

"Human nature." I tasted my coffee. There was even more whiskey in it this time. "Carrick was greedy. Walcott was desperate. It was just a question of putting the right kind of temptation in their paths."

"Speaking of temptation . . ." Atkinson signaled for another beer. "So. What are you going to do next? Are you going to stick around?"

"It's not time for *next*. I'm not done yet. I still have to find Pardew's missing file."

Atkinson slammed his palm against the bar. "And you will. I know it. I wasn't sure before, but now I'm certain."

"Thanks. I guess." I wasn't sure how I felt about his newfound surge in confidence.

"And after that? Will you stay in the city? You can't keep living in a hotel room. But you have that house now, right? Up in Westchester?"

"I haven't thought that far ahead. But I'm not going to live in that house. Not yet. I'll let Mrs. Vincent stay there. My father's housekeeper. It's her home, more than it is mine. Maybe I'll move into the brownstone? That's a nice place. And it's a shame to leave it empty."

"What about work? You can't hang around the courthouse forever. Will you take over your father's business?"

"I hadn't thought about that. It would be nice to honor his memory somehow. But running his business? I'm not sure that would be a good idea. It's in safe hands now. My father's lawyer took care of the arrangements. It may be wise not to mess with it. Better to get the Pardew thing squared away, then decide."

Chapter *Thirty*

ONE DAY, A FORTNIGHT LATER, I FOUND MYSELF BACK IN COURT-room 432.

Being there wasn't part of my original plan. I'd started with two things on my agenda. Clean the section allotted to me. And search a pair of chambers on the second floor. They were the last ones I had left to check, and every time I tried to get into them they were either occupied or there were people in the adjacent court-rooms. I'd tried them first thing on my way up from the janitors' room. A trial was already under way in one of them, and a judge was talking with a clerk in the other. I tried again when I was half-way through cleaning, and still couldn't get in. I tried again when I was done with my section, and still couldn't get in. I figured there was nothing to do but swallow my frustration and resolve to come back the next day, but when I steered my cart out of the elevator in the basement I ran into Frank Carrodus.

"Paul?" He sounded out of breath. "Can you help me? I need

someone to cover for Jane while she's down in Doomsday Day-care. Jas promised to, but she's gone home sick. It won't take long. There's just 428 to 434 left to do."

Why not? I thought. I was happy to do my bit for the kids, and heading back upstairs would give me another chance to check the chambers on the second floor. Maybe I'd get lucky this time.

Room 432 was empty when I arrived. And it wasn't too dirty. I figured it would take me ten minutes to do what was needed. Twelve at the most. It actually took eight, and just as I was finishing a woman emerged from the chambers. I recognized her. She was one of the clerks, but I hadn't seen her in that courtroom before. She normally worked elsewhere in the building.

The woman walked straight past me, heading for the door to the corridor. She was looking down. Moving fast. She didn't acknowledge me at all. But not in the *I'm too important to bother with you* way that some of the judges have. And not in a busy or preoccupied way, like some of the lawyers and jurors and specta-tors. It was more of the stiff, shifty way of a child caught in the midst of some mischief who thinks, *If I can't see you, you can't see me.* But I did see her. And I noticed something. Her shoes. They had four-inch heels. And they were scarlet. Just like two of the pairs I'd seen in the closet when I'd first searched the chambers. I'd held my curiosity at bay on that occasion, but it was too much to ask for me to do so again.

I positioned my cart in the doorway with my broom set to fall if anyone tried to get by, then went inside and crossed to the closet. There were only three shirts hanging on the rail this time, and three ties. Both pairs of men's shoes were there. So was the black pair of women's pumps. But only one of the red pairs. And behind them, there was something new. A padded envelope. It was well stuffed. There were no markings, and it was tied up with string. I pulled it out and loosened the knots. Inside there was a thick manila folder. I checked the label:

The State of New York vs Alexander Michael Pardew.

I reached for my phone. My first thought was to call Detective Atkinson and tell him I'd finally found the holy grail. But old habits die hard. Who knew what was really inside that thing? So I took the folder over to the couch and started to read.

I'd never studied a legal file before. For some reason I was expecting a jumble of incomprehensible documents, full of impenetrable jargon. I thought it might be impossible to make sense of it. But I was wrong. The contents were very logically organized. ADA Dixon had done a great job. The story was easy to understand. I didn't get all the financial nuances, necessarily, but the overall gist was simple to follow. It took ten minutes to get through it, and after my first pass the events seemed exactly as Atkinson and Dixon had outlined. Only with a lot more detail, which I had to believe would be a good thing when it came to ultimately nailing Pardew's ass.

I pulled out my phone, then remembered Atkinson saying he hoped the file would give him something else. An idea about where to look for Pardew. Recurring travel costs, maybe, or utility bills for some remote mountain retreat. Any clue as to where the bastard was hiding. I figured it might be beneficial to spend a little time with him myself, before the police reeled him back in, so I leafed through the file again. Cover to cover. Then I went back to the start. I double-checked some of the dates. Checked for misfiled entries. And photographed certain pages. Not to use as evidence—I remembered Dixon's explanation about the problem with copies. But for my own reference. Because as I sat there reading, I was picking up an echo from my past.

One of our early training modules at Fort Huachuca had covered reconnaissance photographs and how to interpret them. It wasn't one of my favorite subjects. It had been incredibly tedious, cooped up inside a dingy classroom poring over a seemingly endless sequence of boring, virtually identical prints. But it had taught me an important lesson. It had changed the way I looked at things. It had shown me that sometimes it's not what *is* there in a picture that counts. It's what's *not* there. And a couple of things *weren't there* in the image that the documents were developing in my mind.

Pardew had been illicitly reducing the value of my father's assets for over a year. But there was no evidence of any fraudulent activity during the six months before my father confronted him. Had Pardew stopped cheating? If so, why? The business still had more than enough assets to ruin him, based on the formula he'd signed up to. And there were no bank statements for the month when the DUI charges against Pardew had been dropped. That incident also occurred six months before the confrontation with my father. And that was the only period when the financial records weren't complete. Could these things be coincidences? Possibly. But no one in my business—my previous business—believed in coincidences.

The DUI charge had been dropped. The bank records were missing. And the fraud had stopped. All at the same time. Would that be enough to whet Atkinson's appetite? Probably not, based on his track record.

But did it raise a red flag for me? Most definitely.

Instinct couldn't be taught, as my instructors used to say, and I could sense there was something bigger going on here. I needed to figure out whom I could trust before I passed the information to anyone else, so I slipped the folder back into its envelope. Then I wrapped the package in a garbage bag and slid it into my cart. I'd need to find a place to keep it safe. But that wouldn't be hard. I had the whole building at my disposal, after all.

I'd just emerged from the chambers with theories and suspicions about Pardew sparking away in my head like fireworks when the main courtroom door opened and a man came in. I realized it must be Bob Mason, but I hardly recognized him. He looked taller somehow. Younger. Stronger, even. And he was walking without a cane.

"I was hoping I'd find you, Paul." He held out his hand. "I wanted to let you know, you were right."

"About what?"

"You said things would work out. And they did. Like I'd never have believed. A lawyer got in touch, out of the blue. A guy called di Matteo. He said someone had set up a trust to help all the people who lived in our building. It paid for new apartments for all of us, all together, in a much nicer low-rise a couple of blocks south. We'll be moving in a month or so. And it pays for us to have health insurance, too. Which is a godsend for Lydia, because it means she can go to that other hospital and get the new treatment. The doctors there think that soon she'll be able to walk again, before Christmas."

"I'm very happy to hear that, Bob. It's great news."

"It is, but one thing's still bugging me. I don't know who to thank."

"Maybe it's just the universe, working its magic and looking out for good people."

"Or maybe it's *a* good person who's doing the looking out. You. You're the only one I told about our problems. Paul, did you do this?"

"Me?" I picked up my broom. "No. How could I have? I'm just a janitor."

ACKNOWLEDGMENTS

I WOULD LIKE TO EXTEND MY DEEPEST THANKS TO THE FOLLOWING for their help, support, and encouragement while I wrote this book. Without them, it would not have been possible.

My editor, the excellent Brendan Vaughan, and the whole team at Random House.

My agent, the outstanding Richard Pine.

My friends, who've stood by me through the years: Dan Boucher, Carlos Camacho, Joelle Charbonneau, John Dul, Jamie Freveletti, Keir Graff, Tana Hall, Nick Hawkins, Dermot Hollingsworth, Amanda Hurford, Richard Hurford, Jon Jordan, Ruth Jordan, Kristy Claiborne Graves, Martyn James Lewis, Rebecca Makkai, Dan Malmon, Kate Hackbarth Malmon, Carrie Medders, Philippa Morgan, Erica Ruth Neubauer, Gunther Neumann, Ayo Onatade, Denise Pascoe, Wray Pascoe, Dani Patarazzi, Javier Ramirez, David Reith, Sharon Reith, Beth Renaldi, Marc Rightley, Melissa Rightley, Renee Rosen, Kelli Stanley, and Brian Wilson.

Everyone at The Globe Pub, Chicago.

Everyone from Fish Creek Ranch Preserve, Wyoming.

Jane and Jim Grant.

Ruth Grant.

Katharine Grant.

Jess Grant.

Alexander Tyska.

Gary and Stacie Gutting.

And last on the list, but first in my heart—Tasha. *Everything, always . . .*

About the Author

ANDREW GRANT is the author of *RUN, False Positive, False Friend,* and *False Witness*. He was born in Birmingham, England. He attended the University of Sheffield, where he studied English literature and drama. He ran a small independent theater company, and subsequently worked in the telecommunications industry for fifteen years. Grant and his wife, the novelist Tasha Alexander, live on a wildlife preserve in Wyoming.

andrewgrantbooks.com
Facebook.com/AndrewGrantAuthor
Twitter: @Andrew_Grant